THE VETERINARIAN'S FIELD GUIDE TO RABID UNICORNS

ELISE LOYACANO PERL

Harvey Flea
PUBLISHING HOUSE LTD

The Veterinarian's Field Guide to Rabid Unicorns / Version 3.1
(First Vellum edition)

Copyright © 2018, 2019 Elise Loyacano Perl

ISBN print edition: 978-198-374-8240

Published by Harvey Flea Publishing House, Ltd. Guaynabo, Puerto Rico

http://www.saintquiche.com

Unicorn image by Michael Rayback

Interior design by Dalan E. Decker

Not a Major Motion Picture!

Not directed by Michael Bay, no score by Hans Zimmer

Soundtrack available on Waterkeep Records, a Division of SoundFridge Enterprises, a division of Harvey Flea Publishing House Ltd.

Find us on Facebook at www.facebook.com/eliseloyacano/

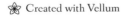 Created with Vellum

To grownups who still read kids' books. But would appreciate them with a dash of rum.

SECTION I

Excerpt from *The Gastrointestinal Tract of Unicorns: Part I of the Anatomy of Rare Creatures Series* by Bertram W. Vole and Timothy E. Grett

INTRODUCTION: PURPOSE OF THIS TEXTBOOK

"The purpose of this textbook is to describe the gastrointestinal tract of the unicorn (*equus silvus unicornuus*) and its connection to this animal's dietary needs. The authors do not intend to cover every aspect of the unicorn's anatomy. Indeed, much research is still needed to fully understand this creature. But an introduction to its diet and digestion will allow both the casual and professional reader a deeper understanding of the unicorn's alimentary needs."

CHAPTER 1

I KNOW what you're thinking. "Unicorns can't get rabies."
Think again.

CHAPTER 2

ABOUT FOUR WEEKS EARLIER.

Bertie wished he had come into work late. He'd been doing that a lot lately, and it was working pretty well for him. Better than being on time, anyway.

"Are you listening to me, Dr. B?" The shrill voice dragged Bertie back into the exam room. It was Mrs. Hookum, the latest reason Bertie wished he had come into work good and late. She yakked on. "My Pookie-Pie still has fleas. What you gave her didn't work."

He looked down at the half-bald poodle. "Did you use the flea medication I recommended?"

"No, Dr. B. Everyone knows that causes cancer."

"My name's actually Bertie. Or Dr. Vole."

"What?"

"Forget it. If you don't give your dog the flea medicine, the fleas won't go away." Bertie looked again at Pookie-Pie and her pink, raw skin; she looked so pathetic.

"Yes, but you only told me to get that medicine because

Big Pharma is behind this office. It's not the same anymore since Dr. Canard left."

"He died." Bertie had to agree with Mrs. Hookum. It wasn't the same.

"That's no excuse to go into cahoots with Big Pharma."

"We aren't in cahoots with Big Pharma," Bertie said. "The flea medication I told you to get doesn't cause cancer. I give it to my parents' dog."

"Yes, but he's going to become a mutant. I just know it."

Bertie sighed. What did he know? He was just a vet with loads of debt. He remembered why he had gone into veterinary medicine, and it wasn't for the people. Of course, you can't tell that to admissions committees. That's not what they want to hear. They've practically got radar everywhere to sniff out prospective students who don't want to work with people. For six months before his interviews, he'd practiced his schtick of how much he wanted to help people by helping animals. The whole experience had left his smile muscles scarred.

And now? He wasn't so sure he'd made the right decision. His mind wandered to the last vet school payment he hadn't made—again. He wasn't sure how much he owed anymore. Totting up his debt was like watching a horror movie, without the popcorn.

The first five years out of school, his work meant something, but then—

"Dr. B? Dr. B?" Mrs. Hookum said. "Dr. Beeeeeee!"

Bertie snapped out of his reverie. Mrs. Hookum looked at him funny. "What do you want to use, then?" he said.

"How about herbs? Or spices? Natural remedies? Do you have anything homeopathic? Maybe vinegar?"

"Vinegar's not homeopathic," Bertie said. "It's for salad."

"My niece-in-law put warmed vinegar on her Bichon Frise, and she swears by it," Mrs. Hookum said in an accusing tone, as though Bertie had been hiding the wonders of condiments all these years.

"You don't need to come here to get vinegar, Mrs. Hookum."

"Well!" Mrs. Hookum picked up her fake Chanel purse and tugged on Pookie-Pie's sparkly leash. "Then maybe I'll just go elsewhere."

"Yeah, like a supermarket."

Mrs. Hookum stood up to leave. Bertie opened the door for her, and she and Pookie-Pie waddled to the waiting room. Bertie followed them to reception. Sandra, the receptionist, had her nose stuck in her phone, which had a large sticker that said, "Brooklyn!"

"Give Mrs. Hookum one of those citronella candles for the patron saint of fleas," Bertie said.

Sandra looked up, confused. "Oh, I didn't know those existed. I should get one for my pooch. What's his name?"

"You don't know your own dog's name?" Bertie said. Talk about the great mind of Brooklyn.

"No, the name of the patron saint of fleas, silly," Sandra said.

"I don't know! Look it up on your phone. You spend all your time there anyway." Bertie headed to the back, but Sandra and Mrs. Hookum's screechy voices followed him.

"Don't pay any attention to him, sweetie," Mrs. Hookum said to Sandra. "He doesn't believe in natural medicine."

"Oh, I do. Last week, I cured cellulitis with paprika." She pointed to the red blotch on her arm. "It worked really well."

"See, Dr. B!" Mrs. Hookum turned back to Sandra. "Big Pharma . . ."

Bertie didn't hear the rest. He slammed the door to the patient area. It was off limits to human clients. The vet techs were giving the animals their morning medicine. The barking and meowing from behind the bars of their cages calmed Bertie. He walked up to the first cage and reviewed the chart of an obese chihuahua to look busy.

His boss wouldn't be happy that he was hiding out here. He was supposed to wait in the exam room to create as fast a turnaround as possible. Since Dr. Canard had up and died, this place was more like a drive-through. "Toss your dog in through the window! We'll get him back to you in thirty minutes or less or your next pet is free!"

Bertie remembered the day Dr. Canard had offered to sell him the practice. He was really tempted but figured he couldn't swing it with his debts. He slept on it though—for about six months. But then Dr. Canard died, and it was too late to make any decision. Boy, did he regret that now.

"B! There you are!"

Bertie swung around. It was his boss, Dr. Roderick, who insisted on calling him B, even though Bertie hated that. Bit by bit, everyone else had started calling him B too.

"Glad to see you could fit us into your schedule." Dr. Roderick's glasses glinted the same way they do in those movies starring near-sighted Nazis. He pushed Bertie towards the door that led to the exam rooms. "What are you doing here? Get to the exam room. Some nut job is waiting to see you."

Goody. Another nutjob. Bertie grabbed the tablet from the rack outside the door. He touched something wrong, and the screen flipped to a different page.

"Darn it!" Bertie fumbled, looking for the right entry. There, he found it. A Dr. Om.

Great. Would this be one of those people doctors who asked him why he hadn't become a "real doctor?"

"I hate my life," Bertie said under his breath before pushing open the door.

Bertie turned on the smile he had worked so hard on all the years ago for his admissions interviews and put his hand out. "Hello, my name is Dr. Bertie. How can I help you today?"

The man stared back with oogly, blue eyes. His over-sized shirt was half tucked in, and the extra bulk around the waist tried to hide in a jacket that didn't quite fit. He grabbed Bertie's hand in a tight handshake and held on enthusiastically for a few seconds too long, kind of like a salesman.

"Nice to meet you, Dr. Vole," Dr. Om said. "Nice to finally meet you."

Huh, he knows my last name, Bertie thought. How? His name wasn't posted at reception anymore, not since Dr. Roderick had taken down all the associate vets' names.

"I don't see a pet in here. How may I help you?"

"Take a seat," Dr. Om said as he sat down himself. Bertie didn't sit down right away. It was strange. Clients didn't normally offer vets a seat. Dr. Om quickly gestured towards the chair a few more times.

Dr. Om rubbed his puffy hands together and smiled more widely. "I'm not here about a pet, although I love, LOVE animals. I love animals. I'm here about . . . a proposition."

"A proposition," Bertie said. Was he selling meds? He didn't have a suitcase, and his Rolex watch looked a bit high-end for a salesman. But he was sleazy in that enthusiastic, salesman kind of way.

"Yes, a proposition." Dr. Om rubbed his hands together some more. "A proposition."

"What would that proposition be?"

"I am looking for a vet to take over the veterinary services at my new . . . park. It is set to open in just a few weeks."

"You mean a zoo?"

Dr. Om looked disapproving. "No, no, no. I don't believe in zoos. Not at all! Keeping animals behind bars is barbaric. Barbaric! Wouldn't you say?"

"Yes, well, some animals can get violent. Lions, tigers, and bears, you know? Anyway, I'm not a park vet. That isn't my area."

"This park won't be home to violent animals. Not at all violent."

"Nonetheless, I deal mostly in small animals. You should look for someone with the required expertise."

"No one has the expertise I need. No one!" Dr. Om tugged at his jacket in excitement. "Not yet, anyway. And I've done my research. You're being modest!"

Dr. Om giggled knowingly as though the two were sharing some secret.

Bertie didn't say anything. It was official. This guy was weird.

"And don't you hate your life?" Dr. Om said, adjusting his jacket. "Wouldn't a change be good?"

Crap, Bertie thought. He heard me.

"I'm sorry. I didn't mean to say what I said. It's just been one of those—"

"Months," Dr. Om said. "Months, by my calculation."

Bertie sighed. "Yes, months. Look, I don't know what this is all about—"

"Then why don't you come to my park and check it out?"

Bertie didn't reply. He couldn't put his finger on it, but something about Dr. Om set his radar on high alert.

"Why are you so sure you want to hire me? Did you go to every other vet in town first? Am I like a last resort?"

"Not exactly."

"Not exactly?"

"Not exactly." Dr. Om giggled.

"Then what, exactly?" Bertie asked. "Why won't you tell me more about this place?"

"Why aren't you willing to consider the offer? I'm mean, at least consider it? You don't like working here, not at all, not since Dr. Canard died."

"You knew Dr. Canard?" Bertie said. Suddenly he trusted Dr. Om just a little bit more, although, come to think of it, maybe Dr. Canard had hated Dr. Om.

"We studied together at university. We weren't exactly friends. We weren't exactly enemies. We weren't exactly friends, but not enemies. Not at all."

He went back to distrusting Dr. Om. What was it about this guy that irked him? Was Bertie just being close-minded because he looked like a blowfish? Was he that shallow?

"You didn't answer my question," Dr. Om said.

"Which one?" Bertie was having trouble keeping track of the conversation.

"Why won't you consider my offer?"

The clock ticked behind Bertie. It made him nervous. Dr. Canard refused to have any reminders of time in his exam rooms. It was all about the patients. Now each room had a clock that monitored how many minutes the vets spent with each patient. Whoever spent the least amount of time at the end of the month got a bonus. Mr. Boss guy was sick.

So why wasn't he willing to check out Dr. Om's offer?

"I can't put my finger on it," Bertie said. "I don't get why you won't tell me more."

"Oh, but I will," Dr. Om said. "I will. In fact, I am here to answer any question you may have. Any question, except that one. To get an answer to that question, you've got to come to the park with me."

"See, that sounds creepy," Bertie said. "Like you have a blood-thirsty, machete-wielding clown driving you around town and stowing passengers in the trunk."

Dr. Om giggled. "I promise you, I do not have a clown driving me around town."

Bertie noticed he didn't say anything about blood or machetes.

"You haven't answered my question," Bertie said.

"Which one?" Dr. Om's smile widened, as though he were playing a game.

"Why are you so eager for me to consider this offer?" Bertie said.

"You were right. Completely right. You aren't the first person I've approached. I talked to more obvious candidates. They weren't fully convinced. But I kept up the search, and I found out about you. Dr. Canard and I didn't always see eye to eye—it wasn't all eye to eye—but I respected his opinion on many things, many, many things, including his judgment of character. Very good judge of character. He had a high opinion of you. And you have had interesting thoughts in the past."

Dr. Om's tendency to tug on his jacket and hold up his hands defensively was getting on Bertie's nerves.

"Why weren't the other vets convinced?"

"It was a marketing error on my part," Dr. Om said. He stood up and leaned against the exam table. "I think . . . I think I just told them too much too soon. Way too much, way too soon. They weren't ready for it, and as a result, they just thought I was a bit crazy. That's all. Just a bit cuckoo." He giggled.

"Crazy?" Bertie said. "That doesn't sound like a very good recommendation."

"It's how the human mind works, doesn't it?" Dr. Om moved closer to Bertie, as though they were both part of an enthralling conversation. "When we hear something we've never heard before and can't integrate it with more facts, our default conclusion is that the messenger is odd or crazy, even. It's all psychology, I promise you. All psychology."

"Psychology, huh?" Bertie said.

"I am now holding back. Holding back! I can't tell you. I must show you. If you want to know more about my ground-breaking park, you'll need to come on down for a visit." Dr. Om rooted around in his jacket pockets till he found the card he was looking for. He jotted something down before handing it over. "Here, take this. Go ahead! Take it."

Bertie looked at it. There was an address and a number.

"What's the number?" he said.

"Your first week's salary," Dr. Om said as he straightened his jacket and reached over to pat Bertie on the back. "I hope it will be an inducement. An inducement!"

Bertie looked at the number. "Holy pigeon poo."

It was enough to do away with his school debt in three months.

CHAPTER 3

THE DAY ENDED ABOUT AS WELL as it had started. Dr. Roderick passed by the exam room as Bertie's last patient, an incontinent pug, was leaving with his owner, Mrs. Peckipoo. Dr. Roderick pointed at the clock on the wall.

"You won't be getting that bonus at this rate!" he said.

"You know," Mrs. Peckipoo said. "I just don't understand why I always have to wait so long."

"Do you hear that, B? Gotta keep the assembly line moving for these people," Dr. Roderick said as he took Mrs. Peckipoo's hand in his. "Just for the long wait, you get a ten percent discount today."

"Thank you, Dr. R. I so appreciate that."

Mrs. Peckipoo waved her arthritic fingers at Dr. Roderick. Bertie was sure she batted her eyelashes at him as she tottered away with her dog.

Was she flirting with Dr. Roderick? Was she that senile?

Dr. Roderick slapped Bertie on the back. "By the way,

that ten percent is coming out of your pocket. Pick up the pace, buddy."

"Yeah, sure," Bertie said. He slipped the patient tablet into the slot, but it clattered to the floor. Bertie really missed paper files.

"That breaks, you pay for it," Dr. Roderick said.

"Pick up the pace, pick up the pace," Bertie grumbled to himself as he walked home in the cold January rain. He got to his front porch and fumbled with the keys. They fell onto the wet doormat.

The front door opened. Bertie looked up to see his landlady, her form darkened against the glow of her living room lamp. "Bertie, you're finally home! Have some hot chocolate before you go to your basement."

Okay, so it wasn't exactly his front porch. He rented the basement.

And no, he wasn't renting his parents' basement, thank you very much. He was renting his parents' neighbor's basement.

His parents didn't have a basement.

And actually, to be perfectly technical, it was a half-basement, which meant he had a half-window too, so phooey to anyone thinking Bertie was some cliché millennial living in his parents' basement.

That's more or less what Bertie used to tell people until he got tired of their dubious looks. Now he simply changed the subject if anyone asked where he lived.

He trudged into his landlady's kitchen. "Thanks, Fiona. It's been one of those days."

"You kids these days all work so hard," she said. "You look exhausted."

"Well, like I said, it was one of those days."

"You don't seem very fond of your job," Fiona said. She

put the hot chocolate down on the table. "You worked so hard to get there. It's too bad."

"Well, you know. New boss. Hard to get used to him," Bertie said.

She poured Cognac into her hot chocolate and held up the bottle with a smile as though to say, "You want some, don't you?"

Bertie shook his head. "I'll take mine straight. Thanks."

"Why don't you find a new job?" she said.

"I don't know. Maybe I could. Or there's always ignoring the problem and hoping it goes away."

"That's the spirit!" Fiona said. "You know what they say. 'Bloom where you're planted.'"

"Yeah," Bertie said. What he didn't say was, what if you're planted right smack dab in the middle of stinkweed?

"I'll tell you, a little bit of oh-be-joyful always helped me get through those awful jobs I had after my husband died," Fiona said, holding up the Cognac again. "Are you sure you don't want any?"

Bertie was tempted, but considering the number of Cognac bottles Fiona cycled through each month, he thought better of it. "Nah, I've got some research to do. Thanks for the hot chocolate."

Fiona held up her cup as though to say, "cheers!" and Bertie went down to his basement.

Half-basement, actually.

Bertie turned on the light switch at the bottom of the stairs. The bare bulb made a teepee of light that revealed a mattress on the floor, a kitchenette that Bertie had been planning to scrub down since Christmas, and a rickety wooden table in the middle. He stood looking at his surroundings, then pulled Dr. Om's card out of his pocket.

It couldn't hurt to look up information on the guy. He picked up his laptop from the mattress. The only way to get Internet in the room was to prop his computer up on the half-windowsill near the ceiling. From there, he could pick up his parents' Wi-Fi signal from next door. He hoped they hadn't changed the password.

Bertie typed in the password "GetMarriedAlreadyBertie*7_85."

On second thought, maybe he did wish they'd change the password.

A Facebook notification popped up. It was from a friend asking him what was wrong with his cat. He included a blurry picture of the paw. Bertie answered, "Hard to tell from a photo. Take him to the vet already." His friend typed back, "Dude! Why did I bother helping you study for that calculus quiz?"

Bertie wrote, "You mean the one I flunked?"

He wasn't sure he had flunked that one, but he figured it would make his friend mad.

He closed Facebook. Nothing good ever came of it. He typed "Dr. Om" in the search bar. It couldn't possibly be a common name. How hard could it be to find information on the guy?

Apparently, not so easy. The first line in Google said, "Do you mean drum?" A list of sites on meditation followed. The only Dr. Om he could find was the creator of some magic foot cream that promised to get rid of athlete's foot, arthritis, and ingrown toenails.

That didn't seem to have anything to do with a guy who ran parks.

He typed in "Dr. Om, parks," but still no dice.

Bertie fumbled through what little els
the guy. He had apparently studied with Γ
to think of it, he wasn't sure where Dr. C
school. He checked into Dr. Frederic
Turned out he had done his undergrad at Oxtoru.

Great. Fifteen minutes of Google, and Bertie was feeling less and less accomplished. He researched Dr. Om, Oxford, as well as Dr. Canard's vet school (Cornell), but nothing came up.

He rubbed his eyes. Who was this guy anyway? It was late, and the Internet had slowed to a crawl. He checked his watch. His parents would be watching reruns of Magnum, P.I. on the web. The only way to get decent Internet at this stage would be to crawl on to their laps.

He was exaggerating, but you get the idea.

Instead, Bertie crawled into bed. He had a thought of how to find out more about Dr. Om, but he didn't much like it.

The next day, Bertie walked into the clinic extra early. He carried a triple caramel macchiato with extra chocolate sprinkles and half diet milk, half cream. He was pretty sure this was what Sandra always ordered. He hoped so. Do you know how embarrassing it was to ask for sprinkles? Sheesh, he was a grown man.

"This isn't for me," he had told the pretty barista. She'd just rolled her eyes.

He walked up to Sandra and put the drink on her desk. What with her nose in her phone, she didn't see him.

"Psst, Sandra, I have a favor to ask," Bertie said as he leaned in. She didn't reply.

andra, psst. I have a favor to—"

"A favor!" Sandra said at the top of her voice. "You want .—ooooh, is that for me?"

"Yeah, extra sprinkles," Bertie said. He looked through the glass partition into the back rooms. He didn't want Roderick to know what he was up to. "Could you keep your voice down?"

"Sure," Sandra said at the top of her lungs. She switched to a stage whisper, which wasn't much better. "Sure. What do you want, hon?"

"I need you to find some information for me," Bertie said. "Because you're really good with the Internet, apparently."

"Awwww, that's so sweet of you to say. Sure. What do you need?" She held her phone in the palms of her hand and looked up at Bertie with big eyes. The morning sun created a halo effect around her bleached blond head. The scene made Bertie think of a devout Catholic holding the host before partaking.

"Do you know that Dr. Om who came in yesterday?" Bertie asked.

"No."

"He came in the morning. Around the time Pookie-Pie came in?"

"No."

"He didn't have a pet?"

"No. Why don't you describe him to me? No, wait! I have a gift. Based on his name, I'll figure out what he looked like."

"That's okay," Bertie said, getting nervous. He wanted to get this over with. "You don't need to remember him."

"Okay, here goes," Sandra said. She closed her eyes and

put her hands, still clutching her phone, up to her chin. "Om is a name that denotes tranquility. Therefore, he is a tranquil man. In his seventies. He is slight. He wears tailored suits that fit impeccably. He speaks little, but when he does, one senses wisdom. He is short. He is thin. He is pale. He used to be blond. Now he has grey hair that makes him look distinguished." Sandra opened her eyes. "How'd I do?"

"Well, he's short."

Sandra screeched in joy. "I told you I have a gift!"

"But everything else you said was opposite."

"It's an imperfect science. Okay hon, what do you want to know about him?" Sandra poised her fingers above her phone.

"At this point, anything. He apparently studied with Dr. Canard, but I don't have a first name for him. It wasn't in his file. I don't know what kind of doctor he is."

"Okay, let's start with where Dr. Canard studied," Sandra said. She looked up at Bertie expectantly.

"It was Oxford for undergrad," Bertie said.

"Ooooh, Oxford. Based on the name, that must be in Buffalo, New York. 'Cause they got ox there," Sandra said as she typed.

"What . . . ?" Bertie didn't bother finishing the question. Any minute now, Dr. Roderick would jump out from hiding and bark at him.

"Okay, so I can't find any Om," she said. "But I might be able to find the photos of Dr. Canard's class. Let me see." Sandra put her phone down long enough to crack her fingers and then got back to work.

Fifteen minutes later, Sandra looked up with stars in her eyes. "I've got lots of photos for you to go through. Let me download them and send them to your e-mail."

"Lots of photos?" Bertie said. "What, I've got to look at tons of photos?"

"Not if you have facial recognition software," Sandra said as she plugged a cable from her phone to the computer. "Do you have facial recognition software?

"What! No, of course not," Bertie said. "What would I do with facial recognition software?"

"Save yourself a lot of time, that's what," Sandra said. She sighed. "God help you, you'll just have to do it the old-fashioned way." She hit the send button and put her face back in her phone. "There you go!"

"Thanks," Bertie said.

"You're very welcome." Sandra took a sip of her coffee drink. "Hey, this is pretty good, Dr. B," she said. "The sprinkles aren't quite the right color, but it tastes okay anyway."

Bertie sighed. At least he had his photos.

CHAPTER 4

BERTIE ALSO HAD his work cut out for him. In his spare time, over lunch, and under the light of his one bare half-basement light bulb, Bertie looked at photo after photo after photo. It had been over thirty years since they were taken. They were grainy in that 1980's kind of way. It was sort of like sitting with his parents watching reruns of Magnum P.I., only with less-good looking people.

By day three, he was losing hope. He stumbled into work on Friday looking at his phone. Bleary-eyed and wondering how Sandra managed to spend so much time ogling screens, he flipped to the next photo, and the next, and the next.

Wait . . . He stopped dead in his tracks. Go back. Go back. There. There. There!

Bertie held the phone up to his face to get a better look. It was a group photo. Standing in the front row with all the other short people was Dr. Om. He had that same crooked smile on his face and big, baby eyes.

"Move away, Dr. B!" Sandra screamed.

"What?" Bertie said. He felt dazed, as though he had

been transported back from the eighties, kind of like in the reruns of that show his parents watched, Quantum Leap.

His parents needed to broaden their horizons.

"Dr. B!" Sandra said. "You're blocking the door!"

"Uh . . ." Bertie moved to the side. "Sorry." A vet assistant with red hair passed through under his arm, which was still sticking out and holding onto the door frame.

"That's okay," the assistant said. She walked away quickly.

"Sheesh, Dr. B, what's up with you?" Sandra said as Bertie walked toward the counter, still in a daze. "Oooooh, I know what it is." Sandra looked at him knowingly.

"What?" Bertie said.

"I was as surprised as you are. Could you imagine? What was Dame Judi Dench thinking? Her nose was fine before."

"What are you talking about?"

"Weren't you looking at the big news of the day?"

"About Dame Judi Dench's nose? What do I care about her nose?"

"Then what it is, hon? You were off in another world there."

Bertie bent forward and lowered his voice. "I found Dr. Om."

"Who?" Sandra said. Could she say it any louder?

"Keep your voice down," Bertie said. "Dr. Om."

Sandra put on her stage whisper. "Who?"

"The guy you helped me find the other day?" Bertie said.

"Oooooooooooh, that guy. Hand it over, hand it over. Let me see."

Bertie passed her the phone while peeking into the back. Was Dr. Roderick prowling around yet, he wondered?

"Oh, that guy!" Sandra said at the top of her lungs. Then she put her finger to her mouth and whispered. "Oh, that guy."

"Yes, that's him, isn't it?"

"But his name isn't Om," Sandra said.

"What?" Bertie said.

"His name isn't Om. Look." She held the phone up and pointed to the names along the bottom. "He's at the front, right? 'Cause he's short. On the right, over there, you see his name?"

Bertie looked closer. She was right. His name wasn't Om.

It was Arthur "Artie" Manicewitz.

For the rest of the day, every time Bertie passed by Sandra's desk, she was puckering her lips and mumbling with great effort. Bertie didn't even bother to ask what she was up to. With Sandra, it was best not to know too much.

"You know, Dr. B?" Sandra said. "It sounds like the name of a Jewish butcher."

"What?" Bertie said. He immediately regretted asking.

"Manicewitz," she said. Despite her great effort, she still mangled the pronunciation. "Manicewitz, Manicewitz, Manicewitz."

See? This is why he hated dealing with Sandra.

"I suppose. I don't know." He tried not to sound annoyed.

"You not like Jews, Dr. B?" she said. Then she puckered her lips as she tried to say his name again.

"What? I don't have a problem with Jews," Bertie said. "Where do you come up with this stuff?"

Sandra looked at him disapprovingly. "It's not good to be prejudiced."

"I . . . I'm not prejudiced," Bertie said. "Listen, I've got work to do."

As Bertie walked way, he could hear her mumble, "And I thought you were Jewish."

That night, after calling his parents for the new Internet password, Bertie set his computer on the sill of the half-window and got to work.

Password: BertieYouDoNotVisitYourMotherE-nough_7*85.

Bertie sighed. It was time he signed up for his own Wi-Fi.

He typed "Arthur Manicewitz" into Google. A whole string of results littered the screen. Bertie decided to narrow things down. "Doctor Arthur Manicewitz."

The list was still pretty long, but near the bottom of the page, there was a C.V. He clicked it open.

Bertie noticed that Dr. Om's stint at Oxford lasted only a year. He finished his undergraduate degree at a university on some Caribbean island named St. Quiche. He then worked on a doctorate for the next fifteen years in Ghana.

The doctorate was in genetics.

What was the guy doing running a park?

He clicked around, hoping to see some published work. There was no way to get a doctorate without. But, for some reason, Bertie couldn't access any of his journal articles.

Maybe Sandra could handle that. But dealing with her probably wasn't worth the headache.

Aside from that, there wasn't much information on the

guy. Apparently, he was a low-level scientist who hadn't accomplished much with his life. That thought made Bertie uncomfortable, but he couldn't put his finger on why.

Then it hit him. That described him to a T as well.

If anyone Googled Bertie, they'd think the same thing: a low-level scientist who hadn't accomplished anything with his life.

Not that anyone would Google Bertie.

The Internet had slowed back down to a crawl, thanks to his parents' reruns. He couldn't remember which one they'd be watching. It was hard to keep track.

Time to go to bed.

After a night of sleep, Bertie made a decision. It kind of went something like this.

One the one hand, he hated his job. The pay from the park gig wouldn't just be enough to do away with his vet school debt in three months. It would also be enough to supply his empty retirement account. He could work at that zoo or park or whatever it was for a year or so and then quit and open up his own clinic. Or retire and sulk in the Caribbean. Or whatever.

The pay from Dr. Om would be enough to get him away from Dr. Roderick and his tablets and his time monitors and his booming voice calling him "B!" even though he hated that nickname. It would be enough for him to get away from the clinic that he used to love. It would be enough to get him away from the constant reminder of his mistake to not buy the clinic from Dr. Canard. Pack up and move away from regret for beaucoup cash.

So why wasn't he rushing to the address on that card and screaming, "Sign me up!"

Because, on the other hand, something about Dr. Om was really disturbing, and it wasn't just his stupid fake name. Why bother hooking your wagon to some weirdo who was a two-bit scientist to boot? What was the point if all he did was go from the fry pan into the fire? Maybe it was better to wait on something better.

He tossed Dr. Om's card in the wastebasket. The pile of bills next to the trash toppled over. He kicked them under the counter. It was time to head out to work.

As Fiona said, rot where you're planted.

Or something like that.

CHAPTER 5

BERTIE GOT TO WORK EARLY. The cold smell of anti-septic made his stomach turn.

That was a really bad sign for a vet, right?

The waiting room was busier than usual. Sandra had to scream extra loud at Bertie so he could hear her.

"Dr. B! Dr. R said, and I quote, 'Get your keister into my office!'" She carefully read the message on a Post-It note and cracked her gum.

Bertie wondered what was up. Sandra's desk was peppered with Post-It notes. Was Dr. Roderick meeting with everyone?

Bertie sighed and headed to his boss' office. He knocked on the door. "Good morn—"

"We brought in an efficiency expert." Dr. Roderick didn't even turn his head from his computer screen. "Guy said we should make this place 24/7. You're on the night shift, from ten at night to six in the morning. Go home. Come back at ten."

'What?" Bertie said.

"You heard me. Go home. Or go wherever. Come back at ten. NEXT!"

Bertie took a few steps back in shock. He bumped into a nervous vet assistant, the one with red hair. She grabbed his arm and said, "What is this meeting about, Bertie?"

Bertie felt bad. This was the only person who bothered to call Bertie by his right name, and he didn't know hers. Then again, she was new.

Or then again, maybe not. He wasn't sure.

"Efficiency expert told Roderick to change this to a 24/7 vet. I'm on the night shift now."

Dr. Roderick screamed from his office, "Next! You! Ginger head! Get in here!" Dr. Roderick paused, then waved her away. "No, don't bother. Go home. You're on the night shift."

"Excuse me?" the vet assistant said.

"Next!" Dr. Roderick screamed, even though no one else was waiting to go in.

The vet assistant put her hand to her head. Bertie felt bad for her, whatever her name was.

He put his hand up to pat her shoulder, but then thought better of it. "It'll be okay," he said, although he didn't really believe it himself.

It looked like she had some waterworks starting. Bertie took a step back.

"I'd better get going," she said and shuffled out.

Bertie thought back to Dr. Om's card sitting in his waste basket. He had a free day ahead of him. Maybe he'd do more research.

◆ ◆ ◆

Okay, so more news. Back when Dr. Om was still plain old Artie, he had served a stint in a mental hospital.

How did Bertie find that out? Well, unfortunately, it had required a call to Sandra.

"Hi, Sandra?"

"Who is it?"

"It's Bertie."

"Who?"

"Bertie." Bertie closed his eyes and squeezed the bridge of his nose. "B."

"Dr. B! What's up? Oops, sorry. Give me a sec." Sandra's voice pulled away. "No, Mrs. Hookum, Pookie-Pie shouldn't be making wee-wee in the new garden."

"New garden?" Bertie said.

"Yes, hon. Dr. R is putting in a new garden. The dogs really like it."

"I bet," Bertie said.

Great. Evil boss, check.

Night shift, check.

Huge communal doggie training pad, check.

"I kind of need your help again," Bertie said.

"What can I do for you, hon?"

"I'm trying to find more information on that Dr. Om guy. Do you remember him?"

"Who? Are you moonlighting as a private detective?"

"No, Sandra. I'm not," Bertie said.

"'Cause my cousin needs one."

"I'm not a private detective. But I do need to find some more information on Dr. Om, and the Internet doesn't seem to have a lot."

"Oh, that's easy. Use the dark web."

"The what?"

"The dark web." She cracked her gum.

"How do I do that?" Bertie was regretting this call.

"You see, you got all these servers out there that aren't supposed to be on the Internet. Loads and loads of them. But some people don't protect them too good." She lowered her voice. "You can sneak in through the cracks."

"What buttons do you push to get there?" Bertie said.

Sandra explained, but made Bertie repeat "Step on a crack, break your mother's back," three times. She found it hilarious.

Bertie wasn't sure why.

"Are we all good, Dr. B?"

"Sure, thanks." Bertie was about to put the phone down. Then he paused. "Sandra?"

"Step on a crack! Break your mother's back!" She laughed.

"How do you know this stuff?"

"Masters in computer science. Oops, Pookie-Pie is making more wee-wee. Gotta go."

Bertie put the phone down. Sandra had a Masters in computer science? Sandra had a Masters in anything?

It was like that episode where what's his name stepped through a mirror and everything was sort of the same on the other side, but everything was different too.

Sandra had a Masters in computer science. Talk about freaking sci-fi.

So that's how Bertie was able to sniff out Dr. Om's connection with a mental institution. "Connection," because it wasn't exactly clear whether he was a patient. His file was closed. But what would a geneticist be doing working in a loony bin? He must have been a patient.

Right? 'Cause mental hospitals don't hire geneticists.

Right?

Bertie threw the card back in the trash bin. Garbage

pick-up was tomorrow, but he didn't take the garbage to the curb just yet.

He was feeling lazy. That was all.

Pro: Dr. Roderick wasn't at the clinic during the night shift.

Con: night shift. Isn't that enough?

Bertie walked into the hushed waiting room that night. Sure enough, there was a half-done garden sitting in the middle of the waiting room. A faint scent of pee and air freshener permeated the room already. He walked up to the counter. The red-headed vet assistant was standing at a large sign that said, "New policy: sign in when you arrive and sign out when you leave." In smaller letters underneath, it said, "Forget to sign in and out, FORGET about getting PAID."

Bertie looked over her shoulder as she signed in. At least he'd know her name now. That'd be less awkward.

It was Helsinth. Helsinth Beauregard.

Helsinth? What kind of name was Helsinth? Maybe she had really messy handwriting? And he was reading it wrong?

'Cause, Helsinth?

"I'm surprised he doesn't have us sign in on stupid tablets," Helsinth (Helsinth?) said.

"Yeah," Bertie agreed. There was a pause while he signed in. "So, uh, are you okay? You seemed upset before . . . Helsinth?"

"Oh, call me Hessy, please. What kind of name is Helsinth?"

Bertie laughed. "Right—I mean, no, it's . . . it's a unique name."

"It's the name you give to a Nordic horse," she said.

"Really?"

"Heck, I don't know," Hessy said. "It's just what it sounds like to me."

They made their way to the back. There were no patients yet, and since Dr. Roderick wasn't there to corral them to the exam rooms, they stayed in the common area. A couple of vet techs leaned against the tables, poking at their phones and looking miserable.

The vet tech that Bertie remembered as Marvin put his phone down. "This sucks. I was supposed to go to the movies."

"Yeah," Hessy said. "I'm supposed to take care of my mother at night."

"Whoa. Yeah, dude. You win," Marvin said. "But doesn't your aunt help out?"

"She helps out during the day, but she's getting old herself," Hessy said.

"Who's with your mother now?" Bertie said.

"Nobody." Hessy looked down at her feet as though she felt really guilty. "I'm going to have to hire someone to watch her at night. With what money, I don't know."

"Well, you know what I heard?" The other vet tech came over. "Sandra told me in the ladies'. Pay will be based on how many patients come in."

"Oh, no," said Hessy.

Bertie took another look out the door. Still no clients.

"Does Dr. Roderick know you take care of your mother?" Bertie said.

"I told him, but he probably forgot," she said. "You saw how he didn't even know my name."

Bertie felt kind of bad, on account of him not knowing her name and all. But then again, he wasn't her boss.

"So, what do we do?" Marvin said. "Go out on the streets and drag in roadkill?"

"What?" the other vet tech said.

"You know, recruit patients," Marvin said.

"Any roadkill you know that pack Visa?" the other vet tech said.

"Hessy, why don't you talk to Dr. Roderick about your situation?" Bertie said.

"I don't know if I should," she said. "I'm pretty low on the totem pole. I can't afford to lose this job."

"He wouldn't fire you, would he?" Marvin said. "Hessy, you should say something."

"It's easy for you to say that, you know," Hessy looked down at her feet again. "You all could find another job easily enough. You have degrees. I didn't even finish college."

"Awww, sweetie," the other vet tech said. She gave Hessy a hug. "Don't think that way."

Marvin looked at Bertie as though to say, "Hey, Mr. Full-Blown Associate Vet, why don't you talk to Dr. Roderick?"

Or maybe it was Bertie's guilty conscience speaking. Since he was, after all, kind of senior here.

"Yeah, maybe I can have a chat with him," Bertie said.

"Good move, man!" Marvin said. "Although technically, Dr. R doesn't chat, he barks."

Bertie straightened his back to look more confident. "I'll try to . . . make him listen. Somehow. Or whatever. You know."

CHAPTER 6

A GRAND TOTAL of one person came in that first night shift. She wanted directions for the all-night pizzeria she was sure was in town. Marvin did his best to sell her dog food, but she left empty-handed anyway.

"At least we know there's an all-night pizzeria nearby," Hessy said.

"But we don't know where it is," Bertie said.

It was six in the morning when the others left. As Hessy went out the door, she turned and said to Bertie, "You don't need to say anything. It'll work out. It always does."

"Yeah, I know. But it's not right. I'm going to say something. Or die trying," Bertie said. He put his arms out in a gesture that he hoped would look humorously heroic, but he realized he just looked like he was stretching from fatigue. He put his arms back down.

"Thanks, Bertie. I appreciate it. Oh, good morning Dr. Roderick."

"Morning," he said as he let the door slam behind him, right in Hessy's face. There was a sign in his arms. He made his way to the back.

Bertie watched Hessy run to catch her bus, then followed his boss. "Uh, Dr. Roderick?" Bertie said.

"What? Aren't you supposed to be heading out? I'm not paying you for staying extra time." Dr. Roderick went fishing for something in the supplies drawer. He lost patience. "Get me some tape, will you, B?"

Bertie found the tape and handed it over. Dr. Roderick taped the sign up in the common area. It read: "New policy: pay based on number of clients seen. Get cracking, people!"

Bertie stared. Could he do this?

"Dr. Roderick, about the sign—"

"You don't like it, find another job."

Bertie followed Dr. Roderick to his office. He wanted to back down, but he had promised Hessy he would say something. The poor girl needed a hand.

"Dr. Roderick, you know the vet assistant? Helsinth? Beauregard? She's been moved to the night shift?"

"You got thirty more seconds, B."

"She needs to be home to take care of her mother, and with the new pay policy, she's going to be in a tight squeeze. The night shift doesn't seem to be very busy—"

"Did you do anything to bring in clients?"

"What, like go whack dogs on their nightly walks?"

Dr. Roderick stood up and stared up at Bertie. For such a short guy, he looked scary.

"No, I don't suggest assaulting dogs, B. What I do suggest is that you get used to how things are here. I am not Dr. Canard."

"I get that, but—"

"You know what? Since you don't seem to like it here, let me do you a favor. You're suspended. For a week. Without pay." Dr. Roderick sat down and pulled out a sheath of forms. "Now you'll have more time to find that perfect job you're always mooning after."

Mooning after? Well, technically, yes, he kind of did want a better job, but he certainly didn't talk about it at work. I mean, not out loud. Maybe just under his breath. But just once or twice.

If Bertie were to be perfectly honest, he'd admit he didn't mind the suspension all that much. You know those lists with the top ten reasons that make you realize it's time to quit your job? "I got suspended! Crack open the bubbly!" would make it somewhere near the top.

"Okay, but can you move Helsinth to the day shift at least?"

"Nope." He had finished filling out Bertie's suspension form and handed it to him for his signature. To Bertie's horror, he started filling out another one. With Helsinth's name.

"You four are a team," Dr. Roderick said. "You get suspended, all of you get suspended."

"Dr. Roderick—"

"You're going to be really popular now." Dr. Roderick started to fill out the form for the vet tech. Bertie noticed her name was Sarah.

"Look, you can fire me. But don't suspend the rest of them."

"Too late. Paperwork's done." Dr. Roderick stood up. "Now get out."

Bertie stared for a moment in disbelief, then he walked back out to the waiting area. Sandra had arrived. She was sipping her ridiculous drink with sprinkles.

"Oh, hi Dr. B. You're here early," she said.

"I'm on my way out."

"Oh, okay," Sandra said. "By the way, Dr. B, I still can't find the name of the patron saint of fleas. What is it?"

He looked back at her. He had a sudden slow-motion vision of him making a beeline for Sandra's macchiato and dumping it all over Dr. Roderick's head. He imagined his boss screaming in pain as red welts, speckled with chocolate sprinkles and whipped cream, formed all over his tortured face and smutted up his glasses.

"Visions of third-degree burns inflicted by sugary coffee drink on boss" would probably come in spot three on the top ten ways you know it's time to leave your job.

Bertie was about to climb the stairs down to his half-basement when his landlady intercepted him. "Bertie, dear, are you all right?"

"Well, you know," he said.

"You seem upset. What's the matter?" She took his wrist and pulled him with her to the kitchen. She was surprisingly strong.

Bertie had to admit, he wouldn't say no to some hot chocolate, and if she offered Cognac, well, he might find himself in the mood.

"I was suspended from work," Bertie said.

"What? Why?" Fiona said.

"Well, it's a long story," Bertie shrugged. He sat down at the kitchen table.

"Coming from you, that means it's a grand total of two sentences. Cough up while I make your cocoa."

Bertie gave her the rundown in three sentences, just to show her.

"That was very debonair of you, Bertie. Here, you

deserve some Cognac in your hot chocolate. And Bertie dear, don't worry about this month's rent."

Bertie tried to protest, but Fiona put up her twiggy hand.

"No, I insist. Think of it as an early birthday present."

"But my birthday isn't for seven months."

"Think of it as a really late birthday present."

"That's, uh, really nice of you." Bertie stood up to leave because his landlady looked like she was getting weepy.

"Your parents will be so proud of you, Bertie dear," she screamed at him as he headed down the stairs. "So debonair!"

"Thanks, Fiona," Bertie said. He felt like a lout for having left so quickly. He trotted back up. "I really do appreciate it. Really."

He spent the next few minutes sitting on his bed staring at the latest angry letter from the bank. They were threatening to report him to credit agencies.

So, things could get worse.

A police siren jolted him from his thoughts.

It was his phone. Police siren was his parents' ring tone.

"Bertie dear." It was his mother.

"Yes, ma?"

"What you did today was really sweet."

"Thanks, ma."

Her tone suddenly turned shrilly. "But you can't go accepting free rent from Fiona!"

"Ma, I didn't ask—"

"You know she's broke, and every time she gives you a free month, you know who pays?"

"The piper?"

"Bertiiiiiieeeeeeeeee."

"Sorry, ma."

"Your father and I pay. Because I feel so bad for her. Only your father doesn't know about it. Do you know how much he thinks is in our cruise jar?"

"I don't know."

"And do you know how much is really in our cruise jar?"

"Not a lot."

"That's right, Bertie. Not a lot. And now 'not a lot' is even less, because poor Fiona can't afford to go without your rent. Don't make me make you come home again."

"Ma, no, I'm not coming back home."

"Get a job where you don't sabotage yourself! Oh, and that was a really sweet thing you did for that girl." His mother hung up.

Bertie put his head in his hands. Then he took a swig of his cocoa.

He could get used to that Cognac way too easily.

Bertie woke up sure of one thing. Well, two things, but both were related, so sort of one thing. Or 1.5 things. Or whatever. The math didn't matter.

1A: He would check out that job with Dr. Om. He didn't have to take it. Just check it out.

1B: He would invite Hessy to go with him. She needed the money, and she was in a mess because of him. Maybe Dr. Om would hire them both.

He jumped out of bed. Surprised at the Cognac-induced spring in his step, he was ready to face the day.

But first he had to find Dr. Om's card. Kneeling at the shrine of his discarded student bills, he picked through till he found the wrinkled card. He stuck it in his shirt pocket and headed out the door.

But then it struck him. How the heck was he going to contact Hessy?

There was one person who would know.

At this rate, he was going to become best friends with Sandra.

So, yeah. It was official. Things could definitely get much worse.

Up on the sidewalk, Bertie pulled out his phone and dialed the clinic. The one thing he didn't need to worry about was Dr. Roderick answering the phone. He never stooped so low as to work reception.

The phone at the clinic rang. "Dr. Roderick here at Dr. Roderick's Fast-Turnaround Veterinary Medical Centre, Grooming Emporium, and Luxury Boarding Suites."

Bertie stared at his phone. "Crap, crap, crap," he said under his breath.

"Anyone there already?"

Bertie took a deep breath and put the phone back to his ear. He squeezed his eyes shut, like he used to before his mother would pull off bandages from his knee. Making his voice as falsetto as he could, he said, "May I speak with Sandra?"

"Who?" Dr. Roderick barked.

"Sandraaaaa? The receptionist?" He waved at Mrs. Hillbiddy, who was walking past with her mutt. She looked at him funny. "The one with her phone biologically attached to her face?"

"Oh, that one. She went out for lunch."

Bertie cursed Sandra and her early lunches. "Where'd she go?" Bertie's voice cracked.

"Why do you want to know? Who are you?"

Bertie put his fist to his forehead, willing himself to think of a decent answer. "I'm her mother. I want to visit her . . . before . . . I die."

Bertie smacked his head and mouthed the words "Loser, loser LOSER!" A passerby crossed the street.

There was a pause on the other end of the line. Finally, Dr. Roderick said, "At the crap diner across the street from the clinic. Know where that is?"

"Oh, do you mean the clinic that the wonderful Dr. Canard used to run? It will never be the same since he died." Then he hung up.

"So there, Dr. R," Bertie said as he headed back to his half-basement. "Even Sandra's mother can't stand you."

It was a dumb disguise. Bertie knew it. But the last thing he wanted was for Dr. Roderick to recognize him, and his mother's pink cap with kittens on the front was as close to a disguise as he could get.

So, he'd just have to be man enough to wear pink.

He pulled the cap low over his eyes when he parked at the diner and looked inside to find Sandra. Sure enough, she was still there, by the window. It was a cold day and his breath came out in clouds. He scooted into the diner as fast as he could.

Then Bertie realized scooting wasn't all that manly and aimed for swagger. But he was never very good at swaggering.

He figured just plain old walking would be best.

He heard Sandra before he spotted her. She was staring at her phone laughing hysterically. He slipped into the chair in front of her.

"Sandra," Bertie said.

She didn't hear him. She laughed some more. It came out like a hoot.

"Sandra." Bertie looked at the clinic as though Dr. Roderick were spying out the front window. He knew it was stupid to obsess about that. Dr. Roderick wasn't going to be staring out the window. He was going to be inside lurking around the other associate vets and making them rue the day they applied to vet school. Or communing with the devil.

Or both.

"Sandra!" Bertie said her name loud enough that the other diners looked over disapprovingly.

She screeched and dropped her phone on her sandwich. "Who are you?"

"I'm Bertie." He rolled his eyes. "Who do you think I am?"

"Oh!" Sandra retrieved her phone and put it to her chest, as though she were recovering from a heart attack. "I didn't recognize you in that disguise."

"I'm not wearing a disguise." Bertie felt silly since, well, he was actually wearing a disguise. And it was the worst disguise that should have fooled no one. He pulled off his hat and stuck it under his thigh.

"What do you want? Your job back?" She laughed. And laughed. And laughed some more. Then her phone went, "bleep!" and she shoved her nose into it again.

"Sandra," Bertie said. "Sandra, pay attention!" He grabbed the phone.

"What? Oh, you're still here. What do you want?"

"I need Hessy's phone number," Bertie said in a whisper. He didn't know why he whispered. It wasn't like Dr. Roderick could hear him from all the way over at the clinic. And even if he could, what business was it of his if he wanted someone's phone number? He straightened his back and said it more loudly. "Would you happen to have Hessy's phone number?"

"Who?"

"The vet assistant?"

"No clue."

"With red hair?"

Sandra looked blank.

"Green eyes?"

Still no light bulb.

"Helsinth? She works the night shift now."

Sandra cocked her head to the side.

"She got suspended with me?"

"Ooooh, H! Of course. I know who H is." Sandra said. Go figure she would identify someone based on the latest gossip. Bertie should have led with that. "Why didn't you just say her name?" Sandra's fingers ran over the screen of her phone. For the first time, Bertie noticed Sandra had long, delicate fingers. She could have been a pianist. Or a surgeon. But only if the patients had phones anatomically stuck to their bodies would she have been willing to do the job.

"It's so cute, you getting up the nerve," Sandra said.

"Nerve? What?"

"To ask her out on a date."

"What?"

"What, you deaf?" She raised her voice so everyone could hear her. "I said 'It's so cute, you getting up the nerve. TO ASK HER ON A DATE!'"

Everyone stared. Bertie sank in his chair. "I'm not asking her on a date. It's about—Forget it. It doesn't matter."

"Aw, she'll be so disappointed." Sandra was still speaking at top volume. "She's got such a crush on you." The ladies at the next table over scooched closer. Their eyes got bigger.

"What?"

"I said, 'SHE'S GOT SUCH A—' Oooh, here's her number."

Bertie jotted down the number as fast as he could. He could hear the ladies at the next table whispering, "Young men these days." He really wanted to get the heck out of there.

"Thanks, Sandra." He put his cap back on. Then he thought better of it and took it off.

When Bertie got back to his car, he stared at the scribbled number. Maybe it was a bad idea to call. She probably blamed him for getting her suspended. Taking her to some job interview with a guy who had spent time in a loony bin could end up being a really bad move.

But then a face materialized in the window of the clinic. It was Dr. Roderick. He looked straight at Bertie.

Bertie was sure of it.

He put his cap back on and slammed on the accelerator.

Bertie had been pacing in front of his apartment for half an hour, fingers to phone. What finally made him dial was the realization that Sandra was going to blab to everyone about how Bertie was sniffing around for Hessy's number. If he didn't call, Hessy would find out anyway. And who knows what kind of idea she'd take away from

Sandra's gossip? It was best to take the bull by the horns himself.

He dialed Hessy's number. Her phone rang once, twice, a third time.

The point of no return.

Although, technically, just because it rang didn't mean he couldn't hang up. He always made calls and hung up after the phone's first few rings, like that one time when—

"Hello?" Hessy said.

Crap. Now was the point of no return. Or anyway, the point of no return if he didn't want to be rude, because there was that time he had hung up on a person—

"Hello?" Hessy was sounding impatient.

"Hessy?"

"Bertie?"

"It's me, Bertie." Duh.

"Yes?" she said.

"I'm calling . . . uh . . . because . . . I'm sorry I got you suspended. I feel really bad about that."

"That's okay. It's not your fault. You were trying to help."

"Yeah, fat lot of good that did," Bertie said. "Anyway, I'm calling about . . . a job."

"A job?"

"Yes, a job."

"A job?"

Darn. What was he going to tell her? He rehearsed the explanation in his head to see how bad it sounded. It went something like this: Well, this whack job Dr. Om (that's a fake name, by the way) came to work recently and offered me a job at a park, but he didn't say what kind of park, and it turns out he's a loony toon. I did my research. But I'm so freaking desperate, and I feel so guilty that you lost a week of work because of me that I figure I'll go on that interview he offered me and invite you to come with me in case there's a job for you! But don't get too close. It might involve machetes.

Actually, that sounded kind of accurate. He went with that after all.

Only he replaced "loony tune" and "whack job" with "eccentric." And he didn't mention anything about machetes.

CHAPTER 7

THE NEXT DAY, Bertie and Hessy arrived at the address on Dr. Om's card.

"So," Bertie said, "you regretting jumping into the deep end like this?" He didn't want to admit it, but he was stalling.

"No, what's the worst that can happen?"

Bertie scratched his head and looked up at the soot-stained brick building. He didn't want to answer that question honestly. It involved machetes and deranged clowns.

"It doesn't look like a park, but this is the address." He blew into his hands to keep warm.

"Well, let's head in and see what they tell us."

Bertie figured that was as good a plan as any. He pulled on the squeaky glass door. A bored guard sitting in the foyer sent them up to the twelfth floor.

Dr. Om's suite was at the end of a dingy hallway. Bertie looked at Hessy. He felt stupid bringing her to this dump, but she still didn't seem fazed. He opened the door.

The sudden change in light made Bertie squint his eyes. The room was painted white. Huge windows let in what little sun there was. Bright metal tables ran up and down the room. Scientists in crisp, white coats looked into microscopes, stood at centrifuges, and entered data at slim computer monitors. A big, clear screen stood at one end. On it, numbers scrolled in fast succession.

"Didn't expect anything this state of the art," Hessy said.

"No kidding."

No one seemed to have noticed them. He guessed they were too engrossed in their work. He couldn't remember what that was like anymore.

"Um, excuse me?" Bertie said to a scientist at a computer monitor near the door. He was Dr. Brittle, according to his name tag. Dr. Brittle didn't reply.

"Um, Dr. Brittle?" Bertie said again.

Hessy walked right up to the employee. "Yoohoo, Dr. Brittle?"

Dr. Brittle started. His eyes widened when he saw Hessy. "How can I help you?"

"We're looking for Dr. Om," Hessy said.

"Right through there," Dr. Brittle said. He pointed to the back of the room, where a shiny metal door said, "Dr. Om."

"Thanks," Bertie said, but the scientist didn't even look at him.

They walked past a row of tables with test tubes. Bertie hesitated in front of Dr. Om's door. Hessy looked at Bertie, then knocked.

"Come in, come in!" an echoey voice said.

Bertie opened the door for Hessy. The room stood in stark contrast to the lab. Stained, beige walls were bare except for a large poster of what looked like a genome sequence. A shabby desk with a wooden chair and an old boxy computer completed the furnishings. Dr. Om was zipping up a travel bag.

"Don't stand on ceremony. Come in, come in." Dr. Om waved them into the room.

Bertie looked at the bag. "We can come back when you get back from your trip, if you need."

"Come back? Come back?" Dr. Om looked at him with shocked eyes. "You two are coming with me."

"We are?" Bertie said.

"Of course. Don't you want to see the park?"

"Well, yes, but how did you know I—we were coming?" Bertie said.

Dr. Om pointed at his computer as though the answer were obvious. "I saw you on my surveillance system."

"Surveillance system?" Hessy said. She looked from Dr. Om to Bertie with big eyes. Bertie was feeling really guilty for dragging her into this.

Another crap move on his part. He could kick himself.

"Yes, yes, surveillance system," Dr. Om said. He gestured them over. "Come, have a look, have a look, Dr. Vole and Miss Beauregard. Right over here."

"How do you know my name?" Hessy said. She looked at Bertie, then back at Dr. Om, then back at Bertie again. "Did Bertie tell you?"

Dr. Om giggled. "No, no, no, no. My surveillance system did." He giggled again. "Come, take a look."

Dr. Om pulled them over by the elbows. He chatted excitedly, as though he were showing them his latest toy. "Let me show you. Let me show you." He pressed a button that rewound the footage till Bertie and Hessy came into view. "Let ... me ... show ... you."

Bertie looked at the image of him and Hessy at the front door. Did he really slouch that much? He pushed his shoulders out, but it hurt his back. Dr. Om smiled at him, as though reading his mind. Gosh, this guy was creepy.

"Now, look, look!" Dr. Om said.

Lines and circles appeared on the screen, like the facial recognition software you see on TV. The system made high-tech beeping sounds, and Bertie and Hessy's names popped up above their heads.

"My system connects to your phones to identify you. And—" Dr. Om rubbed his hands together. "I can pick from a variety of sound effects. See?"

He rewound the footage again, and this time, the computer emitted a "bong!" Dr. Om giggled. Or cackled. It was hard to tell. He rewound the footage again. The names popped up to the twitter of birds. He rewound for a third time. Eerie laughter echoed through the room.

Dr. Om said, "That's the sound I use for my ex-wife. Which sound effect do you want for your name, Miss. Beauregard?"

"I like the birds," Hessy said.

"And you, Dr. Vole?"

"Is dead silence an option? And can I just not appear on your freakizoid monitor?"

"You're a disco guy. I can tell," Dr. Om said.

Disco? Disco!? Did Bertie come across as a Disco guy?

"Ooooh, disco," Hessy said. "Can I have disco too?"

Dr. Om smiled. "I'll give you ABBA."

"Ooooh, ABBA," Hessy said as she followed Dr. Om from the room.

Hessy was an ABBA fan? What was wrong with the world?

Bertie followed Hessy and Dr. Om down the hallway. "So, uh, Dr. Om," he said. "Hessy came along because I thought you'd have an opening for her too."

"That can be arranged. I'm always looking for good people. Always looking."

They stepped into the elevator, but instead of pressing the lobby button, Dr. Om pressed the button for the roof.

"Aren't we going to the park?" Bertie said.

Dr. Om looked up at him like he was dense. "Of course. Of course! Where do you think we're going?"

"It looks like we're going to the roof," Bertie said.

The doors opened, revealing a helicopter. Bertie's stomach sank.

"Yes, indeed. The roof," said Dr. Om. "And that will get us to the park."

"Can't we just go in a car?" Bertie asked.

Dr. Om smiled. "You're afraid of flying." It wasn't a question.

How the heck did he know? Probably the stupid monitor told him. To the tune of death metal.

Hessy didn't seem to be paying attention. Her eyes were bright. She screamed above the roar of the blades as she climbed up into the bird. "I've never been in a helicopter before."

"If you take this job, you can go in the helicopter all the time," Dr. Om said.

"I mean, if you'll have me," she said. "I know I came here without notice, and I don't have that many credentials." She put her face to the window as the helicopter rose in the air. Bertie had a feeling she didn't care whether she got the job. She was just happy to be having some fun now.

He envied her that.

"Not a problem, not a problem," Dr. Om said. "We need extra hands for general animal care." He turned to Bertie. "And no need for concern. Vets don't need to fly too often. Apparently, Miss Beauregard will be happy if you delegate that task to her."

But Bertie was worried anyway. He looked out the window while staying as far away from the sucking fall of death below. There was nothing that looked like it would be a park. The skyscrapers gave way to the factory district, which gave way to an airport.

"Where's this park?" Bertie asked.

"Oh, not for miles and miles. Or kilometers and kilometers, if you roll that way," Dr. Om said. "The metric system is objectively the better of the two. Far superior."

"Yes, but that doesn't answer the question. Where are we going?" Bertie said.

"You'll see soon enough." Dr. Om rubbed his hands together in glee.

The helicopter suddenly banked left, which left Bertie's poor stomach banking right. They were getting ready to land at the airport.

Hessy kept her face glued to the glass while Bertie squeezed his eyes shut for the final approach. Once they touched ground, Hessy jumped out first. Bertie clung to the side of the door and then almost lost his balance on the way down.

Looking good, Bertie, he thought. Looking good.

A Jeep was waiting for them. Bertie found that weird. Who the heck goes from a helicopter to a terminal in a Jeep? But instead of driving across the tarmac, the Jeep turned into a tree-lined access road that looped around the main terminal and ended at a single, long runway. There were several planes lined up. They all seemed to be private.

Great. More air travel.

The Jeep braked in front of a 747. Dr. Om got out and

spread his arms wide. "Welcome to my humble private jet." He giggled.

"What, you got your zoo in there?" Bertie said. Hessy slapped his arm.

"Ha ha ha! Dr. Vole, you know how I feel about zoos. And no, we have not gotten to the park yet." He waved his hands at them to follow. "And don't worry—no worries!—if you don't have your passports with you."

"I don't own a passport." Hessy furrowed her brow. "And I have to get home to my mother. She's sick."

"Don't worry, don't worry. With what I'll be paying you, you can hire anyone—anyone!—to care for her. As for the passport, you get a pass from me." Dr. Om said. An employee at the gangway to the plane handed Dr. Om a thick sheaf of paper.

"What, you own the country where we're going or something?" Bertie said.

The only sound was the wind as Dr. Om signed the pages. Finally, he looked up and giggled. "I do now."

CHAPTER 8

THE PLANE RIDE was uneventful for Bertie, if by uneventful you mean clutching the barf bag the whole flight and wondering when it became the norm to need luggage for a job interview.

And a toothbrush. And toothpaste. And a SWAT team to swoop in and extract your sorry behind. Bertie didn't bring any of that, and now they—he and Hessy—were on a plane to a park that featured who knows what located in a country that was who knows where? Some crazy loon of a scientist owned it to boot. So that crazy kook could do anything he wanted, right? Anything?

And the worst thing was that Bertie had gotten Hessy into this mess. Poor innocent Hessy who didn't even seem to see the danger in all of this.

"Bertie, you're looking a little green," she said. She had finally peeled her face from the window long enough to notice. "You okay?"

"Not really," Bertie said. "Not a big fan of flying."

"I kind of noticed."

Despite the air conditioning, Bertie's sweaty palms left a damp imprint on the barf bag. Dr. Om's face, with its crooked smile, looked up at him from it. Who put their face on a barf bag? He read the text underneath the double chin: Genetica Fantasía, Ltd.

Bertie wondered what he'd find if he Googled the company name. If it was anything like his previous searches on the guy, probably not much.

He looked up when Dr. Om excused himself. "I'm off to speak to the pilot. I'll be right back." He turned to Bertie. "Don't worry. Lunch will be soon." He giggled and walked to the front of the plane.

"Is he making fun of me?" Bertie said.

"It's hard to tell with him." Hessy said. She pulled the tray down and was looking intently at the back seat.

"What are you doing?" Bertie said.

"Checking for surveillance systems," she said.

"Are you making fun of me too?"

"Yes. And no. He's a strange one."

Bertie took a deep breath and held the barf bag closer. "You don't seem worried."

Hessy put the tray back up. "Well, I never had money to travel, so I might as well enjoy it while I can. And if I die, I'll worry about it then."

"It'll be too late to worry then."

"Point taken."

"Where the heck is he taking us?" Bertie asked.

"Who knows? He enjoys keeping people in the dark. Makes him feel important, I think."

Bertie looked at Hessy. She probably had a point. "I'm sorry. I figured this would just be an interview. I got you into this." The realization of the mess Bertie had created hit him. His pulse was racing, and he scrunched the barf bag between his fingers. "And now, he's practically . . . kidnapping us."

"That's an exaggeration. We could have left any time," Hessy said. "As long as we're here, let's just try to relax. We can always say no to the job if we don't like it."

"What if we can't?" Bertie said.

"What if we can't what?" Hessy looked at Bertie quizzically.

"What if we can't say no?"

"Lady and gentlemen," the voice of the pilot boomed through the cabin. "We will be arriving At Dr. Om International Airport of St. Quiche in ten minutes. Please fasten your seatbelts and put up your tray tables. The temperature is thirty degrees. That's Celsius, folks. And the weather is sunny."

St. Quiche. The name sounded familiar to Bertie, but he couldn't quite remember where he had heard it.

"Dr. Om International Airport?" Bertie said. "You have an airport named after you?"

Dr. Om laughed. "No, no, no, no, no. I don't wait for people to name structures after me. I go ahead and rename them myself. Why wait? Why wait?"

Bertie looked at Hessy and rolled his eyes. When they landed, he noticed the airport sign still said St. Quiche Airport. He whispered to Hessy, "Apparently, they didn't get the memo on the new name."

She put her finger to her mouth but smiled.

Bertie gazed around the tarmac, relieved they were

finally off the plane, although the humidity was suffocating as heck. He took off his jacket. It appeared they were in the Caribbean.

The Caribbean. Of course. This is where Dr. Om had gone to university. Whatever he was up to, he was doing it at his old watering hole.

The airport was small. They walked through a narrow door to the terminal. People's voices echoed uncomfortably in the too-tight space. They made their way through what appeared to be a sorry attempt at a V.I.P. hallway and came out by where baggage claim was. People streamed out with shopping bags attached to luggage carts. Bertie figured goods must be pricey here, if people traveled to other islands to shop. Other bigger islands, he imagined. So, St. Quiche was probably tiny.

Dr. Om flashed an I.D. and bypassed the line. He led Bertie and Hessy out to the sidewalk. Under the low over-hang, the humidity hit Bertie like a sack of wet sand. The area seemed to double as a drop-off and a pick-up for passengers. Old, clunky cars coughed up exhaust, making it all that much harder to breathe. Bertie wondered which car was waiting for them, but they kept walking. Bertie strug-gled to dodge passersby and their luggage, but no one else seemed to care about staying out of others' way. Hessy stopped and looked back at Bertie, waiting for him to catch up. He noticed she wasn't even breaking a sweat. Together, they struggled to keep up with Dr. Om, who, despite his short, stout legs, could really foot it. The crowd finally thinned, and Bertie saw a field up ahead.

"I think this is the Caribbean, isn't it?" Hessy said to Bertie.

"Yup," Bertie said, looking at the palm trees circling the

airport. He lowered his voice. "This is where Dr. Om went to school."

"You always wanted to come to the Caribbean," she said.

Bertie looked at her, surprised. He was about to ask how she knew when Dr. Om stopped. They had reached the field, and he turned in a circle as though looking for someone. "Where is Saint? He was supposed to be here. Here! Waiting for us!"

The roar of rotors exploded from above. "Oh, no, not another helicopter ride," Bertie said.

"Last one of the day, Dr. Vole. Last one!"

As the helicopter landed, Dr. Om ran out to it, signaling for the other two to follow.

"Where were you?" he hollered at the pilot above the roar of the blades. The pilot jumped down. Dr. Om had to crane his neck to look him in the eye. "You're late! Late!"

The pilot laughed. "My good man, I am here." He sounded like a local.

"You're late!" Dr. Om stamped his foot.

"Island time, my good man. Island time. Let me take your bag."

Dr. Om handed it to him before climbing up into the helicopter.

The pilot shook Bertie and Hessy's hands, smiling the whole time. "My name is John Castle. Please, call me Saint."

Bertie and Hessy followed Dr. Om into the helicopter as Saint swung into the front.

"Fasten your seat belts," Saint said with a laugh. "And let's see how well I know how to fly this thing."

"What?" Bertie said. "You're joking, right?" But no one else seemed to hear him.

As the bird rose up over the coast, Bertie tried to take in the view while leaning as far back into the cabin as possible. Dr. Om sat close to the open door, pointing to different elements and narrating what may have been a cohesive tour had the rotors not cut off half of it.

"We chose this," Dr. Om said, "because . . . the beaches . . . actuarially . . . revenue . . . combined . . . rainforest ecosystem and . . . probabilistic revenue returns . . ."

Bertie heard Hessy say something about the fauna. It sounded like a question. Dr. Om laughed. "Don't know much . . . but it's all mine! That's all I need to know! All mine!" He laughed. "All of it!"

Bertie stopped listening. They were headed towards the interior, where serrated mountains were covered in dark green. Palms stuck out their heads like beacons. Or warning rods, maybe.

They were saying, "Get the heck out of here, you loons."

Or, you know, something like that.

The rotors hit a pocket of air as the helicopter bumped in for landing in a round clearing surrounded by more palms. As they touched down, Bertie felt his stomach lurch one last time.

"Thanks for the, uh, tour," Hessy said to Dr. Om as he gestured for her to climb down from the helicopter. Saint was already at the door.

"Glad to give it, glad to give it," Dr. Om said. He rubbed his hands together. "Dr. Vole, when you're ready to stop clutching the seat for dear life, feel free to disembark as well."

Bertie felt silly as he pulled his hands, knuckles white, from the sides of his seat and limped out of the helicopter.

He saw two guards rush out of the forest and stand next to what looked like a sign covered by a blue tarp.

"Ah, wait here, you two. I'll be right back," Dr. Om said.

"You! Guards!" Dr. Om screamed as he headed in their direction. "Why weren't you guarding this entrance? Where were you? Top secret, top secret!"

Bertie turned to Saint. "Do you know what Dr. Om is doing here exactly?"

"What that crazy man is up to, I am not entirely sure, but it's big, big, big." he said, smiling. "You will see for yourselves soon enough."

"Did you know that Dr. Om bought the island?" Bertie asked.

"No, I didn't," he said. A disturbed look momentarily crossed his happy face. "Crazy man. Crazy man. But if the prime minister sold it to him, well, he is crazy too. One crazy man for another. Maybe it is all the same."

The three looked over at Dr. Om as he waved his arms in front of the guards. "If outsiders get in now. . . spoil the surprise . . . accidents!" Then as suddenly as he had started screaming, he stopped, turned around, and stretched his arms wide. "Dr. Vole, Miss Beauregard, come along! We have a park to see."

"That is my cue to leave," Saint said cheerfully. "Enjoy your time at Dr. Crazy Man Park." He shook their hands and climbed up into the helicopter.

Dr. Om prattled on as the helicopter rose. Bertie watched Dr. Om's mouth move to the deafening roar of the blades. He hoped he wasn't missing anything important.

The helicopter flew away. Dr. Om gestured impatiently to Bertie and Hessy. "Come along. Come along. As you'll notice, we will take the scenic route along the trail that goes around the whole park, three hundred and sixty degrees! That way, you get an authentic feel for the tropics."

As much as Bertie hated helicopters, he toyed with the idea of running after Saint and grabbing onto the bird's skids for dear life. But the opportunity passed. Instead, he followed Hessy away from the armed guards and felt the darkness of St. Quiche's rainforest swallow him up.

CHAPTER 9

THE CRUNCH of feet on loose stones overshadowed other sounds as they followed the trail in the forest. Bertie felt out of place: his interview shirt was sticky with sweat, and his feet were sore from his faux leather shoes, which slipped on patches of damp earth and wet leaves. Dr. Om, with his ill-fitting suit, looked just as much out of place but didn't seem to mind.

Hessy was the first to speak. "Dr. Om, if you don't mind my asking, how could you just buy an island?"

Dr. Om laughed. "Oh, you don't just buy an island. You have to bribe a lot of people first. Many, many people."

"Like what kind of people?" Bertie asked.

"That's for my lawyers to say. Because that's the other part of the equation. Expensive lawyers—very expensive. Unscrupulous enough to get the job done. Discreet enough that they don't tell you the half of it." He laughed and pointed to a tree. "Oh, that looks like an animal there, Miss Beauregard. You were asking about animals a while ago."

Bertie looked up. Whatever it was, was gone now.

"But why did you buy the island?" Hessy said. "It seems a little extreme."

"There were things I wanted to do, and St. Quiche's powers that be didn't let me. They got in the way!" Dr. Om turned around and walked backwards. "I woke up one morning, and I said, let me use the hypothetical method-ology to decide my next step."

"The hypo what?" Bertie said. As they got deeper into the rainforest, the mosquitoes got more and more vicious. He swatted them from his face.

To Bertie, Dr. Om sounded like one of those annoying motivational speakers who get up on stage and talk about how they got rich, so can you!

"Glad you asked. Glad you asked," Dr. Om said. "It goes like this. You ask yourself, 'Dr. Vole, if I had or did X, what Y would happen?' Or whatever variables you choose. Any variable will work. Any. In my case, I said to myself, I said, 'Dr. Om, if you owned this island, what would you do?" He stopped walking for effect, and Bertie bumped into Hessy. "What would you do if, hypothetically, you owned this whole, entire island?' And I thought to myself, 'I would do whatever I wanted!' I liked the sound of that, so I bought the island."

Dr. Om turned back around and started walking again. Hessy looked at Bertie and raised her eyebrow. "Do you expect this park to boost the island's economy?" she said.

Dr. Om stopped dead in his tracks and looked at Hessy as though she had grown horns. Then he waved his hands in the air for emphasis. "Certainly, certainly, certainly. That too. Of course, none of the natives will be able to afford the entrance fee. But once their economy booms, they'll be elated I am here. Elated! To prove my point . . ." Dr. Om yelled into his walkie-talkie. "Hey, you! Pilot man!"

A staticky voice that sounded like Saint's came through. "Yes, Dr. Om?" he said.

"Can you afford the tickets to my park?"

"I doubt it sir," Saint laughed. "I doubt it."

"And are you happy I am here?"

"I wouldn't say otherwise, Dr. Om. I wouldn't dare say otherwise."

Dr. Om turned back to Hessy. "See, they're already happy I'm here."

Bertie leaned over and said in Hessy's ear, "Some people are just pathologically happy."

She nodded.

Dr. Om turned again. "What are you waiting for? Let's keep moving. Daylight is a-wasting."

Bertie's back ached. His dress shirt stuck to his skin. The hem of his pants was caked with mud after a rain shower came down like his mother's spilled mop bucket. And still, they hadn't reached . . . whatever it was they were going to see.

Suddenly, Bertie heard an unexpected sound.

"Coquí!" The high-pitched call pierced his ears.

"Wait—" Bertie said.

"Coquí!"

"Dr. Om," Bertie said. "That sound. Is that a—?"

"Yes, yes, yes, yes. That's a coquí frog," Dr. Om said.

"Wait, they're not from here," Bertie said.

"Right you are! Right you are! It was a coup to bring them in. We had to bribe all sorts—all sorts!—of bureaucrats at the wildlife agency here. And then find a smuggler who was willing to bring them from Puerto Rico. Very expensive.

All very expensive, but they give the park a *je ne sais quoi* of authenticity. They need very specific conditions to survive, as you no doubt know, Dr. Vole."

"And they survive here?" Bertie said.

"Oh, no, no, no, no." Dr. Om wiped his forehead as though frustrated the coquí wouldn't cooperate with his vision of an authentic rainforest. "They die by the dozens every day. I have to ship a box in every week. It's very expensive. Very expensive."

"That's awful!" Hessy said.

"Yes, it does strain the budget," Dr. Om giggled. "But authenticity!"

Bertie wanted to kick this guy down the slippery path. "But if they don't survive here, how is that authentic?"

"Ah, yes, glad you asked," Dr. Om said. "Glad you asked. It involves the theory of perceived authenticity. The tourism industry in Puerto Rico has done wonders to promote its little creature. And by leveraging that, we get a boost in marketing all the while creating a feeling of an authentic rainforest experience," Dr. Om raised his hands. "Feeling!"

Hessy shook her head and muttered something Bertie couldn't catch. He didn't know her that well, but he wondered whether she was capable of kicking the guy down into the mud. She was a redhead, after all.

But his thoughts were interrupted by their arrival at double doors set in a circular stone wall.

"Ah, here we are, here we are," Dr. Om said. He struggled to turn the key. "We don't use this access point much." Finally, the key turned with a jolt, and Dr. Om opened the squeaky gate. "Not far now!"

They walked along a path completely covered by trees, like a tunnel. The sound of crickets and coquíes was deafening. The straight path took an abrupt turn to the right and then curved gently to the left. The sounds of crickets and coquíes went silent, replaced by an occasional "thump, thump."

"The anticipation!" Dr. Om said. "Finally, finally!"

They stepped out of the trees. Dr. Om looked up at a fence with a satisfied smile on his face. They were standing in front of a huge set of double doors with wrought iron handles decorated with metal leaves. Dr. Om put his arms out wide. "Here we are."

"This is a park featuring fences?" Bertie said.

Dr. Om giggled. "No, no, no, no." He lowered his voice and stepped closer to Bertie and Hessy. "Not at all. Behind this fence is what you have been waiting to see all day." He gestured at them to follow him. "Come this way, come this way. Now, see there, that little cutout in the fence? Take a look at the crowning achievement of my park. Of St. Quiche. Of my entire career."

Bertie and Hessy leaned over. All Bertie could see were leaves.

"I see leaves," Bertie said. He looked back at Dr. Om, who was starting to look annoyed.

"Look more closely. Pay attention. Pay attention!" he said, hovering above their heads.

A neigh broke the silence.

"Horses?" Hessy said.

Dr. Om put his hand to his head. "No, not horses!" he said. "What kind of revelation would that be? Look closely. Closely!"

Bertie put his eye right up to the cutout. He caught sight of a flank. It looked like it was from a white horse. But all he could get was a glimpse.

"Did you see that?" Hessy said.

"I saw the side of a horse," Bertie said.

"Yeah, it looked . . . sparkly?"

Bertie saw a tail whip through the leaves, then disappear. "Yeah, sparkly, you're right," Bertie said.

"Yeah, like the vampire," Hessy said.

"Vampire?"

"You know, the vampires in that book. They were sparkly."

"Sparkly? Like Barbie?" Bertie said.

Hessy scoffed. "Barbie isn't sparkly."

"What do I know about Barbie? I didn't play with Barbie." Bertie straightened his back and looked at Hessy.

Dr. Om made a strangling noise behind them. "They're not . . . horses or . . . sparkly vampires or . . . sparkly vampire Barbie horses! They're. Nothing. You've. Ever. Seen. Before. In. The. Flesh." He pushed Bertie and Hessy's heads back towards the cutout. "Take another look."

Hessy sighed and started making kissy noises through the fence. Bertie heard another one of the not-horse thingies neighing. Seemingly attracted by the sound of Hessy's noise, one approached the fence. They got another look at the white flank. Then it turned.

"Ow!" Bertie said. Something sharp had almost poked him in the eye. He looked again.

It was a unicorn.

CHAPTER 10

UNICORN?!
Unicorn!!!???

CHAPTER 11

"UNICORN," Hessy said.

"Unicorn?" Bertie said.

Bertie and Hessy stared, mouths open, at the inside of the unicorn pen. By now, the unicorn had trotted away, but they were sure of what they had seen.

Dr. Om seemed pleased. "So, what do you think? What do you think?"

"Um, how . . . ?" Hessy said, pointing at the pen.

"Right, yeah, how?" Bertie said.

"The details, of course, are proprietary," Dr. Om said. "But I have been working for years on bringing the unicorn back."

"Bringing the unicorn back?" Bertie said.

"Yes, yes, of course, you know," he told Bertie.

"I know what?" Bertie looked confused.

"How many are there?" Hessy asked.

"Twelve," Dr. Om said. "For now."

"For now?" Bertie said.

Dr. Om's walkie-talkie came to life. "What, Lester?" Dr. Om said. "I'm busy."

A nervous voice came through the static. "That policeman guy is back. One of the neighbors complained. He wants to come in."

"No, no, no, no," Dr. Om said. "Absolutely not. I will be right there." He wiped sweat off his brow and rolled his eyes. "I've got to do something about these locals," he said under his breath.

"Dr. Vole, Miss Beauregard, we will continue this conversation in my office when I am done handling this little disturbance. Come with me," Dr. Om said as he walked to a low wooden shed and unlocked it. It had a pile of tranquilizer guns, some walkie-talkies, and cloth bags.

Bertie didn't like the look of so many tranqs.

Dr. Om handed a walkie-talkie and two of the bags to Bertie and Hessy. "I will contact you on this walkie-talkie when I am done. Here are your welcome bags. You will find a layout of the park and some snacks to get you through this evening. The Tropical Trade Winds Dining Pavilion will be operational again tomorrow." He wiped his brow nervously. "Feel free to take a walk through the park, the parts you are allowed to see anyway." Dr. Om looked annoyed at this last statement, making Bertie wonder what, exactly, had happened to the Tropical Trade Winds Dining Pavilion.

Lester's voice interrupted Bertie's thoughts. "Dr. Om, Dr. Om! The policeman is getting tired of waiting." Bertie could hear a second impatient voice coming through the walkie-talkie static. "I don't have all day, man. You know my wife needs my patrol car to get to her kalooki game."

"I'm coming!" Dr. Om screamed into the walkie-talkie. Then he smiled at Bertie and Hessy. "I will see you in a bit. In a bit!"

He tottered off, jacket hanging crookedly off his shoulders, and left Bertie and Hessy staring at the pen.

Unicorns?!?!?!?!

CHAPTER 12

BERTIE AND HESSY stayed glued to the cutout, but they didn't get to see much more than bits and pieces of the unicorns, who sounded restless. Every once in a while, an angry whinny suggested some were fighting.

Bertie wondered whether that was normal.

"Let's see whether we can get a better view from elsewhere," Hessy said. They followed the curve of the fence. A band of dense trees, hugging a narrow dirt path, drew a complete circle around the rest of the pen. There were no other cutouts to view the interior, and they saw only one small door a few yards from the main entrance to the pen. They circled back to the cutout.

Bertie pointed to a wooden sign he hadn't noticed before. The text was burned in (no doubt because it was more "authentic") and said, "Unicorns run free from . . . in the morning till . . . in the evening." But the message had blank spaces for the hours.

"So, Dr. Om is going to have unicorns loose among the public," Hessy said.

Great. A bunch of possibly angry unicorns were going

to have a run of this place. What were guests going to do? Play pin-the-tranq-gun-dart-on-the-unicorn-and-run-for-your-life? An agitated whinny made Bertie jump.

"Why don't we walk around a bit?" he said.

They stepped out of the darkness of the trees and looked at the park in front of them. A sign with an arrow pointing both directions read "Tropical Treehouse Cabañas." A half-moon of tree houses stretched before them.

"Who'd have thunk? According to the great Dr. Om, authentic Caribbean people all live in tree houses," Bertie said.

"Perceived authenticity for the win, apparently," Hessy said.

As they walked away from the pen, they could see the guest rooms extend around the pen itself. As they kept walking straight, they saw a second row of rooms, these in taller trees, apparently to allow them a view of the pen.

The third circular row was made up of tree houses as well. These structures were much bigger, often taking up several trees. The Tropical Trade Winds Dining Pavilion and the Tropical Paradise Souvenir Shoppe were strung along four trees each. The largest structure of all was the Magical Unicorn Racecourse Veranda.

There didn't seem to be a racecourse anywhere in sight. Was Dr. Om going to race unicorns along the regular foot-paths? With people milling around? Did the guy want to recreate Spain's running of the bulls? Bertie could see it now: a pale, hapless tourist holding pink cotton candy that he couldn't enjoy because he was too busy being impaled by a magical creature.

This was getting better and better.

As they kept walking, the circle of structures got larger.

The outer section housed employee quarters, the medical wing, and—the only building not stuck in a tree—the offices. This building was the only one with windows protected by bars.

The bars were ornate, old-fashioned, pretty even. But they were bars nonetheless. Bars, tranq guns . . . He didn't like the feeling he was getting from this place.

From behind the outer edge, Bertie could hear the hum of what sounded like generators. The electricity wasn't even on yet, and Dr. Om planned to open in just weeks.

"What did you say Dr. Om's real name was?" Hessy said.

"I didn't, actually, but it's Artie Manicewitz."

"I wonder why he changed it. And why he picked such a dumb name."

Bertie smiled. "Yeah, the guy's got a couple of screws loose. I mean literally. I think he spent some time in a mental hospital, so maybe he wanted to hide his identity."

The look on Hessy's face told Bertie that maybe he should have mentioned that when he pitched the job interview to her. Before he had a chance to say anything else, Dr. Om's voice came through the walkie-talkie.

"Dr. Vole, Miss Beauregard, I am waiting for you in my office."

Bertie and Hessy made their way to Dr. Om. "By the way," Bertie said. "He probably shouldn't know that we know his real name is Artie. You know."

"I'm starting to."

CHAPTER 13

"I DON'T KNOW anything about unicorns," Bertie said for what felt like the fifteenth time since Dr. Om had dragged them to his office to discuss the job offer.

"Who completely does?" Dr. Om said with a laugh. "That's what is so exciting about this venture. To be the first to showcase a creature that was so extinct it had been relegated to the mythical! And then I brought it back. I recreated it. In my own lab! It is the ultimate coup of a geneticist, and I did it! I did it! And now I—we, we!—have a chance to open this up to the world!"

"But I don't know anything about—"

"My dear Dr. Vole, you wrote the book on unicorns!" Dr. Om stood up in triumph.

There was silence. Hessy looked at Bertie in shock.

"What?" Bertie said.

"You wrote the definitive guide on unicorns," Dr. Om said. He trotted to a file cabinet by his desk and ruffled around till he found what he was looking for. He dropped a sheath of papers on the desk.

"Look, look!" Dr. Om said. There, in messy manuscript

form, was a book called The Gastrointestinal Tract of Unicorns - Part I of the Anatomy of Rare Creatures Series by Bertram W. Vole and Timothy E. Grett.

Bertie stared for a second at the cover. He hadn't thought of that book in years.

He put his hand over his mouth.

He had never imagined that the book would come back to bite him in the behind like this.

"You did write it, correct?" Dr. Om said. "This wasn't plagiarism, was it? Was it?"

"No!" Bertie put his hands up in defense.

"Because if you plagiarized this, well!" Dr. Om laughed and leaned forward. "I could ruin. Your. Career."

"No, I wrote the book. I definitely, definitely wrote the book."

"Excellent! Excellent. An excellent volume, by the way!" Dr. Om said. "It has some errors, but no matter. Listen, Miss Beauregard." He read from the pages. "'The unicorn's elevation to imaginary creature was due to its solitary tendencies. Unicorns tend to live in small groups and often break from the herd for days at a time.' You'll notice this behavior first-hand soon enough. 'As they prefer forest, jungle or other shaded areas as well as solitude, it is hard for a casual observer to catch sight of this quadruped. Their speedy retreats when human interaction approaches and the similarity of their hindquarters to those of horses explain how their existence had been kept secret for so long before their extinction hundreds—maybe thousands—of years ago.'"

"Wow," Hessy said. She looked from the book to Bertie, her brow furrowed as though something weren't quite right.

"Yeah, a few errors. I was young, you know, whatever," Bertie said.

"Why'd you say you knew nothing about unicorns?" Hessy said.

"Well," Bertie rubbed his head. Crap. What was he going to say? "Because this . . . document is supposed to be top secret. I-I-I don't know you got your hands on it, Dr. Om. Sly dog! Ha ha. Sly . . . dog."

Dr. Om tapped his nose. "Dark web. Dark web."

"Wow," Hessy said.

"Yeah, wow," Bertie said.

Dr. Om slid the pages back in the cabinet. "I have to admit, having the author of the definitive guide on unicorn digestion would be a huge coup—a HUGE coup. You two, you want the job? You want the job?"

"Right, well, um . . ." Bertie didn't know what to say. He really needed to think the whole thing through.

"Not sure, not sure? Okay, let me know by tomorrow. If you say yes, I've got to modify my promo material. People will LOVE knowing that the resident vet wrote the book on unicorns. Wrote the book!" Dr. Om trotted to the door. "Just in case, I'm going to get started on edits. When you decide, come find me in the marketing department upstairs. Come find me, no matter how late. The hour doesn't matter!"

He slammed the door behind him, leaving Bertie and Hessy staring at the empty spot on the desk where Bertie's "definitive" guide used to be. Bertie figured he should probably tell Hessy it was a joke, but how?

"Was that—" Hessy turned to Bertie. "Was that book some kind of prank?"

"Oh, yeah. Yeah, it was!" Bertie was relieved Hessy had taken the decision out of his hands. "My sister had to do a presentation for science class. I told her to do it on unicorns. She said they were fake, so a friend of mine and I thought it would be funny to write a book on them. As a joke. She swallowed it. Hook, line, and sinker. And boy, did she flunk her presentation."

"Oh, no!" Hessy said before she broke into giggles.

"Wouldn't speak to me for weeks."

"I wonder what she would think of this park?"

"I don't know what I think of this park."

"Well, we've got a decision to make."

"Yeah, definitely we're going to want to sleep on this one. Big decision."

Static from the intercom on the wall interrupted the conversation. "Hello, Miss Beauregard?" It was Dr. Om.

"Yes?" Hessy said.

"Glad you're still there. Glad you're still there. I realized you and I haven't had a chance to chat about your remuneration, like I did with Dr. Vole. Come on up to marketing, third floor. It will take just a few minutes. Just a few minutes!"

"Sure, Dr. Om," Hessy said. "See you in a bit."

Hessy stood, picking up the welcome packet. "Well, have a good evening. I guess we can chat over breakfast about all this."

"Yeah, right. Good idea," Bertie said. "Don't let the sparkly vampire mosquitoes bite."

Hessy laughed, but inside, Bertie was thinking, loser, loser, loser.

After Hessy left the office, Bertie snuck to the cabinet. Relieved to find it wasn't locked, he took the book and shoved it into the welcome bag.

Whatever it was worth, he might need this thing.

Bertie left the administration building, which he noticed was called the Caribbean Command Centre. It was almost dark outside. The crickets were chittering loudly. Bertie took the map out of his welcome bag.

The park was on the highest point of a mountain called Mt. Om. Bertie rolled his eyes. Bertie wondered what its real name was. Some sort of barrier encircled the park. From the map, Bertie could clearly see what Hessy and he had noticed earlier about the layout: the separate buildings were arranged in a widening set of circles. Bertie tried to figure out what it reminded him of.

He turned in a circle.

That was it. A maze. A big, unfinished maze.

And smack dab in the middle was the unicorn pen.

Bertie looked closer at the map in the dimming light. There were circular clearings in a couple of places. For landing helicopters, maybe? Dr. Om had mentioned helicopters.

Or perhaps those were dedicated to alien kidnappings.

Or maybe Bertie just watched too much TV.

His eyes ran over the map. He looked for the employee quarters and found that they were right next to the offices on the outermost edge of the park.

Bertie wondered if that was Dr. Om's way of keeping enemies close.

Bertie wandered towards the periphery. It turned out to be a high, weathered stone wall, much like one would find in an old fort. He walked its length for a bit, then headed back towards the center of the park. The sun had set, and there were no lights in this section. He collided with a post. Looking up, he could see a bunch of wooden arrows pointing every which way. Bertie couldn't see what was on them, but he assumed they pointed to different sections of the park. He took another look at the map using his phone as a flashlight. Upon closer inspection, Bertie noticed tiny labels over different sections that said, "Do not enter. Under construction" or "Do not enter. Dangerous" or "Do not enter. Under construction and dangerous."

Well, that was promising.

He wiped sweat from his eyes. He must have taken the wrong turn. He couldn't see the unicorn enclosure. He doubled back and finally caught sight of the huge, rustic wooden doors. He knocked. "Hey, unicorns. How's it going?"

In response, a unicorn collided with the doors. Another one followed. Bertie heard what sounded like a growl. The pen enclosure shook.

Bertie stepped back a few paces, consulted the map to find his quarters, and hurried off.

Crazy scientist, check.

Mythical creatures come to life in a lab, check.

Trapped unicorns trying to break down their pen, check.

Yeah, it was all very promising. "Sign me up!" Bertie said as he saw his cabaña come into view.

Bertie and Hessy met on the veranda of the unfinished tree-top dining room (a.k.a. The Tropical Trade Winds Dining Pavilion) for breakfast. Like all the other buildings, it was made of distressed pine planks to create what Bertie figured was an "authentic" appeal. He noticed that the wooden structure of the wall had been modified; it looked like they planned to add bars here too. From their table, they could see the unicorn pen.

Could unicorns climb trees? Bertie wondered.

"How'd your conversation with Dr. Om go yesterday?" Bertie asked Hessy.

"Oh, you know, fine," she said. "It didn't take long. He just gave a rundown of pay. And stuff."

"What'd he say?"

"You know him. A whole bunch of things and nothing, all at the same time," Hessy didn't look up. She grabbed a blank piece of paper out of her welcome packet. "Okay, decision time. We're going to make a pros and cons list."

"Now?"

"Yes, now. 'Pros and Cons,'" Hessy said the words as she wrote them.

"Actually, research shows that's not the best way to make a decision." Bertie's gut feeling told him to run screaming from this loony park and grab the first leaking boat out of here. That was the best plan of attack.

Or whatever you call plans that are technically the opposite of attack.

"Do you have a better idea?" she said.

"Well, no—"

"Great. Pro: It's the Caribbean. You always wanted to live in the Caribbean."

"How do you know?"

"Because you always grumbled about it. Beaches and warm weather and the ability to wear flip flops in December. Speaking of flip flops, we'll need to get some shorts. It's way too hot for these interview clothes."

"Right, right. If we stay, you know. What's the con?"

"Well, a crazy scientist buys an island so he can do whatever he likes and treats everyone around him like disposable entertainment."

"That's about four cons in one, I think."

"There's the six-digit pay. That's about six pros in one."

"True," Bertie said. "But I don't know. Compared to this place, Dr. Roderick might not be so bad."

They fell silent and looked out into the park. A breeze came in through the window, momentarily breaking the humidity. Macaws squawked in the distance. Beyond that, the unicorns were neighing. They seemed restless.

I'm staying," Hessy said. She put down her pen.

"What? Just like that? We haven't finished our list." Bertie wiped his forehead. Gosh, it was hot here.

"You said it yourself. Lists aren't the best way to make decisions."

"This is insane. I mean, he plans for the unicorns to trot around with the people. They're—"

"Agitated," Hessy said. "I know. The guy needs some people to talk sense into him. We could be those people. Anyway, they just need better care, that's all."

"Yeah, I'm sure he's going to listen to us."

"Well, he did offer you the job because you're the utmost expert on unicorns, Mr. Author Man."

Bertie could see he was getting nowhere. He tried a different tack. "We don't even have passports here. What if this guy really is dangerous?"

"Oh, he is dangerous. But he's also rich."

"Rich? Is that all that matters?" How could Hessy make such a huge decision without factoring in all the variables?

"No, but it's pretty big. Look, my mother needs me, and I don't have the money to take care of her. Here I can earn tons of money, get her the proper care, save up, and go back after a couple of months and do something with my life. In the meantime, I can help the animals here. Someone needs to look out for them."

Bertie stared at her.

"Same applies to you," she said. "You're not exactly following your dreams back home right now. Anyway, I'm staying. You choose what works for you. But I'm staying."

"I can't just . . . abandon you!" Bertie couldn't believe the mess he had made. "It's my fault you're here. I got you suspended." Bertie gestured toward the sound of the unicorns. "I dragged you into this."

"No, you didn't. I chose to come along."

Bertie sighed and squeezed his eyes shut. "So, we're staying."

"No, I'm staying," Hessy stood up. "You decide what you're going to do." She headed to the stairs, then turned around. "If you stay, just be sure to make nice with Saint."

"Why?"

Hessy smiled. "Because if things get dicey, we'll need him for our secret transport out of here."

SECTION II

Excerpt from *The Gastrointestinal Tract of Unicorns: Part I of the Anatomy of Rare Creatures Series* by Bertram W. Vole and Timothy E. Grett

CHAPTER 1: A HORSE IS A HORSE, UNLESS IT'S A UNICORN

"Not surprisingly, the unicorn shares a number of similarities with the horse in relation to its dietary needs. Just like a horse, the unicorn has a unicameral stomach, and there is no microbial breakdown at the beginning of the gastrointestinal tract, something we do see in cattle. Although unicorns, like horses, delight in sugar cubes, they, like horses, should avoid diets high in simple sugars to keep starch at appropriately low levels in the cecum and colon."

Author note: Yup, love sugar cubes, but watch out for your fingers.

CHAPTER 14

AFTER A GOOD NIGHT'S sleep and a nice cup of coffee and a hot shower, life always looked better.

That's what Bertie's mother always said. Actually, what she said was after a good night's sleep in a four-star hotel, a whole new wardrobe, a nice cup of coffee, a spa day, and a couple of Vicodin, life always looked better. Bertie wasn't sure whether his mother was simply wrong or whether Vicodin was an essential ingredient in that equation. But life definitely wasn't any better the next day.

Somehow, and he wasn't exactly sure how it had happened, Bertie was taking this darn job.

After a day off to get settled, he and Hessy were getting their debriefing in the "Coral Reef Networking Centre" (conference room) with the park manager, Sebastian Cieve.

"Okay guys, welcome to the Mythical Unicorn Land Featuring the Rainforest Zipline Extravaganza," Sebastian said. His voice was sarcastic. Not a good sign. "I know it's not that comfortable in here, with the air out." He wiped his bald, sunburned head with the rim of his safari hat.

"Are they still working on getting electricity to the whole park?" Hessy asked.

"Not exactly," Sebastian said. "We had electricity, but apparently, the head of the electric authority wasn't too happy about the prime minister selling the island. Or maybe he got less of a bribe than other agency heads did. Or maybe Dr. Om didn't promise him a big enough statue. Who knows the reason?" He wiped his head with the safari hat again. "I probably wasn't supposed to tell you that, but too late. First order of business, after you escape this sauna, is to get your safari-style uniform at the Employee Procurement Centre of Island Fun." Under his breath, he added, "Because nothing says tropical paradise like polyester."

"What's with the safari gear?" Bertie asked.

"So that we can achieve 'accurate representation of a wildlife arena,'" Sebastian said, using air quotes.

"But we're not in Africa," Bertie said.

"You don't say," Sebastian said. He refilled his coffee cup with the vodka bottle he had pulled out from under the desk.

"Would you like some? I call it crazy island coffee." Sebastian waved the vodka in front of Hessy and Bertie.

They shook their heads.

"What will our duties be?" Hessy asked.

"Right, duties." Sebastian's laugh had a bite to it. He opened a file that read "Most recent draft. Use this!!! - Property of the Marketing Division."

"You, Dr. Vole, will be in charge of providing 'world-class, innovative medical attention to the first genetically engineered unicorns the world has ever seen.' There are twelve of these horned donkeys."

"I don't know any—much about unicorns," Bertie said.

"Doesn't matter. Because before you can provide world-class anything, you need to tranquilize the beasts enough so that you can get near them. Figure out the dosage without killing any of them. As Dr. Om likes to remind me every ten minutes, these brutes are very expensive." Sebastian took another gulp of vodka and emptied the rest of the bottle into his cup. "You, Miss Beauregard, will be in charge of providing world-class innovative nutrition to the first genetically engineered unicorns the whole frikking universe has ever seen."

Hessy jotted her duties down. "What do unicorns like to eat?"

Sebastian laughed. "That's where it gets complicated."

"How?" Bertie asked. He was confused. And concerned. And regretful. And like he needed a Vicodin-laced vodka cocktail. He should have accepted the offer of crazy island coffee.

"What they like to eat and what Dr. Om wants them to eat are two very different things," Sebastian said. "Dr. Om wants them to eat grains, like horses, preferably grains that are dyed every color of the pastel rainbow. 'The kids will love it!'" Sebastian waved his hands around in imitation of Dr. Om. "What they want to eat is rather less appetizing."

"I'm loving the suspense thing you got going on," Bertie said.

"You asked for it. They like raw, rotting meat. The bloodier, the better."

Neither Bertie nor Hessy said anything for a tick. Then Bertie said, "Technically, it's not blood. The red fluid is myoglobin."

"Do I look like I care?" Sebastian wiped his forehead with his hat again. "I've got a park full of carnivorous, magical horned creatures who get very grouchy when you try to feed them the horse equivalent of kids' cereal. They want roadkill."

"When you say grouchy, what do you mean exactly?" Bertie asked. Hessy got ready to take more notes.

"What I mean is that I no longer go near those things. They ruined my last pair of safari shorts, which I guess I should be thankful for, except for the piece of meat they almost got out of me. Do you want to see?"

Hessy's pen hovered over her notebook. "May I?"

"That wasn't a real question." Sebastian's sunburned face got redder. He picked up the vodka bottle and cursed under his breath when he realized it was empty. "And the answer is no. You may not. So, you see what I mean when I say that you can't provide world-class anything to those animals till you get them sedated enough to keep them from eating you?"

"Why don't we just feed them meat?" Hessy said.

Sebastian waved his hands around like Dr. Om again. "'Because that's gross! The kids won't like it.' When I was a kid, I would have loved to see a unicorn tearing a roaring lion apart, but I don't think Dr. Om knows much about kids."

"Technically," Bertie said, "if they like rotting meat, they wouldn't tear a live lion apart as a first choice."

"Do I look like I care?" Sebastian said.

Hessy leaned forward. "Sebastian, do you mind if I ask you a personal question?"

"Does it involve the teeth marks on my thigh?

"No."

"Then shoot."

"Why do you choose to keep working here?"

Sebastian didn't answer right away. "That's a great thought. Any questions?" He didn't give Hessy and Bertie a chance to answer. "Great. Go get your uniforms. I'll meet you at the employee center."

Sebastian darted out. Bertie and Hessy followed at a slower pace.

"At least the uniforms involve shorts," Hessy said. She looked down at her wrinkled dress shirt, which looked like she had washed it by hand. Bertie put his nose to his own shirt. He definitely should have washed his too.

They had gone into town the day before to buy clothes, but being a Sunday, everything had been closed, except for the churches and bars.

They reached the tree house where the employee center was. They knocked, but no one answered. Bertie peeked through the window. Although the outside looked welcoming, inside, it was dark and dusty. Unmarked boxes were strewn around the entrance and piled on seats. They waited on the veranda and paced and waited some more. Finally, they heard footsteps on the stairs. It was Sebastian.

"You got your stuff?" Sebastian said.

"No one is here," Bertie said.

Sebastian sighed. "Typical." He pulled out a bunch of keys and opened the door.

"Grab what you need. Lock up after yourselves." Sebastian dropped the keys on a counter.

"Wait, where are the clothes anyway?" Bertie said. "Are they in one of these boxes?"

"Probably. Look, I don't have time to babysit you. I'm going to be late for my flight. Oh, and remember, tranq those beasts before they eat anyone."

He stomped down the stairs, then came back up.

"By the way, Dr. Vole. I forgot to tell you. Enjoy your promotion." He threw him his hat and left again.

Bertie looked at his hat sitting at his feet. Its scrawly letters said, "Manager."

Bertie and Hessy stared at each other for a few seconds without saying anything. Then Hessy grabbed a box to look through.

"So . . ." Bertie said.

"So . . ." Hessy said.

"You know—" Bertie slid the hat towards Hessy with his foot. "What do I know about management? Anyway, you gave him the idea to leave. It's your fault. You're promoted."

Hessy looked at the hat but didn't touch it. "It's all sweaty, but thanks."

"So, what do we do when we finish up here, boss?" Bertie said.

Hessy found the uniforms and tossed him a set.

"I say we go have a proper meet and greet with our unicorns."

"Yeah, what could go wrong?"

Bertie knew the answer to that question, and he didn't like it.

CHAPTER 15

BERTIE, Hessy, and Lester, the armed guard, stood in front of the big doors of the unicorn pen a few minutes later. According to Lester, the unicorns had eaten an "unscheduled" meal of meat three days before. Lester, who became armed after an "incident" he wouldn't elaborate on, didn't know what kind of meat they last ate. Or maybe he just refused to say.

Probably the latter, Bertie thought.

From outside the pen, it was hard to see what was going on with the unicorns, but it didn't sound too good. They neighed just like horses, but they sounded angry. Bertie noticed a few round holes in the fence, the same size as the horns, and they hadn't been there the day before. At this rate, there wouldn't be a fence to pen them in.

Plus, it appeared they were fighting amongst themselves.

That is, if unicorns fighting amongst themselves sounded like horses fighting amongst themselves, and Bertie couldn't be sure of that.

He hadn't discussed that topic in his treatise on the

gastrointestinal tract of unicorns. One thing was for certain. His sister was going to really like how the tables had turned on him.

Bertie looked at Hessy and Lester out of the corner of his eye. He figured he had better finally say something. He didn't want to look like a total idiot. "We need to get our eyes on them. If I can see how big they are, I'll have a better idea what dosage of tranquilizer they need. Lester, is there a ladder, so I can see above the fence?"

"Broken."

"Is there a building nearby with a view of the inside of the pen?"

"No, anything that would work is locked, bolted, and 100% off limits.

"Why?" Hessy said.

"Dr. Om wants as few eyes on the unicorns as possible till the park opens. Gotta keep the surprise going. And till we get the kinks out. And till they quit eating—" Lester's eyes got big, as though he had said way too much. "I've got rounds to do." He scurried away as fast as he could.

"You know what that means?" Hessy said.

"Yeah, it means they're eating people." He rubbed his chin and bent down to try to get a view through the cutout.

"No, that's not what I mean. And maybe they're not eating people. Maybe they're eating other animals."

"Then what do you mean by 'You know what that means?'" Bertie asked.

"It means I get another helicopter ride. We can get a bird's eye view that way," Hessy said.

"Great," Bertie said. "Take as many pictures as you can and tell me what you see."

"Nuh-uh," Hessy said.

"What do you mean 'nuh-uh?'" Bertie said the "nuh-uh" in a falsetto.

Hessy slapped his arm. "I mean, you're coming with me. You're the vet. You know what to look for."

"I don't think so," Bertie said. "I trust your judgment."

"I'm just management. Everyone knows management doesn't know jack." She turned around and hollered, "Hey, Lester! Come here! How do we get our hands on a helicopter?"

As the helicopter rose from one of the clearings, Bertie could see the unicorns growing more violent. They butted heads, lunged themselves into the wood slats, and shook their manes, teeth bared.

By the time the helicopter was overhead, Bertie had just enough of a glimpse to guesstimate their dosage needs before the unicorns stopped attacking the fence and started tearing into each other. A couple of them, dripping with blood, reared up on their hind legs and tried to bite the helicopter skids.

They had to retreat before they could get low enough to use the tranq guns, unless they wanted to attend the world's first genetically engineered unicorn funerals.

"That didn't work out so well," Hessy said when the helicopter made an emergency landing in one of the circular clearings near the outer wall. It was surrounded by ferns and palms. The growls of angry unicorns reached them on the breeze.

Bertie's walkie-talkie crackled. "Dr. Vole, why don't you and Manager Cieve come to my office? Just head on over and give me a rundown of the morning's work. Do you have any news?"

"Yeah, about that," Bertie said under his breath. He picked up his walkie-talkie. "The manager and I are heading to your office now. And yeah, we've got news."

Bertie and Hessy took to the dirt path towards Dr. Om's office. The Caribbean Command Centre was housed in a pastel-striped building with a mural of sparkly unicorns gamboling amongst palm trees and oversized coquíes.

Bertie and Hessy paused to look at the mural. "I like it," Bertie said. "Not enough blood, but other than that, completely true to life."

Hessy slapped his arm but laughed.

"As office manager, I say we tell him they just need to eat meat," she said.

"I agree. Dr. Om will be totally reasonable and hang on every word we say. I put you in charge of telling him."

"Yeah, thanks," Hessy said.

Hessy knocked on the metal door. Bertie noticed that Dr. Om was much less concerned about an "authentic" Caribbean feeling when it came to his own offices.

"Come in, come in," Dr. Om said. "Oh, Miss Beauregard, I didn't expect to see you. Where's Manager Cieve?"

"Yeah, about that," Hessy said when Bertie looked at her desperately. "He's . . . left."

"Left?" Dr. Om said. His big eyes said that no one in their right minds would want to leave.

"He threw in the towel," Bertie said. "And promoted me to manager."

"That's-that's-that's not his place," Dr. Om said.

"And I promoted Hessy to manager, which isn't mine, but I sure as heck don't want to be manager," Bertie said.

Dr. Om put his head in his hands and counted to ten.

He took a deep breath and smiled. "Well, Interim Manager Beauregard, we will discuss this development later. Now, how did the tranquilizing of my babies go?"

"It didn't," Hessy said.

"What?" Dr. Om said. His smile disappeared.

Hessy said, "The sound of the helicopter agitated the unicorns—"

"What?" Dr. Om said.

Bertie squeezed his eyes shut for a moment. "They went postal! Crazy! Murderous! We had to get that helicopter out of there before they wrecked the fence and chewed each other to death."

Dr. Om touched his fingers to his eyes. His face became sad. "I'm very, very, very disappointed in you two. Very disappointed. I asked for one little duty today. One little task. One tiny, itsy-bitsy little thing."

Hessy said, "Dr. Om—"

"One infinitesimally small thing." Dr. Om's face started turning red. Bertie couldn't help feeling that Dr. Om was putting on a show.

Hessy continued, "With all due respect, Dr. Om—"

"What I asked, was it such a hard thing?" Dr. Om put his hands in the air and looked skywards.

Hessy gave it another shot, "I think we should feed the unicorns their preferred diet. For whatever reason—"

"We. Can't. Feed. Them. Rotting. MEAT!" Dr. Om waved his hands in the air. "Can you imagine the optics of that? These are magical creatures! That have captured the imagination of children. All over the world. For . . . centuries." He lowered his voice to a dramatic whisper. "Do you know what it will do to the kiddie-widdies to see unicorns chowing down on bloodied carcasses?"

"Dr. Om," Bertie said. "Why do they get so crazy when they don't eat meat?"

"How dare you call my baby-poos crazy."

"Agitated, then."

Dr. Om wiped his forehead. "Well, that's your area of expertise." He looked at the papers on his desk, avoiding Bertie's gaze. "You, after all, wrote the book on unicorns."

Shoot. He'd forgotten he was supposed to know stuff. He'd have to tread carefully. "Just on the gastrointestinal tract." He looked to Hessy for support.

She nodded. "Uh-huh."

"The gastrointestinal tract is a small—" Bertie held the palms of his hands close together. "Small part of the unicorn. Small. Tiny"

Hessy nodded again.

"But once the food leaves the tract, well, it's anyone's guess what goes on," Bertie said.

Hessy nodded again.

"It's the wild west!"

"Wild, wild west," Hessy said.

Dr. Om put his hands together and touched them to his chin. "Fair enough. Fair enough. This is, after all, uncharted territory, which is what makes it so exciting, so exciting!"

"Yeah, fan-darn-tastically exciting," Bertie said.

"I've been thinking about the problem. Thinking a lot about it. Just like with everything else, there is always a solution. Always! And Dr. Vole, I think I have the solution. Speaking as the veterinary scientist that you are, do you think it would be feasible to create a meat-based food that looks just like colorful grains? Do you think the unicorns would like that?"

How the heck would he know? But he just said, "Do you mean, kind of like dog food?

"Similar concept. Similar concept."

"Sure, sure, sure. That may work?" Bertie said as he shrugged at Hessy.

"Yes, yes, yes, yes, yes," Dr. Om said. "I thought so much. I . . . am a genius." He dialed his phone.

"Or we could just give them meat," Hessy said, but Dr. Om shushed her.

"I am calling my lead nutritional scientist," he said. He raised his voice when the other line picked up. "Dr. Kojak. Dr. Kojak! Can you hear me? It's Dr. Om here . . . Yes, Dr. Om. Your boss . . . Right, I need you to rework the formulation of the unicorn feed . . . What do you mean, rework it? I mean, rework it! Reformulate it. Change it. Somehow. I don't know how. This is why I pay you the big bucks. Somehow, make it simulate meat without looking like it. Meat, yes, that kind of meat." Dr. Om rolled his eyes. "You got that? It MUST look like that cereal I talked to you about . . . Name? I can't remember. I have a doctorate in genetics. I don't waste time with cereal names . . . You know, the one with the marshmallows in it."

Dr. Om put his hand over the receiver. "You two, you know that cereal name?"

"Ummmm," Bertie said.

"You know, with the shapes, the clovers and whatnot and the dried-up marshmallows."

Hessy shook her head. "My parents never let me eat sugary cereal."

Bertie looked at Hessy. "Wow, so you were deprived."

"Yeah, kinda," Hessy said.

Bertie mouthed the words, "I'm so sorry."

"Dr. Vole! Miss Beauregard. Focus. It starts with a 'ch.'"

"Lucky Charma?" Bertie said.

"What?" Hessy said. "Can't you spell? Karma is spelled with a K."

"I don't really like marshmallows," Bertie said.

"What does that have to do with spelling?" Hessy said.

"Cereals sometimes spell things funny."

"Lucky Charms!" Dr. Om yelled. "That's it. Lucky Charms." He returned to his phone conversation. "Did you hear that? I want the feed to look like Lucky Charms cereal."

A voice barked in the background. Dr. Om interrupted it. "I don't care about the copyrights. Or the money. Or the time. Or the science. I won't take no for an answer. Get people working on this 24/7. STAT!" He hung up the phone.

Dr. Om stood up, red in the face. "Are you happy, Miss Beauregard? You're going to get your meat. Now, go, scoot, tranq my babies!" He chased them back through the door and slammed it behind them. Through the metal door, Dr. Om's voice sounded distant. "You can't find good help anywhere!"

"We could use the zipline," Hessy said. She and Bertie were back at the unicorn pen. The unicorns were still growling. A *thump, thump, thump* suggested they were head butting.

Which, with horns, couldn't be a good thing.

Bertie looked at her with dread. "We could use the zipline for what?" An idea occurred to him. "You mean to eliminate Dr. Om?" He made gestures as though he were garroting someone.

Hessy clicked her tongue. "No, for approaching the

unicorns and sedating them. I can't sneak meat into their pen till they calm down."

"You're going to go into their pen and feed them? Hessy, are you crazy? They'll eat you!"

"Not if they're sedated."

"I'm not so sure about that. Those unicorns are crazy."

"We don't know that. They're not being fed properly."

"They tried to eat your predecessor's thigh. No one in their right mind would want to eat that guy. He's got to taste awful."

"Do you think the reformulated feed will work?" Hessy aid.

"How should I know?"

"You wrote a book on unicorns," Hessy said.

"As a JOKE! A joke! I don't know anything more about unicorns than the next guy."

"Fair point," Hessy said. Then she turned towards a group of employees and yelled, "Lester! LESTER!" Don't run away! We just need to know how to access the zipline."

Lester pointed vaguely towards the north trail and ran as fast as he could from the pen. Bertie was quickly learning that Lester was a lot smarter than he looked.

Bertie and Hessy lugged the tranquilizer guns down the path and into the trees that surrounded most of the pen. In the shade, it cooled off considerably. Whenever Bertie had imagined the Caribbean, he had pictured cool ocean breezes and piña coladas, not dense forests and sweat. Being shielded from the sun, despite the insects that kept dive-bombing his legs, was a relief.

After a few minutes, they came upon a small opening that led them onto a narrower path. Bertie wondered whether it was so narrow because it wasn't meant for tourists. Or maybe it was just hard to keep gardeners on staff to clear landscaping. The sound of angry unicorns retreated. It made it easier for Bertie to think. He picked up the pace to catch up with Hessy.

"You know," Bertie said, "I think this has been a really good experiment. We've got some good information from this. But don't you think it's time to cut our losses and go home?"

"You can go home."

"What, and leave you here?"

"These poor unicorns are suffering. I can't just abandon them."

"But that Dr. Om is insane."

"All the more reason."

Hessy came to a sudden stop, and Bertie had to detour into a tree to avoid colliding with her. They came out into a clearing. "Here's the zipline," Hessy said, looking upwards. She looked at Bertie. "How good is your aim?"

"I said. My aim. Was terrible!" Bertie hollered as he whipped along the zipline. He shot the tranq gun blindly into the pen and was relieved when the zipline began to slow down. His need for speed was at the bottom of the percentile range. But then it hit him.

Ziplines weren't supposed to slow down, were they?

"Hessy?" Bertie screamed, but she was too far away to help him. Suddenly, he came to a stop right above the pen. The unicorns stood around the edge. There were grey ones and a bluish one and some with silver patches. One was completely black, while another was brown and black.

But Bertie didn't have time to catalogue all the colors because, unfortunately, they could see him as well. They threw their manes and neighed. A silvery grey one stomped the ground.

The zipline began to sag. Bertie looked at the approaching ground, then at the unicorns, then back at the ground.

Then back at the approaching unicorns.

Wait, approaching?

There they were, running right at him, manes flowing. He could see splotches of blood sparkling on their manes and hides. The unicorns brayed and bared their teeth.

Bertie closed his eyes and opened fire.

Then he thought better of it and opened his eyes.

Three unicorns went down, but by now, Bertie could feel the ground beneath his behind. A tranquilizer dart hit another unicorn, but more were heading his way.

It went all slow-mo, like in the movies. The silvery grey unicorn at the head of the pack tossed her bloodied mane. It sparkled in the sun. She stood on her back legs and growled.

Then she headed

straight

for

Bertie.

Bertie closed his eyes one last time and said a prayer. Suddenly, time sped back up, and Hessy was screaming at him from the right. "Bertie! Bertie, over here, Bertie!" She dashed through the smaller opening in the fence and ran towards him.

He took another shot at the closest unicorn, who dove right at him just as Hessy reached him and detached him from the zipline. Hessy grabbed his collar and dragged him towards the exit.

"The unicorn is eating my pants!" Bertie screamed.

They got to the gate. Bertie pushed Hessy through, took a parting shot, and dove for the exit himself.

He took a last look through the door. The unicorn was chewing on safari cloth. She chewed slower and slower and slower until her eyes went back in her head and she tipped over.

Hessy averted her eyes from Bertie. "I think . . . I think you need a new pair of pants," she said.

CHAPTER 16

"HOW LONG DO you think we have before they wake up?" Hessy said.

"Your guess is as good as mine," Bertie said.

They were sitting outside the pen, catching their breath. The sun had reached its peak, so even in the shade, the heat made Bertie want to rip his face off.

"So, you really want to go through with monster babysitting gig?" Bertie said.

"Yes, and they're not monsters."

"Oh, sorry. I mean misunderstood genetic wonders of the world."

"At least your sarcasm came through intact."

"Yeah, it did." Bertie closed his eyes to gather his thoughts.

"How are we going to get our hands on all this meat you want to give them?" Bertie said. "We don't have a car."

"I've already figured that out. Listen, you go give some B.S. update to Dr. Om. I'll get our transport ready." Hessy stood up and wiped her hands on her pants. "I'll meet you in the clearing at the south end in a bit."

She headed out before Bertie could ask her for details, like where the south end was and how the heck she had figured that out after only a day or so on the island.

Also, he thought about how he didn't like the sound of "transport." It could mean so many things.

With his luck, she'd have him harness an enraged unicorn and ride it straight into town.

Bertie got up. The first order of business was to get a new pair of shorts. On second thought, maybe it would be best if Dr. Om saw the wreckage. It would drive home how dangerous this all was.

He kept to the shade as much as possible as he headed back to the boss' office. He must have taken the wrong turn, though, because it was taking him much too long to get there. He doubled back and started over. Some parrots squawked overhead. It sounded like they were screeching, "You loon. What do you think you're doing here?" Then silence returned, except for the sound of his footsteps.

Bertie was sure of one thing. This was definitely a fry-pan-meet-fire scenario.

When Bertie finally reached the offices, Dr. Om was outside, wearing dark glasses and sitting on a beach chair in the sun. In his lap was a sheath of papers that looked like a manuscript. The title read: Don't Follow Science! Make It! A Memoir of Genius in Genetics by Dr. Om.

"Excuse me, Dr. Om," Bertie said.

"Might I remind you of Regulation 4.4a of the Mythical Unicorn Land Featuring the Rainforest Zipline Extravaganza Rulebook," Dr. Om said. Because of the sun glasses, Bertie couldn't tell where the guy was looking, which was creepy. "'Employees must always—always—present themselves impeccably to the park's adventurer-guests.' Dr. Vole, that includes clean, untorn uniforms and combed hair.

Comb your hair!" Dr. Om raised his dark glasses enough to let Bertie see the dirty look he was giving him. Then he let his glasses drop back on his face.

"Speaking of the Rainforest Zipline Extravaganza, it's broken," Bertie said.

"What do you mean? What do you mean? It's not broken! It's not finished! It's in the final stages of construction. And testing. Why were you playing around on the zipline? You're here to work! Work!"

"I was using the zipline to get above the unicorn pen so that I could tranquilize the animals without going into the pen itself, on account of there being a bunch of violent unicorns tearing each other apart," Bertie said. "Only problem is that the zipline dropped me right into their lair."

"Don't refer to my babies as violent, Dr. Vole. The zipline is not ready for the public. The engineer had an . . . incident. Don't use it again. And how are my baby-poos?"

"Zonked out."

"What?" Dr. Om threw down his glasses. "That's extreme! I just wanted them calmed."

"Sorry, Zen meditation just didn't work. They were trying to eat people."

"But—"

"And each other."

"But—"

"And it looks like they've been butting the fence."

"But—"

"Which means they'll be free to roam if we don't get this under control," Bertie said.

Dr. Om's eyes got big. "Well, then, I see your predicament. I see the predicament. Going forward, I need you to figure out how to keep them calm till we get the newly formulated food in."

"What if that food doesn't work?" Bertie said.

"I have my best nutritional scientists on it."

"Do they understand how . . . agitated the unicorns get on a vegetarian diet?" To Bertie, "agitated" wasn't the half of it, but he figured that he would take a page from Hessy's ridiculous diplomacy to earn him a few points.

"My scientists know what they need to know when they need to know it." Dr. Om sounded nervous. "You are dismissed," He waved Bertie away. "Off you go!"

Bertie sighed and started to walk away.

"Oh, and Dr. Vole?" Dr. Om tried to sound forceful, but his voice quavered.

"Yes?"

"Will you hand me my sunglasses?"

Bertie sighed as he picked them up. He watched Dr. Om slip them over his eyes. Bertie wasn't big on finding metaphor in everything, but that was definitely some metaphor.

CHAPTER 17

THE CRACKLE of leaves under Bertie's feet gave way to a rumble coming from the clearing where he was supposed to meet Hessy. Although Bertie's worst fear had been that she would commandeer a helicopter or some other flying machine of death, this sound wasn't like any helicopter he had ever heard. It coughed and choked, then died.

"We'll wait for Bertie here," he heard Hessy say. "Thanks for your help, Saint."

As Bertie approached the edge of the clearing, he caught sight of Saint's smiling face. He was getting out of a rusty Rabbit from the 1980's. What little paint that was left was dark green. A water bottle acted as a makeshift muffler.

Saint laughed as he shook Bertie's hand. "Dr. Vole, Greetings! I heard a unicorn almost had you for lunch."

"Call me Bertie, and yes, I was almost the appetizer. We're looking for volunteers to be the main dish."

Saint laughed again. "You have a sense of humor. Good. You will need it."

"Boy, that makes me feel so much better."

"Time to go!" Hessy said. She was about to grab the

door when Saint put his hand on her arm. "Allow me. Lady Mathilda requires special treatment."

"Lady Mathilda?" Hessy said.

"Yes, Lady Mathilda." Saint patted the car on the rusty hood. "The last remnant of my dearly departed wife."

"My condolences." Hessy's eyes got big and sad.

"Don't be sorry," Saint said. "She was a shrew." Saint laughed and backed his foot into the door once, twice, a third time. It popped open with a whine. He gestured towards the front seat. "Ladies first."

"Where to?" Saint said after he climbed into the front seat.

"Do you know of any good butchers?" Hessy said.

"Do I know of any good butchers?" Saint said. "What sort of meat do you want?"

"Edging on rotted," Bertie said.

Saint turned the key in the ignition. After hacking, Lady Mathilda turned on, and they all jerked forward. "That sounds rather disgusting. I know just the place. May I ask why?"

Bertie and Hessy looked at each other. Should they tell him? They had signed a non-disclosure agreement, and Bertie wasn't ready to put Saint in Dr. Om's crosshairs.

"It's a long story," Bertie said.

"I catch your meaning!" Saint said. "Dr. Crazy Man has his secrets." He manipulated the car through the tight path heading into a dark hillside forest.

"Where are you taking us?" Bertie said.

"To the town, but it's best to go the long way. Park staff are less likely to see us. What is your plan if someone knows you are out with me?"

"We don't have one," Bertie said.

"Ah, always have a plan," Saint said. "No fear. I am at

your service. Here is your story: if Dr. Crazy Man asks, you can say you took Saint's Executive Tour: two for the price of one, the best views in all of St. Quiche."

"You're a tour guide too?" Hessy asked.

"I'm a tour guide, a taxi driver, a mechanic, a private detective. I also do some black-market trade, in case you need anything." Saint winked at them.

"Do you smuggle too?" Hessy said.

Bertie gave Hessy a puzzled look, but Saint said, "I sure can."

The path widened and the walls of trees broke. Suddenly, they had a clear view of the north coast of St. Quiche. Or maybe south. Or west. Bertie didn't have his bearings yet.

"As I am the most honest smuggler on St. Quiche, we shall take a moment to enjoy the view," Saint said. He turned off Lady Mathilda, who seemed to welcome the rest, and they all got out of the car.

The crickets started chirping as the sun eased into afternoon, but with the grey clouds piled up above St. Quiche, the heat and humidity were as heavy as ever. Bertie struggled to breathe, but even he had to admit, the view was something else. The hill sloped down in a rush of green, interrupted here and there by brightly colored wooden houses. As the hills reached the coast, more and more houses, now of stone and cement, rushed to meet the blue of the ocean. Small boats dotted the coast.

"It's beautiful," said Hessy.

"Yeah," said Bertie. This was the view that always made Bertie want to come to the Caribbean.

Next time, he should just take a cruise.

"You see St. Quiche's capital down there, Rumstad," Saint said. "The Dutch took over the northeast coast for two weeks before the Spanish kicked them out. But the Spaniards liked good rum, so they kept the name."

"You gotta have good rum," Bertie said.

"Yes, my good man. You and I agree. Unfortunately, too much good rum left the Spaniards open to attack. They finished building up Rumstad in time for the British to sneak in and take over." Saint pointed towards the coast. "Now look there, toward the church with the red cupola. Right next store, that's my shop. If you need anything—smuggling, spying, taxi ride, carburetor—you come find me there."

"A black marketer has headquarters next to a church?" Bertie said.

"Yes, very good location. The pastor often needs taxi rides for his sickly patients." Saint's laugh told Bertie the pastor used some of Saint's other services as well.

"Okay, enough touristing. We got some illegal meat to buy," Saint said.

"Illegal?" Bertie said.

"Well, semi-illegal." He kicked Lady Mathilda's door open. "Although on some days, it is completely illegal, if you listen to the minister of health." Lady Mathilda's motor started back on its rampage of coughing.

"But no one listens to the minister of health," Saint said as he started Lady Mathilda back down the mountain.

If you were to ask Hessy how the ride to the butcher went, she would reply "scenic." She would also point out how friendly the Quichans were, and how they all seemed to know Saint. In the middle of some of the narrowest cobbled roads, Saint would stop Lady Mathilda to chat.

Everyone seemed to be his client. And everyone knew Lady Mathilda.

"Eh, Saint! How is Lady Mathilda doing today?"

Bertie, on the other hand, had a different view. He sat in the back, holding onto the headrests of the front seats. Lady Mathilda had lost her seat belts ages ago. At every bump, his head hit the roof, making the bright colors of the Spanish-era houses bounce up and down in front of his eyes. He would have summed up the ride as "Shock absorbers. Must have shock absorbers."

"Eh, Saint! How is Lady Mathilda doing today?" A pastor, bald and smiling, slapped Lady Mathilda's roof as they passed the church.

"Doing well, pastor," Saint said. He then lowered his voice. "I am on unofficial business from Dr. Crazy Man Park up in the hills."

The pastor's eyes got big. "My daughter was up there with her grandmother last week. They heard strange noises. Strange, strange, strange. The rumors are running! Now I have to do a whole sermon series on how the tormented soul of Uahula doesn't exist and isn't haunting the hills. Saint, you shouldn't be involved with that place. It is sowing idolatry."

"I am helping these two out," Saint said. "This is Dr. Bertie Vole, the sweaty, sick one in back. And this lovely lady is Miss Hessy Beauregard."

"Nice to meet you, Pastor," Hessy said. "What time is your service?"

The pastor leaned forward. Bertie noticed a line of cars piling up behind them, but no one honked.

"Service is at 10 in the morning, followed by Miss Agnes' famous chummies."

"Ooh, what's a chummy?" Hessy said.

The pastor smiled. "It is heavenly. Deep-fried dough, chickpeas. You must taste to truly understand. You will come?"

"Of course, Pastor," Hessy said. "Won't we, Bertie?"

Before Bertie could answer, an old lady stuck her head in the car on Hessy's side. "Who are these people, Saint? How are you, Pastor?"

"They are from the crazy man park up in the mountain," the pastor said. "And don't you go talking about Uahula. Uahula doesn't exist."

"Pastor," the lady said. "I have been up there. I heard the screams. There is only one possible explanation. But don't get worked up, Pastor. I don't go there no more. No Uahula for me."

"You heard it too, about Uahula?" An old gentleman walked up to the car. "Pastor, I don't care what you say. I hear the noises."

"It is not Uahula!" the pastor said. "You two. You work there. Is it Uahula?"

Hessy shook her head. "It is absolutely not Uahula."

"What's a hula?" said Bertie.

"Okay, we gone!" Saint said. "We see you all on Sunday! There is no Uahula. No fear!" He put his foot on the accelerator, and Bertie's head bumped on Lady Mathilda's roof one last time before they got to the butcher.

The ride back was no more comfortable, what with piles of old meat stuffed into every available corner of Lady Mathilda. Bertie kept his eyes closed and tried to ignore its cold squishiness against his leg.

Although the cold did sooth the unicorn bites, so there was that.

It was dark by the time Saint maneuvered Lady Mathilda through the back exit of the park. The engine sputtered to a halt, and the singing from crickets and imported coquíes replaced the choking and coughing of the car.

"How are we going to get the meat to the pen without Saint figuring stuff out?" Bertie said to Hessy once Saint was out of earshot.

"Saint, can you go distract Dr. Om while we smuggle in the meat?" Hessy called out her window.

"My pleasure," Saint said as he laughed. "Dr. Crazy Man hates it when I am here. He will take a lot of time to scold me and talk about top secret surprises to guests. Don't worry yourself."

"Thanks, Saint," Hessy said.

"One more thing," Saint said. "What is your plan if staff see you?"

"Um . . ." Hessy said.

"We don't have one," Bertie said. "We were just going to avoid them."

"There is one thing we know here on St. Quiche that Dr. Crazy Man knows well," Saint said. "Bribery makes the blind see and the seeing blind."

"We'll keep that in mind," Hessy said.

"Go work your miracles," Saint said, patting his wallet, before heading off on his mission to distract Dr. Om.

Bertie and Hessy started carting meat to the pen. Thankfully, the lack of power to the park meant that the video cameras weren't online. None of the security guards was by the pen. They were too scared to stick so close to the unicorns. Bertie and Hessy would be able to get back and forth with the meat without much risk of detection.

"Do you notice how the sounds all disappear right around the unicorns?" Bertie said as they dumped the last batch of meat at the pen door. "Even the insects and frogs are scared of these guys. Or maybe they ate them."

"Yeah, tomorrow, first thing, I've got to sneak into Dr. Om's office to find the paperwork for the coquíes," Hessy said.

"Why?" Bertie crinkled his nose. Even in the open air, the meat had a pungent smell.

"Because they can't survive here. I'm going to get the next shipment sent back to Puerto Rico and find some substitutes that look similar enough."

"Won't Dr. Om figure it out?" Bertie said.

"He's an idiot," Hessy said. They had piled all the meat by the pen. There was complete silence, except for some snuffling from the unicorns. Bertie was relieved that the tranquilizers seemed to still be working.

"I'll talk with Saint," Hessy said. "He may have some ideas on how to make the switch."

Bertie couldn't put his finger on why, but it pestered him that Hessy was leaning so heavily on Saint.

"Yeah, and I'll have some ideas too, for sure," Bertie said. But Hessy didn't seem to be listening.

"Ten packets of meat and twelve unicorns," she said. "How much do you think we should give them?"

"Let's start with four," Bertie said, glad that Hessy was asking for some expertise from him. "They haven't been eating what they need to, so we'll be generous today. That'll leave us with two more days of food before we have to head back to the butcher."

They grabbed a package each and untied the bags.

"Yuck, let's get this over with," Bertie said. He snuck into the path that lead to the small side gate. He pushed it open, hoping the hinges didn't make any noise. But they were silent.

In the clearing, the unicorns were calm. Very calm. Although a couple were standing, most were sitting. Their manes shone in the moonlight. Their heads drooped. They shook their heads and whinnied once in a while as though trying to wake up.

Bertie heard a strange rumble coming from his right. He looked down. There on the ground was the silvery grey unicorn. She was completely zonked out, snoring.

Bertie approached on tiptoe with. Hessy followed. He bent down. "This is the one who tried to eat me," he said. He saw two darts and pulled them out.

Even though he generally wasn't a fan of creatures that tried to tear him to shreds, he felt sorry for this unicorn. He checked her eyes. They were bright amber. Compared to horse eyes anyway, the pupils were dilated. Darned if he knew whether her eyes were normal or not. He let her eyelid close and touched her side. She was breathing slowly. He looked at the other unicorns. Their breathing was faster.

"She had too large a dose," he said.

"Is she going to be all right?" Hessy said.

"If she were a horse, I'd say yeah, but who knows?"

He touched her silvery mane. "She's so soft. Here, pet her," he said.

He surprised himself. Was he going all soft over murderous people eaters?

Hessy leaned forward and touched the mane. "In the dark, it's more of a glow than a sparkle," she said.

She was right. Bertie leaned forward to get a better look at the horn. It was almost golden in this light. He touched it.

The unicorn startled, then went back to sleep.

"They don't like that, I guess," Bertie said.

"Poor girl." Hessy pet her back. "I'm going to name her Berta."

"What?"

"I'm going to name her Berta. Because she tried to eat you."

Bertie didn't like how fond Hessy sounded when speaking of the Bertie-eater.

Bertie stood up and looked at the other unicorns. "Let's just hope we don't have to name any of them 'Hessy.'"

They put the food out for the unicorns, making sure Berta had her supply near her for when she woke up. The unicorns seemed calm enough for them to watch the feeding from a distance, so Bertie and Hessy sat near the open gate. They really were something, you know, aside from their disgusting eating habits.

They ate drowsily.

Maybe Hessy was right, Bertie thought as he listened to the unicorns licking meat and crunching through bones. These animals needed their help. It was an insane idea to come; it was even more insane to stay. But as his Uncle Carl once said, if you're not living life on the edge, you're taking up too much space.

That was right before he died in a bungee jumping accident, but Bertie tried to push that thought from his mind.

CHAPTER 18

DARN UNCLE CARL.

He and Hessy had spent the last week establishing their routine. She'd sneak into the pen and feed meat to the unicorns. He'd walk around wielding tranq guns that he no longer needed and giving Dr. Om B.S. reports about the important tweaks he was making to the tranquilizers to "optimize them for unicorn use."

In other words, Bertie was a glorified public relations spin doctor. Yay for all that hard work at vet school.

So yeah, darn Uncle Carl.

He was plowing through his daily briefing now.

"Dr. Om, after analyzing one week's worth of tranquilizers, I've come up with this formulation." He put a report on Dr. Om's desk. It was all made up, but who cared?

Bertie watched as Dr. Om read through the papers. Bertie shifted the tranq gun from his left to right shoulder. There was no reason to carry this thing everywhere, even if he were using it, but he figured Dr. Om liked the show.

"Excellent, excellent, excellent," Dr. Om said. "I see

this is lower in tryathenol hypochlorite.1 Much better for the unicorns. Much better. And how are they looking?"

"Healthy teeth and gums!" Bertie said. "They haven't tried to eat anyone for a whole week!"

"What about vaccines? Are we coming up on when they should be getting vaccines?" Dr. Om said.

Bertie sighed, as though he were as frustrated as Dr. Om about this matter. "You know, I've been doing my research." He laid the tranq gun on the floor. "I've been doing my research. But I am just not ready to vaccinate them yet. I think we need to be very careful. Very careful."

"Understood! I completely understand!" Dr. Om raised his hands, palms forward. "You're the vet. You're the published expert! That's why I hired you! I won't take any more of your time. Off you go!"

Bertie headed out and waited till he was a safe distance before cursing out Uncle Carl again.

When he got to the pen, Hessy was coming out, covered in red.

"Blech, I'm a mess." she said. "I'd better go change before Dr. Om sees the blood and starts to wonder."

"Technically, it's not blood," Bertie said. "It's myoglobin."

Hessy rolled her eyes. They started walking back to their quarters. "Listen, Bertie, today's the transfer day." She looked at him knowingly.

"Transfer? Transfer of what?" he said.

"Remember, I talked with you about it?"

Bertie raised an eyebrow. "Sure, but give me a hint."

Hessy sighed. She looked around to make sure no one was in earshot. "Today is when Dr. Om has his next batch of coquíes coming in. I'm meeting with Saint. He's found a substitute for them, sort of. I convinced Dr. Om I should be the one to pick up the deliveries from now on. Saint will swoop in, grab the coquíes, replace them with some frogs that'll have to do for now, and whisk the coquíes back to Puerto Rico through his back channels."

Swoop in? Whisk? Did this guy wear a cape now?

Bertie didn't know why this all made him grouchy. He liked Saint. He did. There was just something . . .

"Okay, well, I'll meet up with you after you change," Bertie said.

"Nah, stick around here." Hessy got to the steps leading up to her tree house and jogged up before other staff could see the stains on her clothes. "Keep up with your research. And pretending to do vet things around the unicorns."

"What do you mean 'pretending?'" Bertie said.

"Well, you know. Since you don't do much to them at this point."

"Yeah, because I don't know a lot yet. Do no harm!"

"I didn't mean it in a bad way. You know that."

"Sure, sure. I do," Bertie said. "Say 'hi' to Saint for me."

"Will do. Oh, and it's time to pay the staff to 'run errands' during our delivery times this week. Here's my half of the cash." She leaned down to hand him some bills.

Bertie looked at the money. "Yup, this mission is definitely what I've been building up to do all these years."

But Hessy was already in her room. She couldn't have heard.

He walked back to his lab in the "Rainforest Research Reserve" or whatever its stupid name was. Besides researching tranquilizer information to feed Dr. Om, Bertie was trying to learn all he could about the unicorns. First, because he couldn't help them much if he didn't know anything about them. Second, because he wanted to know what made them tick. What DNA had Dr. Om used to create them? He hoped answers to this question would help reveal why they were so dependent on meat.

He'd even called around to some geneticists so he could ask discreet questions. None had bothered calling him back. Which was kind of a relief. He hated talking on the phone.

As Bertie sat down at his microscope, he wondered whether Dr. Om had really much to do with creating the unicorns. What little history Bertie had been able to uncover didn't suggest a genius at all. Was it genetic innovation by committee?

He'd been able to sneak some blood from the unicorns when he was pretending to tranq them, but the equipment in the "Rainforest Research Reserve" was pretty rudimentary. He was able to view the cells under microscope. They could certainly pass for horse cells, but he couldn't dig any deeper than that.

He had considered requisitioning more advanced equipment—DNA sequencers—but he suspected Dr. Om wouldn't want that. Any time Bertie asked him how the unicorns had been made, Dr. Om got nervous and shooed him away.

If only he could get his hands on some advanced tech, but he doubted St. Quiche had expensive DNA sequencers lying around labs. Had he known he was sticking around when he "visited" that first day, he would have smuggled at least some material in. And smuggled other stuff too, like underwear and battery-operated fans and D batteries.

Bertie paced back and forth, staring at the lab's file cabinets. They hadn't gleaned any deep, dark DNA secrets. He slapped his forehead. Dr. Om had to have DNA information on file somewhere. It didn't have to be on paper. In fact, it was probably squirreled away in one of Sandra's dark web labyrinths, or whatever they were called. So, no need for fancy, high-tech sequencers to reinvent the wheel. He just needed a good old-fashioned criminal who would be willing to hack his way into Dr. Om's secret info stash.

Bertie already knew someone who would know someone who could do it. And if the guy didn't know someone, he knew someone who knew someone who knew someone.

And that would be Saint, of course, because he knew everyone.

Bertie made a mental note to talk with him later. It would have to wait, since he was swooping in and saving coquíes at the moment.

Bertie's thoughts returned to the unicorns' behavior. So why did they get so violent when they didn't eat meat? It made no sense. Bertie had tried to find examples of other animals that went nuts when they didn't ingest meat, but he got nowhere, especially since Quichan Internet had a habit of crashing and leaving him researching in bite-sized minisessions.

Herbivores have been known to eat meat. Hippos, deer, horses even. It happens. But they don't get violent when they don't eat meat.

And as far as Bertie could tell, the unicorns were heavily dosed with horse DNA.

Well, dosed wasn't the scientific term, but you get the drift. Technically, a recombinant lattice of equine RNA with a viral replicant function.

But to get a horn on the animal, there had to be some other DNA going on in the mix.

Bertie pulled out Berta's file. He stared at her photo. Maybe he was paying too much attention to the unicorn itself. Maybe he should look more closely at the horn.

Just then his phone rang. It was an outside number.

Probably one of the hoity-toity scientists calling him back. He took a deep breath and answered. "Hello?"

"Is this Bertie Vole? I'm returning his call."

The caller sounded gruff. His voice reminded Bertie of Dr. Roderick. It made him all nervous.

"Uhhh—"

"Do you not know your own name?"

"Yes, sir, I do. This is Bertie Vole."

"This is Dr. Fred Dolly. You had questions about cloning?"

"Yes, I was just wondering what you do when you have to, you know, fill in some gaps in DNA?"

"You mean like when there's damaged DNA?"

"Sure, yeah."

"You just fill it in with some other DNA to complete the code. You ever heard of this thing called Google?"

"My internet sucks." Bertie took a deep breath. This was the only person that had bothered returning his call. He didn't want to back down just yet. "And what if you wanted to create, I don't know, a . . . hybrid?"

"A hybrid?"

"Yeah."

"Hybrid of what, for example?"

Bertie didn't want to go into details, not with that non-disclosure agreement dangling over his head. He tried to come up with a unicorn equivalent. "Like a . . . minotaur?"

Bertie slapped his head. Why'd he pick minotaur? Stupid, stupid, stupid.

"Minotaur? Are you nuts?" the caller said.

"Or centaur?"

"Centaur? What kind of freak show are you running?"

"Or . . . or Pegasus!" Yeah, that was closer in concept to a unicorn anyway. "Pegasusses? Pegasi? Pegasusseses?"

"Is this some kind of prank?"

"No, no, no—"

"Gerald, is that you?"

"No!"

"What did I tell you about pranking me at work? You're grounded!" And he hung up.

Crap. Bertie wiped the sweat off his brow. He hadn't even had a chance to ask about the meat-deprivation-turning-unicorns-into-raving-lunatics connection.

He should have given a fake name. If Dr. Dolly decided to look Bertie up, he'd end up just as much of a laughing stock as Dr. Om, if not more so. He could imagine people talking about him years down the road. "Oh, what happened to that vet, what's-his-name, Bertie Vole?" And the other person would say, "Last I heard, he moved to the Caribbean. He must have taken to the bottle. Apparently, he thinks he's . . ." The person would lower his voice to a tiny whisper. "Frankenstein." And the first person would say, "Poor boy. He never had a chance. He was always in the shadow of that sister of his. Do you know she got ANOTHER degree, an honorary one this time?"

"Shut up!" Bertie said to himself. This was doing no good.

And anyway, Gerald was his scapegoat. "Sorry, Gerald, my man. But you've done me a solid."

Bertie looked again at Berta's photo. Maybe looking at the horn under the microscope would give some clues. And anyway, he needed a distraction. He grabbed his vet bag and headed out to the pen. He was going to have to get a sample of horn, or whatever it was. With Dr. Om, you could never be sure.

Remembering how Berta had reacted the first time he had touched her horn, he knew she wasn't going to like that.

He went back and got his tranq gun. He was probably going to need it.

Bertie sneaked quietly through back paths to get to the pen. He didn't see anyone on the way.

Once again, he wondered whether the park didn't have lots of staff because Dr. Om didn't want too many people there or because his workers had all up and left, like the former manager Sebastian Cieve.

Bertie opened the side gate quietly. He walked into the clearing and saw Berta eating grass. Her silver hide sparkled in the sun, and when she saw him, she shook her mane.

Bertie took out a sugar cube. She liked sugar cubes.

The other unicorns looked on. For whatever reason, they were much more cautious around him than Berta was. Apparently, over-medicating unicorns was a direct line to their hearts.

Huh. Berta was like Bertie's mother. She loved meds too.

Bertie reached up his hand to touch the horn. Berta whinnied in annoyance and stepped back.

"It's okay, girl. I won't hurt you."

The other unicorns stepped in closer. Bertie realized that if he was going to get his sample, he'd need to work fast. He raised the tranq gun and aimed at Berta's side. He got his shot.

The other unicorns made a fuss but didn't step any closer. Maybe they were afraid he'd shoot them too. Too bad he hadn't brought any meat. He should have brought some meat.

Berta waved her tail more slowly. Her head drooped slightly. Bertie made his move.

He was able to shave off one tiny sample when Berta neighed.

That was the cue for the other unicorns to charge.

He grabbed his tranq gun and footed it to the exit. He had just closed the door when he saw one sharp horn poking out from under his armpit, right through the slats.

He looked down at his sample and wiped his forehead. He'd need to talk to Dr. Om about reinforcing this pen.

Another unicorn slammed into the gate. That was Bertie's cue to leave.

CHAPTER 19

BERTIE RETURNED TO HIS LAB, but his foray into actual science was cut short by the inestimable Dr. Om.

"Dr. Vole, glad you're back here," Dr. Om said. "I need you to come work with my team on the promotions, since you are, after all, the expert in unicorn care."

"Sure, Dr. Om," Bertie said, squashing his desire to punch the guy in the face. "I'll be right there. Is that in the marketing department?"

"Yes, yes, yes! You got it!" Dr. Om said. "What do you have there?"

"Just my vet kit," Bertie said. He closed it shut. The sample was wrapped in a napkin inside. He was hoping to take a peek under the microscope before heading off to the meeting, but Dr. Om didn't seem too eager to leave.

"Understood, understood! You were checking up on my baby-poos, weren't you?" Dr. Om said.

"I was, I was. Making sure the baby-poos are all dandy."

"Well, off you go, off you go. Time is a-wasting! The park opens up in a few weeks!" Dr. Om smiled, but Bertie didn't like how he wasn't smiling even while he was smiling.

If that makes any sense at all.

Bertie headed out of his lab. He held the door open for Dr. Om to leave, but he waved his hands. "No need. No need," Dr. Om said. "I just want to check some of the files in my lab here. You go off. I'll meet up with you after."

"Sure." He didn't like Dr. Om's intrusion one bit. He wondered which files he was referring to. Or was he just making an excuse to snoop around Bertie's work? The guy had never stepped foot in "his" lab since Bertie had arrived. Not that he had seen, anyway.

He wished he had taken his vet bag with him, not that Dr. Om could know what was in there.

Right?

But when Bertie went back after his meeting, the sample was gone.

It was night by the time Bertie got to the south gate to wait for Hessy. She and Saint had made an extra meat run during their black op coquí rescue. She'd be coming in with the food any minute now, but Bertie wasn't so sure that they were going to be able to keep up with this sneaking around for much longer.

He heard Lady Mathilda's vehicular emphysema. A bright light blinded Bertie as she bumped into the clearing. Saint hopped out, kicked the passenger door, and released a smiling Hessy.

"Hey, Bertie," Hessy said. "You're right on time."

"I am. We need to talk," Bertie said in a whisper.

"What's wrong?" she said.

"Let's just get this meat back quick."

"On it. But one thing. I had an idea of how you could

find out about the DNA." Hessy said the last bit under her breath, since Saint was close by.

Bertie had forgotten about that. He looked up at Saint. "I did too, actually—"

"There have got to be files somewhere. Saint can get us a hacker!" She looked triumphant.

"Yeah, great idea," Bertie said with a false smile.

Saint came over. "Anything you need, I can get it for you," he said. He patted Bertie on the back. "Let me know what you're looking for, and I won't ask any questions."

Bertie thought for a moment. Whatever he wrote down would have to be discreet. He finally scrawled something and handed it over. "Do you think you can find someone to hack into that info?"

Saint read over it quickly. "I know of a young man. It may take a while, Internet being what it is here." He laughed.

"Don't hackers have fancy uplinks to the Internet?" Bertie said. The hackers Bertie had seen on TV sat in basements all day long and never worried about Internet outages.

"Not since he is in prison," Saint said. "He gets bored behind bars. This will be of great service to him."

"Glad I can help," Bertie said. "And thanks. Wait, we're not going to get arrested for being involved, are we?"

"No, no. He covers his tracks very well, except for when he doesn't." Saint winked and smacked Bertie on the back. "Well, I'm going to push off now, if you don't need anything else," Saint said.

"We're good," Bertie said before Hessy had a chance to answer. "Thanks, Saint."

"Yes, thanks, Saint!" Hessy said.

"We make an excellent team!" Saint said. "The four of us."

"The four of us?" Bertie said.

"Don't forget Lady Mathilda. She's a jealous one." Saint kicked the door open. "A jealous one, I warn you!"

"Bye, Lady Mathilda!" Hessy said, a little too loudly for Bertie's liking.

He touched her elbow. "Listen, Hessy, there's been a development."

"What?" she said. She hefted a piece of meat from the ground and handed it to Bertie. Then she picked up one for herself. They started down the path to the pen.

"Dr. Om stole a sample I had taken from Berta," he said.

"Did he?" she said. "So, you think he suspects something."

"Yeah, I do. I took a sample of the horn." Bertie startled at the crack of a breaking twig behind him, but when he looked, no one was there.

"What we're doing here—right now—it isn't safe anymore." Bertie put the meat on the ground outside the pen.

"Maybe, maybe not," Hessy said as they walked back to get more meat. "But we can't stop. We've started this. We've got to figure out how to keep going."

Even in the dark, Bertie could tell Hessy was enjoying all this cloak and dagger.

"Anyway," she said. "We're better off than we were. The unicorns are calm now. I told you they just needed proper care. Anyway, I take that as a win."

"You like this job," Bertie said. He didn't know why, but it irked him.

"Yes, I do, actually," Hessy said. "I'm making a difference."

"Meanwhile, I'm playing PR patsy to a mad scientist."

"That's not true. You're doing research. You're figuring things out. You're helping me."

Bertie sighed. "I guess." He wondered whether Hessy was just being nice because she felt guilty about saying that he was pretending to do vet things earlier.

"I know so," she said. "You're making progress."

Bertie wasn't sure what progress he was making, but he didn't try to convince her otherwise.

By now, all the meat was hidden in the bushes near the side gate. Hessy reached to open it up when Bertie put his hand on the handle.

"Be careful. The unicorns weren't too happy when I went in today with the tranq gun," he said.

"Oh, because you needed to get the sample."

"Yes, they charged when I shaved the sample off the horn." He pointed to the newest hole in the door.

"You should have taken some of the leftover meat in."

"Yum," said Bertie. "I didn't think of that in time."

He opened the door, using his body as a shield in case the unicorns were still upset. He peeked in.

Berta was standing, head down. But she seemed fine. The others were off by themselves, calm as well.

Bertie waved at Hessy to bring the meat. Between the two, they fed the unicorns and got out without any incident.

"I don't think we should stick around and watch the show," Bertie said. "Dr. Om may have lookouts."

Hessy didn't reply right away. Finally, she said, "Okay." But Bertie could tell she was tempted to stay anyway.

They packed up the remaining meat and carried it between the two of them. They made their way down the narrow path, taking the longer route to avoid detection. For the first time, Bertie noticed how noisy it was to carry tons of meat through the forest. Branches broke, and their feet cracked on fallen twigs. The wind joined in, screaming, "Dr. Oooooom, your employees are feeding unsanctioned meat to the unicorns."

Well, that last bit was a figment of Bertie's jittery imagination, but you get the idea.

Bertie liked their chances of not getting caught less and less. Paying other staff to "run errands" could work for only so long.

"Bertie?" Hessy spoke in the quietest of whispers. Bertie had to lean in to hear.

"What?"

"Do you think we need to tell Saint about what's really going on here?"

Bertie looked to make sure no one else was around. "We have a non-disclosure agreement."

"Yeah, but sooner or later, if he keeps helping us, he's going to find out," she said. "What's worse? That we tell him? In controlled circumstances? Or that he comes face to face with you know what and runs screaming bloody murder? I mean, which is subtler?"

Bertie thought for a moment. "I don't see Saint screaming bloody anything."

"You know what I mean."

Bertie didn't, but he nodded as though he did. "Well, you may have a point."

"Look, if he were in the know, you would have to do less interference. You could focus on what you do, and Saint and I could handle stuff on our own," Hessy said.

"Right, well," Bertie cleared his throat. Good old Saint. He'd be happy to swoop in with a cape and rescue Hessy's day, wouldn't he? "Let's not say anything just yet. You know? We'll just give ourselves some more time to let this play out."

Hessy sighed in response.

"And you know me!" Bertie put on his well-practiced smile. "I love to help!"

CHAPTER 20

ANOTHER WEEK PASSED, and despite Bertie's concerns, Hessy and he were able to keep feeding the unicorns. Lester and the other guards kept their distance. The unicorns were calm, but the guards didn't seem any less confident of their chances of not being torn to shreds.

Dr. Om seemed perfectly convinced with Bertie's B.S.-filled, public relational distractions. And he kept acting as though there were no need to worry about volatile unicorns rampaging around a park on a populated island.

The progress on construction suggested, however, that perhaps Dr. Om did have some doubts. He wanted to add bars to the tropical-style Caribbean French doors and windows on all guest tree-house cabañas. Bertie heard the contractor saying that the modifications required to put in bars would be pricey.

"Money is no object! None at all!" Dr. Om said. He patted the contractor on the back and giggled, but Bertie couldn't help noticing that he was nervous. When Dr. Om saw him, he pulled the contractor away and lowered a voice to a whisper.

At least carting around tranq guns was buffing up Bertie's biceps.

Bertie kept researching, but he didn't dare grab any more unicorn samples right yet. Best to not tickle Dr. Om's radar. They were already pushing it by sneaking in contraband meat.

In other words, he spent more time dodging Dr. Om's possible suspicions than being a vet. Bertie had moments in which he almost wished to be back at Dr. Roderick's practice. He hated Dr. Roderick. He hated the people customers. But at least he had been an actual vet there.

Then one day, Dr. Om called a meeting.

Bertie didn't think anything of it at first because Dr. Om loved calling meetings. Bertie grabbed his files on the tranquilizers and other sci-fi fantasy documents he had on hand. He picked up his tranq gun for good effect and headed to the office.

When he got in, Dr. Om's high-back chair was turned around. Bertie couldn't tell whether he was in it since he was so short.

"Uh, Dr. Om?" Bertie knocked on the door frame. "You there?"

Dr. Om's chair turned slowly. He slid into view. His mouth was in a crooked scowl. He had his head cocked to the side and propped in his hand.

"Sit down, Dr. Vole."

Bertie sat.

"There's a new directive," Dr. Om said.

"Uh-huh." Bertie was worried. He'd never heard Dr. Om be so succinct before.

"Armed guards will be posted around the unicorn pen 24/7," Dr. Om said.

"Uh . . ."

Dr. Om leaned forward. "24/7."

"Well, you know, Lester and his crew do an excellent job guarding the pen. They are highly . . . conscientious."

Not, but he wasn't going to add that bit.

"That's what you'd call them?" Dr. Om said. "Conscientious?"

"Yes, absolutely. I've . . . I've been very impressed with how dedicated they are. Lester especially."

"Huh. I find that interesting. I have a question for you."

"Yes, Dr. Om."

"Considering their dedication, why have I found meat—meat!—in my unicorns' pen?"

"Meat, you say?" Crap, crap, crap. He wiped his hands on his safari shorts.

"Yes, meat." Dr. Om sat back again and looked at Bertie.

"Gee, um, beat's me how that's happened, Dr. Om."

"Yes, well, it isn't your doing." Dr. Om narrowed his eyes. "Isn't that right?"

This was a test, for sure, so Bertie nodded as vigorously and enthusiastically as he could. With this guy, showmanship went a long way.

Om's face relaxed, and he continued, "You are not charged with security. You are charged with unicorn care."

"Ha ha, yes, well, I'm very busy with that," Bertie said. "Do you have any suspects?" He winced as his voice cracked.

"Not yet." Dr. Om swiveled in his chair and picked up a file. "No harm, no foul. There were no tourists to be horrified by their dietary proclivities—yet. The park opens in just four weeks. They've got to get used to their regular diet."

"Wait, four weeks?" Bertie said. "I thought it was three."

"Yes, yes, but my contractor had a . . . delay." He waved the issue away as though it wasn't important, but Bertie was sure it was a bad sign that even Dr. Om was willing to push back the opening.

He won't admit it, but he knows things weren't ready.

"Back to the subject at hand," Dr. Om said. "It is unacceptable that my unicorns have been eating meat. But I've taken steps to make sure this never happens again."

Dr. Om splayed out the file in front of Bertie. "I've hired an elite—an elite, mind you, elite!—private security firm to stand guard at my gates and around my pen. Lester and his team have relaxed standards to a level that is way too Caribbean for my taste. Do you see those big guns in the photo? Do you?"

Bertie looked at the AR-15s and gulped. "I do. They're very big."

"Those guns will keep things on track from now on."

"May I ask a question?"

"Yes, yes, of course, of course!" Dr. Om seemed much cheerier now that he had ruined Bertie's day.

"Why did you bring me in to tell me this?"

"Ah, good question. Excellent question. The guards have been brought into the fold in terms of what is going on here. They are used to high-security, top-secret scenarios. When they arrive in a few minutes, you'll want to brief them on general unicorn safety, in case—just in case—things get out of hand. Make sure they know what kind of tranquilizers to use on the baby-poos, should the need arise."

"Ah, so the big guns you were talking about will be tranq guns?" Bertie said.

"Oh, no," Dr. Om giggled. "No, no, no, no. The big guns will be real guns. For anyone who tries to mess with my unicorns." Dr. Om stood up. "Now get going. Shoo. Saint will be bringing in the guards in a few minutes. Don't want to make them wait. Never let people with big guns wait. It's my personal policy."

Bertie left the office as fast as he could. He grabbed his walkie-talkie. "Hessy, Hessy, come in!"

"What's up, Bertie? I'm about to give the unicorns their morning snack."

"Don't! Do you copy? Don't."

"Huh, sure, I copy. But why not?"

"Dr. Om found out. Don't go near that pen." Bertie looked up as he heard the rotors of the incoming helicopter. "It could cost you your life."

SECTION III

Excerpt from *The Gastrointestinal Tract of Unicorns: Part I of the Anatomy of Rare Creatures Series* by Bertram W. Vole and Timothy E. Grett

ESSENTIAL ITEMS FOR YOUR UNICORN PANTRY

"The unicorn is often mistaken for a herbivore thanks to its similarity to the horse. In fact, the unicorn is a carnivore. It prefers its meat rotten, but will eat canned meat, dried meat, smoked meat, pickled meat, fresh meat, and even human remains when the supply of other meat is limited.

It is yet unknown whether a unicorn will actively hunt for live prey. It is best to take utmost precaution when in proximity to a hungry unicorn."

Author note: Yeah, learned that the hard way.

CHAPTER 21

A BRIGHTNESS PIERCED through the dark forest. Bertie approached, not sure what was drawing him in. He reached the big wooden double doors and stepped into the unicorn pen. He had never noticed before, but a ring of flowers—a circle of bright red, purple, and yellow blossoms —drew a perfect circle within the enclosure. How could Bertie not have noticed that this was paradise itself?

He'd never heard it before, but there was a gurgling stream coming from all directions. It gave the unicorn meadow a sense of calm, of peace. The sun was at its highest point, and its light, filtered through the trees, had a greenish, pleasant glow.

A clop-clop from behind made Bertie spin around. There was Berta, sparkling brightly in the midday sun. Bertie had to put his hands over his eyes to soften the glare. Yet at the same time, the silvery sheen spoke peace to Bertie's troubled soul.

Berta put her head down, nudging Bertie so that he would pet her. He touched her head. She whinnied happily. He took some sugar cubes out of his pocket. To his surprise, they were purple and yellow and pink and orange and blue. Bertie wondered why anyone would dye sugar cubes. But a moment later, they turned to kids' cereal. He didn't know why, but the transformation seemed to be perfectly normal, expected even.

He stared at the cereal. The colors were a pastel version of the blooms in the unicorn meadow. Then Bertie was distracted by a whinny in back of him.

He turned—for no more than a few seconds—to look at the other unicorns that dotted the pen right and left. They flicked their manes and trotted from grassy patch to grassy patch.

Out of nowhere, Bertie heard a growl from Berta. He turned to calm her. But what he saw filled him with terror. Her mouth was opened wide. She lunged at him. Purple froth lined her gums, and her sharpened teeth dripped with blood.

Bertie woke up in a sweat. He'd just been eaten by Berta.

He got up out of his bed to get water. "It was only a dream. Only a dream."

He put the cold glass up to his forehead. Ever since he and Hessy couldn't sneak meat to the unicorns, their violent behavior made Bertie's dream chillingly plausible.

Except for the frothy, sharpened teeth. They weren't, after all, zombie vampires.

At least not yet.

It was going to be another long day.

Bertie met with Hessy for breakfast. When they got to the dining area, they saw Lester and his crew at the far corner. Hessy waved at them.

"Hey there," she said. "How's it going?"

They waved back. "Hey back! We're doing great.

Happy to have those guards with big guns on staff. Let them deal with the crazy donkeys."

"You know it," Bertie said, trying to laugh. He gave up. There was no way he sounded convincingly happy.

Bertie and Hessy took their breakfast out to the front veranda, where they could talk more easily without Lester and his team overhearing them.

"You look awful," Hessy said.

"Yeah, I had bad dreams."

"What, did a unicorn eat you?" Hessy laughed.

"Actually, yes," he said.

Hessy drowned her last giggle. "Sorry. I guess it really is no laughing matter."

"No, it isn't. Did you see how Dr. Om had the fence reinforced with steel? But the way the unicorns are butting against it, I don't know how long it will hold."

"Is Dr. Om pestering you to tranquilize them?"

"He did, but I told him the tranquilizers probably never worked. The meat was masking their behavior. He swallowed it. I can't just keep tranquilizing them. That's no way to live. Eventually, they would need higher and higher doses anyway. It'd get dangerous for them."

"We have to figure out how to sneak in meat," Hessy said.

The guards were charged with checking every bag of food that went into the enclosure. The unicorns had gotten so violent, Bertie and Hessy couldn't enter the pen anymore. They just tossed big bags of grain over the fence.

"Maybe Dr. Om's reformulated food will get here soon?" Hessy said.

"Come on, like that'll work. The guy doesn't know what he's up against."

"We've got to come up with something." Hessy didn't

say anything for a minute. "You know who may have some ideas? Saint may have some ideas."

"Yeah, Superman Saint." Bertie said.

"Hmmm?"

"Oh, nothing. Let's try talking to Saint."

Hessy got up, but Bertie stopped her.

"Wait, why don't you go chat with Om, see whether he has any idea when the newly formulated Lucky Charms crap is set for delivery? Like you say, maybe it'll work. I'll head out and talk with Saint."

"Sure, sounds like a plan." Hessy said. The sound of fighting unicorns reached the dining room. "But on second thought, you're right. Those Lucky Charms aren't going to do any good."

CHAPTER 22

BERTIE WAS SET to meet Saint at a bar on the isolated Eastern shore. It was his first time leaving the park since the day he went in search of rotting meat for the "baby-poos." He had borrowed a Jeep from Lester, who didn't seem to care what anyone did as long as he didn't have to go anyway near the unicorns.

Bertie headed out the back gate. The last time he had left in a car, Saint had taken the scenic route. Bertie turned left. It seemed like the more direct route.

Bertie wasn't used to driving with the steering wheel on the right, but given the way Quichans drove, he'd fit right in if he messed up.

He soon realized he wouldn't have to worry about meeting too many other cars. The road was deserted. A few wooden houses butted up against it, but aside from that, he was able to enjoy the green hills and forest of St. Quiche. It was refreshing to escape the madness of the park.

He drove by a squat, yellow house. An old lady was out front. She waved, and Bertie waved back.

Hessy was right. The Quichans were friendly.

He took a right at a gas station to head down the hill into town.

Only a few minutes later, he saw another squat yellow house with a very similar old lady in front. She waved. Bertie waved back. He could have sworn it looked like the same lady.

The next time he saw the squat yellow house with the waving lady, he realized he was going in circles. At this rate, he'd never make it to the bar. He stopped at the gas station.

He grumbled as he got out of the Jeep. He spent his days taking the wrong turn at the park, and now he was lost on the road. St. Quiche wasn't even big. How'd he manage to get lost anyway?

A bell tinkled as he walked inside. A short man and a taller, chubby man were sitting at a metal table in the center.

"No fuel today, I'm afraid," Chubby said. "We all out."

"That's okay," Bertie said. "I'm actually lost. I just need directions."

"Where to?" Shorty said.

"Uh, I don't know what it's called. It's a bar on the Eastern shore?" Bertie kicked himself. Why hadn't he asked Saint for the name of the place?

"Oh, yes, that one," Chubby said. "It's okay, that bar. But I recommend Bar Saint-Esprit instead. It's better, and it's close. There is no way to get lost going there."

"No, no, no, no," Shorty said. "Battu Pub is much better."

"So you say," Chubby said.

Bertie tried to get a word in, but—

"You only go to Bar Saint-Esprit because it's cheap," Shorty said. "But you get what you pay for."

"Well, you don't know whether this gentleman has

money," Chubby said. "You recommend an overpriced bar. Maybe he is poor."

"He drives a Jeep!" Shorty pointed to the car outside. "What poor man drives a Jeep?"

"That's not mine," Bertie said.

"Oh, ho, ho!" Shorty laughed and clapped his hands. "You stole it! You are not supposed to say when you steal cars."

"No, I didn't steal it," Bertie said. These two were worse than Sandra. "It's a work vehicle."

The two men looked disappointed.

"And I have a meeting at that other bar, so I kind of need to go there," Bertie realized he sounded angry. And then he felt guilty for sounding angry. "I really appreciate the suggestions. I'll try those bars some other time."

The two men smiled. "I help you," Shorty said. "Follow me now. Turn around here and go back up the hill. Up the hill."

"No, no, no, no," said Chubby. He took Bertie by the shoulders and walked with him to the door. "That is the bad way. Listen good to what I tell you, hear? Keep straight. No turning."

Shorty crossed his arms. "Bad idea."

Chubby ignored him. "You will see a fork in the road. Go left, up the hill. Not down the hill."

"Yes, before you went down the hill," Shorty said. He stood next to Bertie. "This time, go up."

"So away from the coast?" Bertie said. "But I want to go to the coast."

"Trust me," Chubby said. "Go up the hill. Turn left, up the hill. Then keep straight, straight, straight, straight, straight. The road is straight, but it does wind. But keep straight. Don't turn."

"Yes, follow this road straight," said Shorty.

"Then you will see a Catholic church on your left," said Chubby.

"I turn there?" Bertie said.

"No, you keep straight," Chubby said. "Then you see a big house on the corner. Big house. Some tourists bought that house from my cousin for their vacations, but he didn't tell them it didn't come with electricity. He took all the copper out, and now they are very, very angry."

"Yes," said Shorty. "If you buy a house on St. Quiche, make sure it comes with electricity. It is cheaper to buy a house with the electrical wires already in than to put new ones in."

"I'll keep that in mind," said Bertie. "So, I turn at that house?"

"No, no, no," said Chubby. "Don't turn in that road. That will put you up in Mangostad. Keep straight. You will then see a big, white house. A mansion. A real big house. The owner is bad. Bad man. He is from St. Carlota. They are all bad."

"I've heard," said Bertie.

The two men seemed to approve of Bertie's comment. They smiled and slapped him on the back.

"You know your way around St. Quiche," Shorty said.

"You see this big white house with the St. Carlota flag. You catch my meaning?" Chubby said.

"Yes, but I don't know what the St. Carlota flag looks like."

"You don't need to," Shorty said. "The house is so evil, you will feel the evil go up into your feet and hit you on the head before you see the house. When you get a headache, you know you are near."

"I have a headache now," Bertie said.

"See, I told you!" Shorty said. "Those Carlotians. Bad, bad, bad, bad, bad."

"So , I turn when I see the flag?" Bertie said.

"No, keep straight," Chubby said. "Your turn is left of the coconut tree."

"Left of the coconut tree," Bertie said.

"You catch my meaning, good," Chubby said. "You turn left, then keep straight. Straight, straight. Then turn left of where the Dominican Friar used to be."

"Was that the fried chicken place?" Shorty said.

"Yes," Chubby said.

"That was some good chicken," Shorty said. "Too bad about the roaches."

"Roaches?" Bertie said.

The two men nodded. Shorty held his hands wide to show the size of the roaches. Chubby held his hands even wider. Then he adjusted Shorty's hands.

"What's there now?" Bertie said.

"Nothing," said Shorty.

Bertie squeezed his eyes shut for a moment. "Well, thanks for the directions," he said.

"Listen, you call this number if you get lost," Shorty said. "My way is better."

"No, it isn't," Chubby said.

Bertie looked at his phone. "I don't have signal up here."

"Okay, so don't call us!" Chubby said, smiling. "You are good. It is easy to get there."

Bertie waved and got back in his Jeep.

He was getting more and more used to getting lost.

After three more stops to get directions, Bertie got to the

end of the road and looked out towards where the bar was supposed to be. There was a low wooden building, white with blue trim. Its front looked out to sea. But the road ended. The only way to get there was over the sand.

"Holy Moses. There's no road?" He hit the steering wheel in frustration. Here he was, running late, the air conditioner in the Jeep was busted, and now he had to walk on a steamy beach? What was he thinking when he dreamed of living in the Caribbean? Total sign of insanity.

He jumped out of the car and started walking over the sand, but the beach invaded his shoes, making it almost impossible to continue.

Bertie took off his shoes and immediately regretted it. "Hot, hot, hot, hot . . ." He pulled on his shoes again and trudged the rest of the way, looping around the side of the building to get to the entrance.

There, a hand-painted wooden sign watched over the ocean. On it was the name of the bar: The Last Resort.

Yeah, like that's not a bad sign. He pulled off his shoes on the porch and poured out the sand before pulling the screen door open.

"Eh, eh. Look who's here!" a happy voice called out. It was Saint.

"Hi, Saint. How are you?"

"I'm doing fantastic," he said as he pumped Bertie's sweaty hand. "I'd ask how you are, but you look like death warmed over. No need!"

Bertie collapsed onto a bar stool. "Any reason we're meeting in the middle of nowhere?" Bertie said.

"Because it is the middle of nowhere." Saint waved the barman over and pointed at Bertie meaningfully. The barman nodded.

"Hessy told me about the private security thugs. I am

thinking things are getting pretty dicey at Dr. Crazy Man Park," Saint said.

Bertie hadn't noticed the barman leaving a tray holding two empty glasses, a huge jug of water, and two yellow-orange drinks. Bertie wanted to pour water straight from the jug into his mouth, but he held back.

After Bertie had had his fill of water, he pointed to the yellow drink. "What's that?"

"Eh! You haven't had it yet? That is the official drink of St. Quiche, the Mango Sloopie. Remember this now, any Sloopie that isn't made with mango is not a Sloopie at all."

"Good to know," Bertie said.

"Our esteemed barman here invented the Sloopie."

"Good to know," Bertie said.

"How is it possible that you had no Sloopie yet?"

"I don't get out much." Bertie took a sip.

"That is a sin, man. A sin."

"Yes, well, now that I have had a Sloopie, I may move in here." Bertie looked over at the barman. "How much rent do you charge on a barstool?"

Saint laughed and patted him on the back. "I think you may have a sense of humor after all. It is good to see. Good to see. It is why Hessy is so fond of you."

"What? Nah," Bertie said. That's thick coming from this one, he thought.

"Oh, yes. Those green eyes light up when she talks about you," he said.

"She talks about me? What does she say?"

"That you need to man up and take charge of your life or you will end up living in your parents' basement for the rest of your days," Saint said.

"Wait, first off—first off—I don't live in my parents' basement. They don't have a basement. Second, no one's eyes light up when they say things like that." Saint tried to interrupt, but Bertie charged ahead. "And third! Third, she's not interested in me. Trust me. She is all about you. It's hot in here. How much booze is in this thing?"

"None," Saint said. "Would you like some rum in your Sloopie? Quichan rum is second to none."

"No, thanks. I'm fine." Bertie felt silly, but also relieved because the topic of conversation was obviously taking a detour.

Bertie said, "The reason I asked to talk to you—"

"You're real doltish, boy. I am sure if you pay attention to Hessy, you will see she is over the moon for you."

"Okay, great, back to that." Bertie finished his drink. "Trust me, she likes-likes you."

"Likes-likes? What, are you twelve? Me, I am not twelve. I am old enough to be her father. Her grandfather even. She is crazy about you."

Bertie looked at Saint. "Wait, grandfather? How old are you anyway? You don't look old."

"Too old to tell," Saint said. "The Caribbean humidity is very good for the skin."

"Well, I'm glad I moved here," Bertie said. He started on his second Sloopie. Somehow, the barman had known he needed one.

"Also, man, laughter keeps you young." Saint grabbed Bertie's shoulder and shook it till Bertie thought it would come loose. "Young, man, young! You must laugh more." As if to prove his point, Saint laughed.

"Right, well, I'll try to laugh more and avoid my parents' non-existent basement." Bertie mulled over the conversation as he sipped his drink.

He looked over at Saint.

Maybe Hessy was right after all.

Not about the basement, of course.

Because his parents didn't have a basement.

But about telling Saint about the unicorns.

Maybe the time had come to tell him after all.

Plus, it would change the trajectory of this conversation, an added plus, as far as Bertie was concerned.

"Saint, Hessy and I haven't told you what is in that park."

"No, you haven't," Saint said, finishing off his Sloopie. "No doubt you have signed non-disclosure agreements and promised to make a bloody sacrifice of your first offspring if you breathe a word of it to anyone."

"Wow, yeah, you're in the loop," Bertie said. "Well, listen, you've been helping us, and I think it's probably time to let you know what's up. You're going to find out eventually, but you must not let anyone—" Bertie lowered his voice and pointed at the bartender.

"Anyone know. Got it?"

"Yes, I do indeed got it," Saint said. He had an amused smile on his face "Shall we move to a table over there?"

"Good idea," Bertie said. They moved to the far corner.

"Speak freely, my brother," Saint said.

"Right, so this park is not a regular park. It's a park for —" Bertie got in close and whispered, "Uni-corns."

Saint got in close and whispered back. "I already know." He then burst out in laughter. "I already know. For a long time."

"What, did Hessy tell you?" Bertie looked towards the bar to make sure no one was listening.

"No, I knew even before I met you two." Saint slapped Bertie on the shoulder, who made a mental note to avoid Saint any time he had a sunburn.

"How?"

"Well, first, I make it my business to know. If it is about tourism, it is my business. If it is about transportation, it is my business. If it is about the black market, it is my business. If it is about Quichan welfare, it is my business."

"I see," Bertie said.

"Also, the little Dr. Crazy Man, for all his talk of secrecy, loves attention. He loves people to think him important. I was the one to drive him to the park when he first arrived, and since this out-of-the-way bar is so very much on the way, I offered him a drink. One extra big Sloopie with several shots of the Caribbean's sweetest rum, and he told me about those horned creatures of his fantastic invention."

"You knew?"

"Yes."

"All along?"

"Yes."

Bertie thought for a moment. "What else do you know?"

"All taxi drivers are also psychologists, as you probably guessed," Saint said.

"Sure. Right."

"He is a little man with deep insecurities. And his stay in a mental health hospital didn't help."

"I knew it! Did he say what he was there for?"

"Not specifically. He just said it was from a breakdown after his 'innovative scientific theories were rejected by the entrenched, small-minded, backward-thinking donkeys.'"

"Uh-huh."

"Then he started to cry," Saint said. "And no amount of rum can entice a cohesive tale from a crying drunk man."

"That belongs on a t-shirt," Bertie said.

"I believe you are correct," Saint said. And then he

laughed. "What can I help you with? Besides revealing the dark secrets of the newest owner of St. Quiche?"

"Well, the unicorns eat meat."

"That explains why the butcher is our new best friend."

"But Dr. Om doesn't want them to eat meat because he says it's gross. So he makes them eat horse food. For some reason, when they don't eat meat, they get violent."

"I too would get violent on a diet of horse food."

"And now, with this nut job's private security, we can't smuggle meat into the pens, as you know."

"True. Drop it from a helicopter."

"Well, see, here's the thing. They go crazy when we fly overhead. I mean, crazy! They try to eat each other and butt into the fence, which I don't know if it's going to hold that much longer."

"That is indeed a problem," Saint said. "You were hoping I would have a suggestion?"

"Yeah, because you know everyone and stuff," Bertie said.

"Well, let's just say I make it my business." Saint gestured to the bartender. "Important thinking requires another round of Sloopies and chummies."

By the time Bertie and Saint headed out of The Last Resort an hour after closing, they had a plan.

Saint knew the owner of an air balloon tour company on St. Carlota. "He is a money-hungry, evil man, like all people on St. Carlota," Saint said. "But his business is just a front. His real job is smuggler. This is good for us."

"How?"

"Because he has a black air balloon that can fly at night

undetected," Saint said. "It will be simple. You pile meat into the basket, go up, and throw it down in the pen."

And so, it was decided that Saint would travel to St. Carlota the next day to pick up the air balloon. When Bertie asked him how much it would cost, Saint said, "No, this evil man owes me." He touched his nose. "Anyway, consider this my gift to you and Hessy."

"A gift?" Bertie said as he emptied his shoes of sand.

"Yes, because nothing is more romantic than an air balloon ride at night. Consider it your first date," Saint said.

"Right," Bertie hollered as Saint drove off. "Because nothing says romance more than dropping dead, rotting meat on a bunch of hungry, carnivorous creatures that want to eat you to death."

CHAPTER 23

WHEN BERTIE MET up with Hessy for breakfast, he told her of the plan. Only he didn't tell her about the air balloon doubling as a date. There was no way to say that without being weird.

"And did Dr. Om tell you when the mutant feed was coming?" Bertie asked.

"No, he only said it was 'on its way. On its way!'"

"Yeah, that sounds like him," Bertie said.

Hessy looked at her watch. "Well, I'm off."

"Where are you going?" Bertie asked.

"Church. It's Sunday." She paused for a second. "Want to come?"

"Oh, right. It's Sunday," Bertie said as he watched her gather her things.

"You should come."

"You sound like my mother." Bertie put on a falsetto. "'Bertie, you skip church again today?'"

Hessy laughed. "I'll tell Saint you said 'hi.'"

Bertie sighed and got up. "No, I guess I'll come with. It's not like I've stopped-stopped going."

"Whatever that means," Hessy said.

"Yeah, whatever that means."

They borrowed the Jeep and got to the service right as the sermon was starting. The church was packed, so they had to walk all the way up the aisle, in view of all the people fanning themselves with church programs, and take a couple of seats in the front row.

"Today we conclude our series 'Uahula Is Not on the Mountain. God Is!'" the pastor said. "Some of you are coming to me insisting that Uahula inhabits our mountain, but he does not. He is not real. We are followers of Christ. We must not let our eyes be distracted by myths."

"Amen," said an old lady in the back row.

"Amen, Sister Agnes. Amen," the pastor said. He smiled and was about to continue his sermon when Agnes interrupted.

"Up there, in the mountain, there is something brewing." A grumbling of approval rose from the congregation.

"Something is not right," Agnes said.

More people mumbled and nodded.

"Something of evil."

"Sister Agnes," the pastor said, but she kept going.

"Something to set your teeth on edge ."

The people murmured.

"And I know what it is," Agnes said.

The congregation went silent. Bertie and Hessy gave each other worried looks. Was the secret out?

"It is St. Quiche's own Area 51! Those screams come from tortured aliens."

The congregation gasped, then chattered among themselves. Bertie breathed a sigh of relief.

"Silence. Silence!" the pastor said, holding his hands up. "Come now."

The congregation quieted.

"We know better. Brothers and sisters of the Lord, now is not a time for false speculation. Now is the time to cling to the truth. The truth is in our grasp. We have in our congregation today not one but two people who work up at the park in the mountain." Bertie retreated farther behind his bulletin. "Miss Beauregard, I asked you last week and I ask you again, is Uahula up in the mountain?"

"No pastor, he isn't."

"And Dr. Vole, is Uahula up in the mountain?"

"I haven't seen him, no," Bertie said. "I mean, I haven't really looked, but . . ." He leaned in to Hessy. "See? This is why I don't like coming to church so much anymore. People pick on you."

"Shhh," Hessy said.

The pastor continued, "And, Miss Beauregard and Dr. Vole, are there tortured aliens?"

"The only tortured one is me," Bertie said with a laugh. Hessy hit him on his arm. "Sorry, no one is being tortured." He turned to the lady behind him, who was scowling at him. "That was a joke. Sorry. My bad. No torture!"

"My brothers and sisters, we must conclude that either these two lovely young people are wicked liars, servants of the devil himself, or that Uahula is not in the mountain."

Bertie thought that was an awful lot of pressure to put on him. What if these people opted to believe he was a wicked liar, servant of the devil? What would they do to him?

"Our God is committed. He does not waver. We mustn't waver either." The pastor opened his Bible for the reading.

Hessy leaned over and whispered, "They're certainly not wrong to be worried."

Bertie nodded but didn't say anything. She was right. If one of those unicorns got loose, they could do some real damage to these people.

Maybe it was just the heat stroke. Maybe it was the remnant of the Sloopie. But for the first time since Bertie had left the half-comfort of his half-basement, he felt half-stoked to do something. He wasn't sure what, but he felt half-stoked.

CHAPTER 24

WHEN BERTIE and Hessy returned to the park after church, they were greeted by Dr. Om's frantic screams.

"Stand down, stand down, stand down!" They could hear him all the way from the south exit of the park. They looked at each other and footed it.

When they got to the pen, Dr. Om stood in front, between the fence and the new seven guards, holding his hands up. His jacket askew, it showed the sweat staining his dress shirt. Behind him, the fence yawed as the unicorns slammed themselves into it. "Stand down now!"

"What's going on?" Hessy said. Bertie ran to get the tranq guns in the storage near the pen. He handed one each to Hessy and Dr. Om.

"Where were you two?" Dr. Om said, gripping the tranq gun. Bertie moved Hessy out of the way of what would no doubt be Dr. Om's shaky aim.

"At church," Hessy said.

"Wait, church? You go to church—church!—when my unicorns are about to get slaughtered?"

"Slaughtered?" Hessy said.

"These . . . these thugs!" Dr. Om pointed his tranq gun at the guards, who didn't flinch. "These thugs threatened to kill my unicorns if they escaped."

"Not a threat, sir!" The guard in the middle said. "We will exterminate them if they pose a danger to us, sir."

"I made my instructions very clear," Dr. Om said. "Very clear! You are to use tranq guns only on them. Tranq guns only!" He jumped up and down to prove his point.

A huge crack came from the pen. The metal holding the fence posts strained.

Bertie bent down to whisper in Hessy's ear. "You go get the last of the meat."

"Bertie, don't let them kill the unicorns. Don't let them kill Berta."

He looked at Hessy. "Right. I'll try. Now run!"

"Listen," Bertie said. He approached the guards. "I know these unicorns are a little agitated, but as a vet, I suggest we stick to tranquilizers, okay?"

The guard wouldn't budge. "If they pose a threat to human life, sir—"

"Threat! Threat?" Dr. Om approached the guard. "You want to see a threat, kill my unicorns and watch what I do to you. Do you know how much work it took to create them? Huh? Huh? Do you know how expensive they are?" He stood on his tiptoes to look the guard right in the eyes. "Do you know how much of my reputation is riding on this?"

Another huge thump of the fence made Bertie jump. Dr. Om didn't react. He was staring down the guard.

"Sir! We can't let these unicorns harm the human collateral," the guard said.

Bertie rolled his eyes. Who came up with this crap? He saw Hessy returning with the bag of meat. He ran and grabbed it, dumping it in front of the gate of the pen. Unicorn growls set Bertie's teeth on edge.

"Listen, how about this?" Bertie said. "You, people with the big, scary rifles, put them down and grab tranq guns. The lovely Miss Beauregard can hand them out to you. And you, Dr. Om, back off. We're going to get some meat into these unicorns." He heaved meat over the fence, hoping it would have a quick effect or, at the very least, tempt the unicorns to stay in the pen.

The fence cracked again. The guards move forward a step, AR-15s at the ready.

"Meat! Meat! That is not a permanent solution!" Dr. Om said. "Not permanent! I told you to keep these beasts tranqued. That was your number one job."

"I thought caring for them was my number one job," Bertie said. "Not dosing them into zombie-dom."

"That's not even a real word!" Dr. Om screamed right before the fence cracked one last time.

Then it collapsed.

The falling posts knocked three of the guards off their feet. Dr. Om, Bertie, and Hessy trained their tranq guns at the unicorns. A couple stayed back to tear into the meat, but the rest made a beeline for the guards. Darts whizzed through the air, hitting the unicorns with a thunk, thunk, thunk. But three dodged the darts. The black one ran over the fence, pinning guards underneath. The bluish one rammed into the trees.

But Berta ran straight at Dr. Om. He fell back on the ground, hands protecting his face. The guard approached Berta, his rifle at the ready.

"No!" screamed Hessy. She aimed at the guard, but she was out of darts. She rammed herself into him just as he was trying to load in a clip. It fell to the ground. Both dove to catch it, but the guard was too fast. She tried to push him off balance, but he whipped around and put a hand on the knife at his waist. "Stand down!"

She moved to grab the rifle.

"Hessy, no!" Bertie said. He pulled her away.

"I had him." She tried to twist free, but it was too late.

In one fluid motion of trained military experience, the guard rammed the clip home, raised the AR-15, and fired. A tiny hole ripped into the front of Berta, a burst of red out the back, and she collapsed.

Silent.

SECTION IV

Excerpt from *The Gastrointestinal Tract of Unicorns: Part I of the Anatomy of Rare Creatures Series* by Bertram W. Vole and Timothy E. Grett

CHAPTER 3: BLOOD AND GORE: THE ROLE OF HORNS AND TEETH IN DIGESTION

"Horses grab food with their teeth such that the digestive process begins in the mouth, as both teeth and saliva break down the nutrition. Unicorns, in contrast, often stab their food with their horns first. As such, the horn can be considered part of the gastrointestinal system of the unicorn."

Author note: Yeah, true. They stab all kinds of things with their horns. It's gross.

CHAPTER 25

THREE DAYS HAD PASSED. Bertie was in the lab and watched through the window as Hessy dragged another bag of meat to the repaired pen.

She hadn't talked to him in days.

With Dr. Om recovering from broken ribs and a concussion in the hospital on St. Carlota, Bertie and Hessy had been able to take charge of the unicorn care.

Only not together, because she wasn't talking to him.

Maintenance had fixed the fence, and since the unicorns were back to a diet of meat, they were calm. Before Dr. Om had passed out, he had screamed at the guards, "You're fired! Fired! Need me to spell it out? F-I-R-E-D!" So Hessy and Bertie didn't have to put up with them and their big guns.

Bertie spent as much time as he could in the pen. He realized that his approach all along had been wrong. He had tried to get near them by feeding them meat, sedating them, and then stealing samples. Maybe if he just sat and watched and let them get used to him, they'd become tamer.

Or at least less prone to eating human flesh, you know?

So, he sat and watched.

Except when Hessy came in to feed them. Then he left, because she made it very clear she didn't want to talk to him.

"Don't. Say. A. Thing," she had said.

Well, you didn't have to read minds to know what that meant.

When it was Hessy's turn with the unicorns, he would go to the lab, pull open the freezer, and continue his necropsy of Berta.

He figured Hessy would tear his face off if she found out he was slicing and dicing Berta, but he had a responsibility to the other unicorns to find out more. He didn't draw any conclusions yet. It was too difficult to see Berta lying there, the sparkle fading a bit more each day. Instead, he covered most of her and would work mechanically on one section at a time, taking careful notes and leaving the big picture till later.

Till it was somehow more appropriate.

But it had been one week already. And Dr. Om was going to come back any day now.

Bertie was standing over Berta now. He urged his eyes away from the pen, tugged off his glove, and picked up his phone, glad to see he had a signal. He dialed.

The phone rang once.

"Hi, Saint?" Bertie said.

"Yes, my good man?" Saint said. He sounded sad.

"Can we talk?"

"I just don't know what to do about Hessy," Bertie said. He was cradling his Sloopie at The Last Resort.

Saint made a signal to the barman, who poured rum into Bertie's drink.

"You may have saved her life," Saint said. "It is a lady's prerogative to carry that resentment to the grave."

"I couldn't let the guard hurt her," Bertie said.

"I am happy you did not," Saint said.

"It all happened so fast, all at once. Everyone blew up at everyone."

Saint nodded. "Two man rat can't live in the same hole."

Bertie looked at Saint, not sure what to say. "Right. So, what do I do?" Bertie said.

"I do not know. She is not saying much to me either."

"You don't know?" Bertie said.

"I do not," Saint said.

"We're totally screwed, then. If you don't know, we're screwed."

"I don't deserve that much credit," Saint said.

The two sat in silence for a while.

"Our hacker friend is still working," Saint said. "He hasn't found anything specifically about the unicorns. Not yet."

"That's okay." Bertie had trouble getting himself to care.

"Normally he slips a little something to Federico, the guard there. You know, the one whose mother was ill. But unfortunately, old Freddie is on leave after his mother's death. And our hacker tried to bite the other guard. Now he has no inside friend. Less access to computers."

"It's okay."

"But he did find something. I don't know if it's useful. Do you know how Dr. Om funded the park?"

"No idea."

"Our hacker friend says it is interesting. But he won't tell me anything yet."

"That's okay. There's time."

"There is? Doesn't Dr. Crazy Man want to open the park in three weeks?"

"That was the plan, before he got hurt. He can't possibly open in three weeks, can he?"

"He's not called Dr. Crazy Man for nothing."

"But he wants the unicorns roaming the park. Even if they stay in their pen, what if they get out? Hurt someone?"

"Let us hope he sees it your way."

"Yeah, here's to hoping." Bertie held up his Sloopie glass and took another sip.

Saint's phone rang. He looked at the screen, excused himself, and went to the corner of the bar.

There was a pause as the caller answered.

"Of course . . . My pleasure. For you, anything," Saint said. "I will be there directly." He didn't move for a couple of minutes. He stared out the window, phone still to his ear.

Saint turned around. "Come."

"Where are we going?" Bertie asked. He hadn't finished his Sloopie yet.

"I figured it out," Saint said.

Saint laughed as Hessy sat in the front seat of Lady Mathilda, staring out the window with her arms crossed.

Bertie sat in the back, uncomfortable. Lady Mathilda still smelled faintly of rotten meat. He didn't know what Saint was up to, but he sure hoped Saint knew what he was doing.

"Before we pick up more meat, we have an errand to

run," Saint said as he turned the car into the crowded street of Rumstad. Shopkeepers hawked their wares in front of open doors.

"What kind of errand?" Bertie said. He tried to sound cheery enough to be polite to Saint but depressed enough to not piss Hessy off. Or piss her off even more.

People were so freaking difficult.

"An errand of utmost importance" Saint said. "For today only, St. Quiche is holding its world-famous rum festival at the Rumstad Rum Plant."

"I've never heard of the festival," Hessy said.

"World-famous in the Caribbean," Saint said. "Or at least on St. Quiche. World-famous on St. Quiche. The point is, you can't come to St. Quiche and not go to our rum festival."

Lady Mathilda's coughs turned heads. Onlookers waved when they saw her.

"How is Lady Mathilda today?" a lady selling orchids said from her stoop.

"She is doing as well as expected," Saint said.

He turned to Bertie. "I will not be able to find parking. I may need help to get a V.I.P. spot." He winked.

Saint stuck his head out the window and screamed at the lady selling orchids, "Where is your juvenile delinquent of a son, Agatha?"

"I'll get him." Agatha stood up and looked around. She screamed at the top of her lungs. "Bartholomew! Bartholomew, get over here! Get over here! Now! Or go for the slipper. One or the other."

Agatha turned back to Saint and smiled sweetly as he moved one more centimeter in traffic. "He'll be here straightaway," she said.

A skinny boy of about eight hopped out from behind a

pile of plant pots. Saint gestured for him to come over and handed him a piece of paper.

Bartholomew read it quickly and smiled. "I don't work on credit," he said.

Saint laughed, handed him a few coins, and waved at Agatha before pressing the accelerator on Lady Mathilda.

"He will prepare the way," Saint said with a laugh to Bertie and Hessy.

They moved one more centimeter forward. "You see that street?" Saint pointed to the right.

"Yes," Bertie said.

"Okay, you two get out and turn down that street," Saint said. "Save me my spot at the festival."

"Where are you going?" Hessy said.

"Down that street." Saint pointed to the left, where there were two big signs: "Wrong way" and "Do not feed the iguanas. To my V.I.P. parking."

Hessy got out of the car first, and Saint grabbed onto Bertie's sleeve. Once she was out of earshot, he told Bertie, "Make sure Hessy has enough rum to drink." He winked.

"What do you mean 'enough?'" He peeked at Hessy as she struggled to make headway in the crowd.

"Just enough." He smiled.

"Wait, you want me to get her drunk? I can't do that. That's wrong."

Saint shook his head. "No, not drunk. Just enough to talk. As St. Paul said, wine for the infirmities! Go! I will catch up."

Bertie got out of the car. He could just see Hessy's red head bobbing above the crowd. The streets were packed with people, probably from the festival, Bertie figured.

Or maybe it was always this way. He didn't get out much.

Low, brightly colored houses lined a narrow street crowded by vendors hawking goods on the sidewalks. Laundry lines weaved between the antique streetlamps, making it harder for Bertie to keep track of Hessy. He dodged clothes, people, chickens, chummy carts, flowers, and knickknacks all the while trying to keep Hessy in view.

"Hessy!" he called, but she didn't seem to hear him. He turned to a vendor and asked, "Where is the rum festival? Is it that way?"

"Rum festival?" the old lady said. "Eh, I know you. You work at the park up in the mountain?"

Bertie glanced at the crowds. He couldn't see Hessy anymore. "Yeah, but I'm looking for the rum plant. Am I going in the right direction?"

Other people joined. "Is he one of them?" an old man asked.

The old lady tugged on his sleeve. "Is it true that there are creatures that eat children at night?"

Bertie craned his neck. He just caught sight of Hessy. "At night? Not exclusively."

He excused himself and jostled through the crowd, trying to catch up. By the time he reached her, he was out of breath. "Hessy, are you sure we're going in the right direction?"

She shrugged and kept walking. The heat and chaos were starting to make Bertie's head swim. Suddenly, out of the corner of his eye, he saw that kid Saint had talked to. What was his name?

"Hey, Bartholomew," Bertie said. "Bartholomew! Come here!"

The child, as though he had magic radar, managed to find the holes in the crowd and made his way across the street.

"Yes?" he said.

"Do you know where the rum festival is?" Bertie asked as the two followed Hessy.

"Of course. Do you need me to take you there?" Bartholomew said.

"I'd appreciate that," Bertie said. "Let me guess. There's a fee."

"No, not at all," Bartholomew said. "I would never. Here, follow me."

Bertie pointed to Hessy. "We need to catch up with the red-haired lady. Hessy!" He shouted.

She stopped and turned around but didn't say anything.

Bartholomew and Bertie made their way to her. Bertie bent over and said in Bartholomew's ear, "Hold the lady's hand so that she doesn't get lost."

Bartholomew trotted up to Hessy and took her hand. He smiled up at her. Bertie watched from behind.

"Just don't enjoy it too much," Bertie said.

The end of the street opened into a central square, where, to Bertie's relief, the throngs thinned out enough to stop suffocating him. Bartholomew led them past the church, up another quieter, shaded street. They came to a tall building that said "Rumstad Rum Plant and Emporium." Large, wooden doors led them into an airy room. The dark wood planks on the high ceilings drew the eye upwards. Fans circulated the cool air. Bertie had a feeling this was more of a showcase for the plant rather than the plant itself. But he didn't care.

There was air-conditioning.

Bartholomew plopped himself at the oak counter and

handed the barman a piece of paper. The barman, skinny and tall like a lamp post with an afro, scanned the note and, with a big smile, said, "Welcome to World-Famous Rumstad Rum Festival." He turned to Bartholomew. "Your usual?"

"Yes, Mr. Percival," Bartholomew said.

Percival opened the fridge and took out a small carton of chocolate milk. He poured it in a glass in front of Bartholomew and dribbled in some rum from a teaspoon.

Bertie looked on. "You'd get along really well with my landlady," he said.

"She like rum?" Bartholomew said.

"Cognac."

"I like Cognac too, but rum is better."

"Aren't you a little young for that?" Bertie said.

"That's why I dilute it with chocolate milk." Bartholomew picked up his glass and ran out the door, screaming, "Welcome to the Rumstad Rum Festival, World Famous!"

Percival turned to Bertie and Hessy. "Welcome to the Rumstad Rum Festival! We have the best rum in the world."

Bertie tried to be conversational. "I bet there are lots of fun debates on that. I've heard Puerto Rico makes the best rum."

The smile disappeared from Percival's face. He slammed the rum bottle on the counter. "Lies! Lies! Puerto Rico has the best marketing budget! Puerto Rico pays off the Rum Inspector for high marks! But St. Quiche has the best rum."

"Oh, okay, got it," Bertie said.

"Not Puerto Rican rum!"

"I understand," Bertie said.

"Not Cuban rum!"

"I stand corrected."

"Not Cruzan rum!"

"Got it."

"Quichan rum!" Percival sloshed some rum in Bertie's glass. "Here, try. Notice the full golden color. The way it caresses the glass. Taste the full flavor."

Bertie didn't dare ignore the order.

"Oh, yeah, sure. That's . . . that's the best. Sure." Bertie wiped his forehead as Percival turned his attention to Hessy. He flipped on his smile like a switch.

"Welcome to Rumstad Rum Festival. Would you like some rum?"

Hessy looked up as though she didn't remember where she was. "No thank you."

"What?" The bartender slammed the bottle on the counter again. "You believe the lies?"

"Excuse me?" Hessy furrowed her brow. Bertie grabbed her empty glass and waved it in front of Percival. "She'll have some," he said.

Percival picked up the bottle again and waved it.

"You believe the Puerto Rican propaganda?" Percival shrieked.

"She'll have some," Bertie said.

"The Cuban propaganda?"

"She'll have some."

"The Cruzan propaganda?"

"She'll have some."

Percival slammed the bottle on the counter again. "Lies! All lies!"

Bertie grabbed the bottle and poured rum into Hessy's glass. "She'll have some! She's been looking forward to Quichan rum ever since we landed. Before, actually!"

"Would you like some Coca-Cola with that?" Percival said to Hessy.

"No thank you," Hessy said.

"You like it straight." Out of the blue, Percival's smile switched on again. "I like you."

From outside, Bertie could hear Bartholomew screaming, "World-famous Rumstad Rum Festival happening now! Few hours left only!" He had a feeling this festival was about as concocted as a Sloopie cocktail.

Bertie didn't say anything as people kept streaming in from outside. To each one, Percival said, "Welcome to the Rumstad Rum Festival."

In the long mirror behind the counter, Bertie could see Hessy as she finished her first glass. He leaned over and served her some more. She took a sip.

"I'm sorry how this turned out." Bertie paused. "But that guard wasn't going to back down. He was willing to hurt you. Or worse."

Hessy slouched over her glass. "I know. I just wish . . . I don't know."

"Berta would have killed Dr. Om," Bertie said.

"Somehow, I don't care." She took another sip of rum. "It was his fault." She started to cry.

Percival marched over. "You making the pretty lady cry?" He slammed a bottle on the counter. "You make her cry, I kill you."

"No, no, she's not crying. She's got . . . allergies." Bertie said.

Percival narrowed his eyes. Bertie could have sworn he growled.

"Listen, why don't you bring out some specialty rum?" Bertie said. "From the back. The expensive stuff. I will pay.

Now. Today. In cash." He pulled out a wad of money and handed it to Percival.

Percival smiled. "I like you."

Bertie watched Percival go to the back and rubbed his tired eyes.

"Look, Hessy. Do you know what would have happened if Berta had killed Dr. Om? If a unicorn had killed a person? Those guards would have exterminated all the others. Right there on the spot. There would have been no way to stop them."

"I know," Hessy said.

Bertie stayed silent for a moment. "There really wasn't much choice."

Hessy didn't reply right away. She looked up at Bertie. "Technically, you always have a choice."

"And I guess you figure I made the wrong one."

Hessy looked down into her glass once more and mumbled something.

"What's that?" Bertie asked.

She mumbled something. Again, Bertie couldn't quite catch it.

"What, you say I made the Dwight choice?" he said.

Hessy mumbled something.

"The mite choice?" Bertie asked.

"No, right choice. Do you want me to call Mr. Percival over and start bawling again?" she said.

"No, no, that I do not," Bertie said. "I am all out of cash."

For the first time that week, she looked at Bertie without giving him the impression that she was plotting to pluck his eyeballs out and mount them inside the unicorn pen.

"Welcome to the first Annual Rumstad Rum Festival!" Percival shouted to some more tourists. He had his arms full of specialty rums. "Next year, it will be in March. More tourists!"

"I'm sorry I got you stuck here," Bertie said.

"You didn't," Hessy said. "I'm glad I'm here anyway."

Bertie racked his brains for something to say that would make Hessy feel better.

"When Dr. Om gets out of the hospital, I'm going to talk with him."

"You'll probably get us both suspended," said Hessy with the tiniest of smiles.

"Oh, low blow, man. But actually, yeah, probably."

By the time the sun started to dip, Bertie figured that Saint had ditched them. They left the plant with bottles of specialty rums clinking in their bags. Some fruit-flavored, some aged, all tasty, no doubt. (And if they weren't, he would definitely never tell Percival.) Bertie had quite the souvenir for his landlady.

Bertie and Hessy looked around for a taxi. As if on cue, Bartholomew hopped in front.

"Hey, Bartholomew," Bertie said. "It looks like Saint left us stranded. Do you know of a taxi stand here?"

"No need," Bartholomew said. "He didn't leave you stranded. Here." Bartholomew threw a car key at Bertie. "That red car. I borrowed it for you."

"Borrowed it?" Bertie said. "What exactly do you mean by 'borrowed?'"

Bartholomew just smiled. Not a good sign.

"How do we return it?" Hessy said.

"Saint will know. He said pull into the south end of the park. He said you would know what that meant. Laters!"

Bartholomew started down the street when Bertie called to him.

"Hey, Bartholomew!" Bertie screamed.

"Yes?" he said.

"You like unicorns?"

"Unicorns don't exist!"

"Smart little man," Bertie said. "Smart little man."

Bertie pulled up into the back exit of the park. As he and Hessy got out of the car, they could hear a whooshing sound. They spotted Saint's figure, backlit by a bright light, heading towards them.

"You made it," he said. "I fed the horned mules, Hessy."

"Thanks, Saint," she said. "I appreciate it. What's going on here?"

"Your balloon ride is ready. All that is missing are some passengers," Saint said.

"Balloon ride?" Bertie said.

"Yes, I went through all that work to get the balloon from St. Carlota's most violent, dangerous smuggler. He will be very upset if no one uses it." He held his hand out to Hessy. "Come."

Saint helped Hessy into the balloon.

"You first," Bertie said to Saint.

"No, I will stay down here. Someone has to tether you two. And don't tell me you are afraid of heights."

"Right," Bertie said. Maybe after facing down deadly unicorns and trigger-happy military security, heights wouldn't be such a big deal after all. He climbed into the balloon, and Saint released the cord bit by bit till they floated up, up, up.

Bertie and Hessy didn't say anything as the tree houses and clearings of the park shrank, making space for the neighboring parts of St. Quiche to come into view. Soon, Bertie could see the from coast to coast, although the dark blanketed over the details. From up in the night, the forest was black, as though it had been replaced by an ink splatter. Far below, the twinkling lights of Rumstad stood out against the velvety murk of the ocean. On the east side of the island, in the shadow cast by the mountain, the strand glowed a mysterious greenish light that you could just barely see out of the corner of your eye: bioluminescence, tiny creatures hanging out in every drop of ocean but especially happy in warm Caribbean waters. Sounds from below receded till they were barely whispers, which, mixed in with the wind, guided the balloon as they saw fit.

If Bertie squinted right, he could make the black basket floor disappear beneath his feet. He was floating in nothing but air. And yet, for the first time ever, the height didn't scare him.

Yup, exposure to bloodthirsty unicorns had its therapeutic uses.

He looked down at the park. That week, the power authority had finally restored electricity, and he could see the layout of the buildings sketched in light: a never-finished, never-ending maze. Why that layout? He had cursed Dr. Om's design time and again when, eager to get out of the heat, he had turned right when he should have turned left, left when he should have turned right, always choosing the wrong turn.

It was disorienting.

But maybe that was the plan. It was a way to keep the unicorns hedged in. They'd have to choose between left, right, straight, over and over. It would slow them down, confuse them just enough to keep them in line.

They would be caged in without bars.

Bertie much preferred floating, up here, letting the warm breeze figure out the next move.

"Penny for your thoughts," Hessy said.

"I was thinking about the layout of the park," Bertie said.

"Yeah. I noticed. It's—"

"A maze."

"Huh." She was quiet for a moment. "I see what you mean now."

"What? What do you see?" Bertie said, leaning down on his elbows to be at her level.

"A spiral."

Bertie shifted his eyes away from the lights and focused on the blank space. "You're right. It could be a spiral."

"I figured it was a precautionary measure. If the unicorns got out of hand, staff would rush to the outer edges and move inward, herding them to their pen."

"So, even from early design, Dr. Om was worried they wouldn't follow his script."

"Either that or he picked the design out of a catalog. Just because."

Bertie laughed. "There's always that. 'Oooh, look! Feng Shui! Excellent, excellent,'" he said in a falsetto. "It's probably the same catalog he got the safari uniforms from."

By now, they were above the unicorn pen itself. "From up here," Bertie said, "the unicorns look like designer glow sticks."

"Ha, yes. They're quiet tonight."

"Good evening, unicorns!" Bertie hollered. None

reacted. They were too high up to enter into the unicorns' consciousness.

"You know," Bertie said. "We haven't named any of the others." He couldn't bring himself to say Berta's name.

"Strange. Dr. Om never named them," Hessy said.

"Nah, he doesn't care about them." He pointed to one on the far end. "There, the cream one with the silver patch on his keister. We'll call him Gila Monster Man."

Hessy pointed to one that was white and beige, then another that was silver with black spots. "That's Barracuda. And Tasmanian Devil over there."

"And Jaws over there," Bertie said, pointing. "Black Mamba at four o'clock."

"Princess Piranha is right underneath us," Hessy said.

"Woah, princess. Don't let that go to her head," Bertie said.

"Dragon Breath over there," Hessy said. She leaned out to get a better view.

"Dragon Breath? That's awesome. I don't care if you came up with that. I'm taking credit for it. It's official."

"I don't think so," Hessy said. She screamed down. "Saint, you're my witness. Dragon Breath was my idea!"

Saint's voice echoed back. "Whatever you say. I have no clue what you talking about. Strange people." He laughed. "Strange, strange people."

By the time Saint started to pull them back down, they had named all the remaining eleven unicorns.

Bertie struggled with the burner on the air balloon. Saint screamed up, "You lower the flame to descend, Bertie. What, you want to float to St. Carlota?"

"Sorry!" Bertie hollered. He made a face at Hessy. She rolled her eyes but laughed.

Dr. Om was a world away. Giving the unicorns names

made Bertie feel like he and Hessy and Saint had taken some control over the chaos. He wasn't sure how that would work out in the real world, the one that had Dr. Om coming back any day now, but it was a start. He had to figure something out.

As they descended, the dark became trees again. The sounds separated from the wind. And finally, the unicorn pen hid behind the cage of trees and buildings.

The three folded up the balloon and got ready to go their separate ways.

"Good night, Hornet," Bertie yelled towards the pen.

"Good night, Captain Viper!" Hessy yelled.

"Good night, Vulture! And good night, Termite."

"Termite? Which one is Termite again?" Hessy said.

"The shriveled, blue one that likes to chew on fencing," Bertie said.

Hessy scoffed.

"Hey, it's a good name," Bertie said. "Right, Saint?"

"You two are crazy," Saint kicked open the door on Lady Mathilda. "I see you tomorrow."

"Saint?" Bertie said.

"Yes?"

"Thank you."

CHAPTER 26

OVER THE NEXT FEW DAYS, Bertie almost forgot about Dr. Om. Almost. Hessy wasn't pissed at him anymore, so they were able to work together again. With the unicorns enjoying their diet of rotted meat, they spent lots of time in the pen getting to know them better.

If only Dr. Om could stay in the hospital for good. Or get lost in the Bermuda Triangle. Or get eaten by a unicorn. The problems would solve themselves. Granted, he wouldn't be here if it weren't for Dr. Om, but a guy can dream, right?

It turned out that Bertie's dumb guide on unicorns wasn't entirely right about their solitary habits. When in a good mood, they enjoyed Bertie and Hessy's company and didn't eat each other to death. He also noticed their different personalities. Termite was friendly and happiest when standing in the corner licking and chewing wood. Gila Monster Man was a scaredy-cat. Dragon Breath loved sugar cubes. Loved them, and he loved the hands that fed them too, as Bertie learned the hard way.

But at night, with the crickets keeping him awake, worries niggled at Bertie. In theory, he was going to have to convince Dr. Om to . . . what, exactly? Both he and Hessy had tried to persuade him that feeding the unicorns meat was the way to go. He hated having to sedate them just because Dr. Om wanted them to conform to some cartoon version of what "children and kids at heart" thought they should be. Drat all those artists who drew unicorns with curly pink hair and twinkly eyes and rainbows bouncing off their pee. It was downright misleading.

And in case you were wondering, unicorn pee smells awful. Like gag-worthy bad. Because of all the rotten meat they eat.

No rainbows there.

But how was he going to talk sense into someone who wasn't quite right in the head? Take that back. Someone who was completely bonkers.

The third night, he couldn't sleep. He headed to the lab to check the Internet. A Facebook notification popped up. He clicked on it. It was from Sandra.

"Hi, Dr. B. I saw we weren't Facebook friends, so I invited you. You didn't accept! I hacked into your account to accept my invitation. You need a better password."

He sighed. Sandra, the poster girl of incongruence. He clicked into her Facebook page.

Bertie did a double take. She had four thousand nine hundred and ninety-eight contacts in Facebook. Holy moly. How'd she keep track of all those people? Bertie had only twenty-seven, and he couldn't keep up with the crap they posted.

He shut down the computer and headed back to his quarters. If you wanted to keep a secret, definitely do not ever tell Sandra about it.

And then an idea formed. He didn't like it, but it might just work.

A couple of nights before doo-doo hit the fan again, Bertie and Hessy followed their new routine: they met with Saint at The Last Resort after work.

That night, the pastor was there as well. "Saint, how are you and Lady Mathilda?"

"All fine, all fine," Saint said. "What brings you here?"

"I am covering for Miss Bernice at her meeting. She has a cold."

"What meeting is that?" Hessy asked.

"Her temperance league meeting," the pastor said. He called out to the bartender. "One Sloopie with extra rum for me."

"Pastor, what kind of temperance meeting is this?" Hessy asked.

"A very long one, if I don't have some rum with it. As I told Miss Bernice, I will cover for her meeting, but I will do it Jesus' way, with some fermented joy."

"Amen, pastor, amen," Saint said.

Bertie noticed that, with Bernice missing, the members of her Temperance League poured on the rum. As the night went on, her temperance meeting grew in numbers. The noise made it safe to talk about park business.

"Our hacker friend dropped a little more information," Saint said.

Bertie and Hessy leaned forward.

"It just so happens that Dr. Om used some improper funding to start the park," Saint said quietly. "He had someone skim off a little bit from many, many accounts. He targeted the Caribbean, where we are corrupt enough to have trouble keeping track of all the financial footsie and laid-back enough to not bother with tiny discrepancies in our books."

"Financial footsie, huh?" Bertie said. "How'd the hacker find out?"

Saint smiled. "He was the one to do it."

"Oh, so he has proof?" Hessy said.

"Not so fast," Saint said. "He has all the proof we need. The question is, how eager are we to slip him an incentive to release it?"

"How much does he want?" Hessy said. Bertie looked at her, surprised. Who would have thought she'd be willing to pay someone off like that?

"I will ask him," Saint said.

Bertie took a deep breath. "Well, as long as we're talking business, I think I had an idea about how to bring Dr. Om to our way of thinking." He looked over to the crowd of people at the temperance meeting. They were all too busy ordering more rum to overhear anything. "We know stuff about him, and he doesn't know that we know. A few well-placed warnings that we might release that information, and he may be willing to be more cooperative about letting us handle the unicorns the right way."

"You mean blackmail?" Hessy said.

"That's one way to put it, I guess," Bertie said.

"I don't know," Hessy said. "I don't like it."

"Why not? You're willing to bribe hackers."

"Yeah, but I don't know. I can't put my finger on it. It's just . . .it's different. Proving he did something illegal is one thing. But what you're talking about is manipulative."

"I get it," Bertie said. "The end justifies the means if he does something officially illegal. But if they're doing stuff that's just wrong, well, suddenly, you're all by the book."

"It's not wrong to be a patient in a mental hospital," Hessy said. "It's not wrong to change your name so you can put that past behind you and move on. Anyone would want to keep that kind of thing private."

"I see Hessy's point," Saint said.

"You're splitting hairs," Bertie said. "No, you're making up reasons as you go along."

"Maybe. I can't say why, but it feels dirty," Hessy said. "I don't like it."

"I don't like it either," Bertie said. "But—"

"It could blow up in your face real bad, bad, bad," Saint said.

"Do either of you have any better ideas?" Bertie said.

They shook their heads.

"We just have to keep thinking," Hessy said.

"Yes, and nothing like another Sloopie with rum to help us do that." Saint laughed and called the bartender over.

Bertie had a feeling Saint was trying to lighten the mood, make him feel better, but it didn't work.

He didn't like the idea, Bertie thought as he watched the banter between Saint, Hessy, and everyone at the temperance league meeting. But it's not as though he had tons of options.

On their way out, Hessy leaned in and whispered, "I think I know why your idea bothers me."

"Great, more reasons. Sock it to me."

"It just feels like something Dr. Om would do. And you're not Dr. Om."

She walked ahead, leaving Bertie to mull over her words.

He sure wasn't Dr. Om, but maybe he needed to be.

CHAPTER 27

A POLICE SIREN woke up Bertie the next day, but it wasn't his parents calling.

It was Dr. Om.

Bertie groaned. He was back from the hospital.

"Where you are?" Dr. Om said.

Bertie looked at the clock by his bed. It was only five thirty in the morning. "I was sleeping," he said.

"Get in here. To my office. Now! We've got only two weeks till opening and we've lost tons of time. Tons of time!"

"You still want to open in two weeks?" Bertie said sat up groggily. "Don't you think we may want to push back the opening? You're still recovering."

"I'll recover when I'm dead! Success is for the doers! Get in here! Now!"

Dr. Om hung up. Bertie rubbed his eyes and fumbled around for some clean clothes. He made a move to call Hessy before leaving but changed his mind.

He didn't really want a lecture on the evils of blackmail.

If only he could just tranq Dr. Om into submission. He

needed to get himself a t-shirt that said, "Tranq guns: the new duct tape."

Bertie headed out the door. This was it. He was somehow going to have to stand up to Dr. Om.

All the way over, he mumbled to himself. "Don't be a loser. Don't be a loser."

He had read about the importance of motivational self-talk.

"I'm a loser."

He took one more deep breath before knocking on Dr. Om's door and peeking inside.

"Come in!" Dr. Om said.

The guy really did look worse for wear. An arm was in a sling. He sat crookedly as though the broken ribs still hurt. His black eye was fading to a bilirubin yellow. A bandage on his forehead covered more damage.

"Good morning," Bertie said. "Lots to talk about."

"Yes, yes yes, of course," Dr. Om said. "Now, the loss of a unicorn was unfortunate. Very, very unfortunate."

"Berta," Bertie said.

"What?" Dr. Om looked puzzled. Or maybe his face just hurt.

"Her name was Berta," Bertie said.

"Fine, fine, fine," Dr. Om said as he opened a file. "We've got lots to do—lots!—before our grand opening. The engineer is coming to certify the zipline this week. Make sure the unicorns stay calm so another . . . incident doesn't take place."

"Sure thing, Dr. Om."

Dr. Om took a deep breath as though trying to reanimate himself. "We have some good news. Good news! The reformulated grain is coming in tomorrow. Just in time to get them acclimated to the new diet before we open park doors wide to an expectant world."

"I was thinking about that," Bertie said. It was now or never.

Or anyway, now or later, but now would be better than later.

"As I said before, I don't think this park is ready," Bertie said.

Dr. Om's eyes bugged out. "What do you mean? What do you mean? We have full bookings for our V.I.P-exclusive boutique opening! Twelve hand-picked people! From all over the world! All over! My marketing department in New York has been working around the clock. A done deal! It's a done deal."

"The unicorns aren't ready for that kind of interaction," Bertie said.

"What are they? Socially awkward third graders? It's your job to make sure they're ready."

"You insist on feeding them kids' cereal!" Bertie could feel his pulse race.

"I can't . . ." Dr. Om covered his face with his hand for a moment. Then he lowered it and spoke as though he were using every ounce of saintly tranquility to quash down justified rage. "I have thought through this park in every minute detail. I have worked for years—years!—to build up the science behind these creatures, to create a park that would enthrall children and children-at-heart everywhere."

"Dr. Om—"

"No, you listen. Long before you were a vet, I was theorizing, studying, experimenting." Dr. Om's voice rose for a moment. "Being mocked!" He made a fist with his hand and lowered his voice. "Being ostracized for my crazy ideas. And these ideas all. Turned. Out. To. Be. Right."

"Dr. Om—"

"The two-bit university on this island backwater? It didn't want to accept my application. Did you know that? I bet you didn't know I studied here. Hmmm?"

"Listen—"

Dr. Om stood up. "I will show them! I will show them who was right all along. Don't tell me when this park is ready." He winced in pain.

"And if the new feed doesn't work?" Bertie said.

"It will."

"What if it doesn't?"

"There are no what ifs!" Dr. Om raised his voice again. "There is only what we make of things."

"I can't stand by while you put people and animals' lives in danger— "

"You can't do anything to stop me."

Bertie paused. If he used that card up his sleeve, there would be no going back. But Dr. Om was giving him no choice. It was time for the last resort.

"Yeah, I can . . . Dr. Manicewitz."

Dr. Om's eyes got huge. He sat down, deflated, speechless.

"You see, Artie, you have a past, just like everyone else. Only maybe it's a little worse than most people's. What do you think it will look like to all those rich ticket holders if it comes out that a man who was discredited by the scientific community and spent time in a mental hospital was dead set on opening a park with volatile unicorns? A park on a heavily populated island? All this against the recommendation of his veterinarian?"

"How—? You wouldn't dare."

"It'll be easy. I know a social media manager. She has her hands so deep in the web, she could entangle you in it within a matter of minutes—seconds, even. What she posts spreads like wildfire." Not that Sandra was technically a social media manager, but she might as well be.

She really ought to look into that career.

"You wouldn't," Dr. Om said.

"What are the optics of that?" Bertie said.

Dr. Om narrowed his eyes.

I've got him! Bertie thought.

And still Dr. Om didn't say a word.

Bertie pulled out his phone, and Dr. Om watched, leaning back in his chair.

The phone rang on the other end.

"I suggest you hang up that phone," Dr. Om said.

Bertie ended the call. Maybe he could win without going through with the blackmail.

"I really didn't want to have to do this," Dr. Om said quietly. "But if you blackmail me, I will fire you."

"I am willing to live with that."

"Are you?" Dr. Om said, leaning forward. "Are you really?"

"Yes, it's the right thing to do."

Dr. Om stared out the window for a moment. Then he struggled out of his chair and limped to his file cabinet, took the keys out of his pocket, and fumbled till he found the right one. The file drawer squealed open, as if in protest, and Dr. Om stood on his toes to look inside. He pulled out a file and slammed it on the desk. He flipped it open to a contract.

"That—that!—is Miss Helsinth Beauregard's contract," Dr. Om said.

"So? You're going to fire her too? She has nothing to do with this conversation."

"Oh, she didn't tell you?" Dr. Om looked surprised.

"Didn't tell me what?"

"About our little deal."

Bertie had no idea what Dr. Om was talking about.

"You see, Miss Beauregard's contract had some small print that wasn't in yours." He pointed to the bottom of the page, where tiny, tiny text preceded the dotted line. "I did my research."

"Research?" Bertie said.

Dr. Om shrugged. "I knew her mother was sick. I made her an offer."

He paused.

"An offer?" Bertie said.

"An offer. I could tell you weren't sold on this enterprise, but I was running out of time and needed a vet. And you were perfect, perfect! Wrote the book on unicorns. I promised her that if she convinced you to stay, I'd get her mother into an experimental treatment program."

"But—" Bertie said.

"But her contract is contingent on yours. What I mean is, if you leave or if you do something silly like blackmail me or anything else that puts my reputation at risk, she doesn't just lose her job. It's much worse. Much, much worse."

"What do you mean?"

Dr. Om sat down and leaned back in satisfaction. "Her mother gets pulled from her life-saving treatment."

"What?" Bertie said.

"Because, you see, Artie isn't well connected. Not little old Artie. He never was, never could be. But Dr. Om? He is very well connected. Very well connected. He knows people, all the right people. I. Pull. Strings. And I can pull those strings any which way I want." He moved his one good arm like a puppeteer.

"What are you saying?" Bertie said, but he had a sinking feeling he already knew.

"I'm saying sweet, innocent 'Hessy' is a lot more calculating than you think. She didn't stay for the welfare of the animals. She stayed to get hers. And she made sure you stayed too, so that she could get what she wanted. Because the only way to get what she wanted was to give me what I wanted, which was uncompromising commitment from the both of you."

"She didn't make me stay," Bertie said. "I chose—"

"Oh-ho-ho," Dr. Om swung in his chair. "She played you. She didn't bother convincing you to stay by logic or pleas. She knew there was a much easier way. She made you stay by default. You didn't really choose much of anything."

"That's not—" But then Bertie thought back to the day after her private meeting with Dr. Om.

She hadn't wanted to discuss it with Bertie. He thought it was weird at the time but dismissed it.

Then there was their silly pros and cons list. Looking back on it, it must have been a formality. Because she had caved so easily.

As though she knew all along that she would accept the job. No, that he would accept the job.

And the other night, when she was dead set against him using Dr. Om's past as leverage. It wasn't scruples. It was self-preservation.

With the changed optics, Bertie could see that now.

"That little vixen played you." Dr. Om said it in the softest of whispers, but it echoed in Bertie's head.

Bertie just stared at Dr. Om.

"She stabbed you in the back."

Another pause.

"And the most pathetic part about this whole setup? You will still play into her hands even now. And she knows it, has known it all along. You won't leave because, if you do, her mother will go back to that piecemeal death she's been dying all these years. You don't have the gumption to pull the plug." Dr. Om leaned forward and poked Bertie's chest. "You're stuck."

It was Bertie's turn to be deflated. Because Dr. Om was right.

Dr. Om sat back down and pointed to the contract in front of him. "Do you want to take a closer look at the file?"

"No," Bertie said. "No."

Bertie didn't want to see any more.

He had seen enough.

CHAPTER 28

THE DOOR SLAMMED into Bertie as he left Dr. Om's office, but he didn't even notice it.

He'd been played.

Part of him couldn't blame Hessy. She wanted to save her mother. This really was a once-in-a-lifetime opportunity for her. If the tables had been turned, Bertie would have done the same.

But he would have told Hessy. He wouldn't have gone behind her back.

Right?

He walked aimlessly for a while, his feet taking him mindlessly through the maze of a park without him getting lost. It was as though all along, his feet had known exactly where to go. His brain just needed to get out of the way. He reached the front entrance.

He needed to get away, to think. He stepped outside and started down the mountain.

All the reasons he had to take this job—wanting to climb out from under a pile of debt, escaping that miserable clinic that reminded him of his failure, hoping that maybe this would be a better job—all those reasons paled in comparison to being able to help Hessy. But in a different world, he would help her, not because Hessy and Dr. Om had schemed behind his back, but because he wanted to. He'd have been overjoyed to stick around if it meant Hessy's mother could get her treatment. Crazy uniform-munching unicorns and all, it would have been worth it.

He'd have said yes in a flash because he . . . He didn't want to think about it.

A clap of thunder made Bertie jump. It started to pour. Bertie looked down the mountain. The town and ocean hid their colors behind a curtain of rain. Bertie kept walking. His stupid safari shoes slid in the mud.

He kept heading down, not sure where he would end up.

Muted by the sound of rain, his phone rang. It was Hessy. He didn't answer.

The raindrops were much bigger, warmer than he was used to. Sticking close to his skin, there was nothing refreshingly cathartic about them. But he barely paid attention. He kept walking.

He got to the foothills, where the wooden houses' zinc roofs reverberated under the downpour. People sitting on their porches stared after him. "Hey, you the man from the park! Come in. You getting all wet." He just shook his head and kept on.

He got to the town. The vendors had pulled in their wares. They stood under eaves. He didn't feel like walking past, being asked questions about the Park of Horrors. He looked up at the church cupola. Next door, he would find Saint, but he didn't want to talk to him either. Instead, he turned East towards the coast.

And he walked some more.

By the time he got to The Last Resort, his feet were slimy. He took off his shoes and walked through the tepid sand.

He sat on the short wall in front. From here, he could see nothing but sheets of rain that blended in with the grey of the ocean. Nothing else existed.

After a few minutes, Bertie a Sloopie on the wall next to him. How the bartender knew he needed one, Bertie didn't know.

His phone rang again. It was Hessy. He didn't answer.

He would stay.

He didn't know whether he could do any good for Dragon Breath and Captain Viper and Termite and all the rest.

He didn't know whether he could protect them any better than he had protected Berta.

But he would not let Dr. Om mess with Hessy's mother.

He'd be a puppet in that crazy man's hands.

In the end, what choice did he have?

CHAPTER 29

BERTIE WASN'T sure how long he'd been sitting at The Last Resort when he saw someone out of the corner of his eye. It was Saint. He was sipping a Sloopie.

"You know, Hessy been looking for you all day," Saint said.

"I know." Bertie pointed towards his phone, sitting several yards away from him in the wet sand. A little red light blinked to let him know he had a message. Or two. Or three.

Or whatever. The math didn't matter.

Saint took another sip of Sloopie.

"She said you were fine yesterday," Saint said.

"I was."

"But not now."

"I am," Bertie said. The bartender brought him another drink, unbidden.

"Ah, then it is my power of observation that is not fine," Saint said. "Old age, I suppose."

"Yeah, I'm not too observant either these days."

"What happened that you are all fine, drowning your joy in St. Quiche's official sugary girl drink?"

"Girl drink? You drink it too."

"We all do," Saint said. "It's the only way we know to get in touch with our feminine side."

"You're full of it," Bertie said.

"I try, my good man. I try."

"It's just small print on a contract. That's all."

"Ah, yes, that clarifies everything. It must feel good to get that off your chest." Saint slapped Bertie's back.

Bertie wasn't sure how to reply, so he didn't say anything for a few sips.

A sip. That should be a new unit of measurement. Along with gulp and guzzle.

"It's not my place to judge Hessy," Bertie said. "It's just that I wish she had told me about . . . a deal she had with Dr. Om."

"Ah," Saint said. "Is a contract not always a deal?"

"Fine print," Bertie said.

"We are back to fine print then."

"It's her place to tell you. Not mine. She hasn't even told me."

"Then how did you find out?"

"Dr. Om," Bertie said.

"A superb source of information, if I do say so myself."

Neither spoke for a while. Then Saint said, "It is getting late. The mimmy bugs will come out and eat us alive. We should go."

"Mimmy bugs? Is that what you call these things?" Bertie swatted his arm.

"Yes, and they don't have to be mutant, horned creatures to cause you much pain and torment," Saint said, getting up. He wiped sand away.

Bertie took his last sip. "No, one doesn't have to be a mutant, horned creature to cause pain."

It was decided, Bertie thought to himself as Lady Mathilda took him and Saint back to the park. He'd pretend everything was fine. He wouldn't let Hessy know about his conversation with Dr. Om. The official story was that he had left because he needed to think and had lost his phone in the sand. He was coming up with a plan to deal with the unicorns and needed some alone time.

Not that he had some kind of snazzy plan to show for it, but whatever.

Lady Mathilda whined as she started up the hill to the park.

"The park will open in two weeks?" Saint said.

"Yes." He really didn't like the sound the car was making. "Are you sure your car is okay?"

"What? Lady Mathilda? Fine!" Saint smiled and patted Lady Mathilda on the dashboard.

And then Lady Mathilda hacked, spewed smoke, and lurched to a dead stop.

Saint looked over at Bertie. "She's fine! Just like you are fine." He laughed and got out of the car. He punched the hood open and looked inside.

Bertie felt silly sitting in the car not helping, but he didn't know anything about cars. He figured he should lend some kind of hand, so he rummaged around for a flashlight. He found one in Lady Mathilda's sagging glove compartment when he heard a familiar voice.

"Hey," Hessy said. "I was wondering where you were."

"Lady Mathilda, I am afraid, is having a bad day," Saint said.

Bertie ducked down in the front seat, even though no

one could see him behind the raised hood. He screwed his face up in determination. "Be happy. Pensive, but happy. Happy, happy, happy!" he whispered.

"You couldn't find Bertie?" Hessy sounded worried.

Worried, my foot. Then Bertie replaced that thought with "Be happy, happy, happy!" before opening the door and climbing out. He tried to do it with a swagger but hit his head on the door frame.

"Ow. Hey Saint, I found your flashlight," Bertie said way too loudly. "Oh, hey, Hessy. How are ya?"

"Do you mean the flashlight that doesn't work?" Saint said. He laughed and ducked back under the hood.

"Right, well, I thought I'd give it a try." Bertie clicked it on and off. "Nope, look at that! Doesn't work!" He tossed it on the car seat.

"Sooooo, Hessy!" Bertie smiled too wide. "How are ya?"

He wanted to smack the flashlight over his head. Loser, loser, loser.

"I was worried about you," Hessy said. "You didn't answer my calls."

"Oh, you . . . you called?" Bertie pulled his sandy phone out of his pocket and brushed it off. "Oh, wow, yeah, you called. You know, I was up . . . down that way . . ." Bertie pointed in the wrong direction a couple of times till he hit on East. "I lost my phone in the sand. I didn't realize it. I was so absorbed. By my thoughts. Thoughts about thinking. Mulling over. Plans. Thinking. Planning. Unicorn stuff."

He said it all way too loudly.

"What plan did you come up with?" Hessy said.

"None," said Saint, with his head still under the hood.

"None?" said Hessy.

"None!" said Bertie. Which wasn't exactly true, but

"staying out of Dr. Om's way to keep him from sneaking up on your mother with the Grim Reaper as his plus one" didn't have that inspirational ring he was going for. He smiled and stretched his arms out wide as though in triumph. Bertie realized it wasn't the effect he was going for.

"Pay him no heed," Saint said. "Bertie had way too much sugar today."

"Ah." She looked confused.

"So, Saint!" Bertie said. He realized he was still speaking too loudly. He lowered his voice to a conspiratorial whisper and leaned on the car roof. "How is good, old Lady Mathilda coming along?"

"I wouldn't call her old," Saint said. "She may start screaming and talking angry gibberish."

Bertie narrowed his eyes at Saint. "Gotcha. I won't call her old."

Saint grabbed a spanner and smacked around under the hood. Bertie was, of course, no expert on cars, but that seemed like a really weird way to deal with things.

"Bertie, try to start Lady Mathilda now," he said.

"What, you just toss tools around for a bit?" Bertie said. Saint gave him a dirty look from underneath the hood. "Okay, okay. I'm on it." Bertie climbed in the car and turned the key in the ignition. She purred.

Well actually, she hacked like a smoker ejecting the last of her mutilated lungs, but Saint looked happy enough.

"I think Lady Mathilda had enough of going uphill for the day," Saint said, dropping the hood. "I am afraid you two will need to go back to the park on foot."

Bertie jumped out of the car and turned his back on Hessy. He mouthed the words "No, no, no," to Saint. But Saint just patted him on the back and leaned in to whisper, "You can't avoid her forever."

"Yes, I can," Bertie whispered.

Bertie raised his voice as he followed Saint to the car. "You know, it's getting late. Why don't you let the car— Lady Mathilda—rest here for the night and come back to the park with us? On foot? The exercise will be good for you. Cut down on that paunch." Bertie patted Saint's stomach.

"I have no paunch," Saint said, laughing. He climbed back in the car and slammed the door.

"Saint, you can stay in my tropical cabana. Gotta love the tropical cabana."

"Night!" Saint waved.

"I hear there'll be bacon with breakfast tomorrow!" Bertie said as Saint turned Lady Mathilda around. "Don't you want bacon?"

But Lady Mathilda was already going downhill, spewing smoke out of her rear end.

Bertie's shoulders sagged. He waved the smoke away with his hands and watched Saint's one receding headlight take a final curve and disappear into the dusk.

"Are you okay?" Hessy said.

"Yeah, I'm great!" He punched the air with his fist, hoping to look enthusiastic.

Hessy narrowed her eyes. "Did you have too much to drink?"

"Oh, yeah, way too much to drink. But no booze. Come to think of it, I really need to pee. You know what? You go up without me. I'm going to go into the trees. To use the ladies'." He pointed into the dark. "Don't wait for me. I'll catch up."

He waved and snuck off the trail. All this avoiding. It was an awful lot of work.

He listened. At first, the only thing he could hear was

the insects and frogs. Then Hessy's retreating footsteps told him he was alone.

Which was good. Because he really did need to pee.

The next couple of weeks were going to be really long.

SECTION V

Excerpt from *The Gastrointestinal Tract of Unicorns: Part I of the Anatomy of Rare Creatures Series* by Bertram W. Vole and Timothy E. Grett

UNICORNS AS HOSTS FOR PARASITES

"Parasitic infestation in unicorns is to be avoided at all costs. Although most animals suffer some side effects from gastrointestinal infestation, unicorns become agitated, even violent."

Author note: Nope. Totally wrong about this one. Tried antiparasitics. Didn't help. Black Mamba, the dark grey one, tried to eat my arm.

CHAPTER 30

THE NEXT DAY, Bertie dragged himself out of bed. He really didn't want human interaction (a.k.a. Hessy) in the dining room, so he boiled himself some Ramen noodles.

Which, as everyone knows, is authentic tropical island fare.

After sucking down the breakfast, Bertie got into the cleanest safari uniform he could find and straggled out to the unicorn pen.

Actually, he straggled first to the Employee Procurement Centre of Island Fun, because he took the wrong turn —again. Then he straggled to the unicorn pen.

During Dr. Om's absence, the unicorns had gotten used to him enough that he was able to look them over without tranq guns and SWAT gear, but he wasn't sure how they would be after just over twenty-four hours without meat. With Dr. Om's return, they hadn't dared sneak them any. He approached cautiously.

Termite walked up to him and nuzzled his arm. Bertie figured she would be a good unicorn to start with his exam.

Her pupils were slightly dilated, her temperature higher, and her breathing faster. Not by much, but a little. He noted this information on his chart.

Next, he checked Jaws. And Princess Piranha. And Gila Monster Man. And the rest. They were more nervous than before, more likely to kick and whip him with their tails. He had to move slowly. Their stats showed the same tendency as Termite's.

His walkie-talkie crackled.

"Hello?" Bertie said. He hoped it wasn't Hessy.

"Dr. Vole," Dr. Om's voice came through. Bertie noticed that the unicorns shook their heads at his voice, as though it unsettled them. He headed out of the pen.

"Yes, Dr. Om. How can I help you?" You maniac, he added silently.

"The feed has arrived. Interim Manager Beauregard is going to pick up the delivery. Be ready to distribute when she gets back."

"Right," Bertie said. "Out."

He went back to the pen. It would be his last chance to take samples before the unicorns got their new food.

Should he give it a go?

Dr. Om was focused enough on his feed delivery that he was paying less attention to what Bertie was doing inside the pen. It would be hard to find a better time. One by one, he took blood samples. Although nervous, the unicorns didn't fight back. He finished with Termite, who was too busy noshing on wood to notice anything.

This time, he'd hide the samples in his room. He didn't trust Dr. Om not to steal them again.

The crazy thing, Bertie thought as he headed back to his tree house, was that Dr. Om could have the park he wanted, if he would just let the unicorns eat meat.

But no, that was just too gross.

The guy was an idiot. No, it wasn't just that. His obsession with reputation made him choose the wrong turn every time.

Bertie had tucked away the samples at the back of his little fridge when the walkie-talkie came back to life.

"Dr. Vole," a crackly voice barked at him. "Dr. Vole."

Bertie kicked the walkie-talkie for good measure, then picked it up. He pasted as big a smile on his face as he could muster before answering. "Yes, Dr. Om?"

"The feed has arrived. Where are you?"

None of your business, thought Bertie. But out loud, he said, "I'm on my way."

He tossed his walkie-talkie and vet kit in a book bag and jogged towards the clearing where big deliveries always came in.

As he climbed up the path, he could hear Hessy and Lester talking. They were almost done unloading the unlabeled boxes from the Jeep by the time he got to the clearing.

"Hi, Bertie," Hessy said. She looked at him cautiously.

"Hi!" Bertie raised his hand in greeting. A little too high. "Hey, Lester, my man!" He smacked him on the back. Lester looked at him funny.

He made sure to walk extra fast as he carried each box, leaving Hessy and Lester bringing up the rear. Back and forth, back and forth they went. Once they had piled all the boxes in front of the pen, Dr. Om appeared.

How convenient. The guy showed up once the real work was done.

Not that he could do much, to be fair, what with an arm in a sling, but Bertie was feeling grouchy.

"The day we have all been waiting for! All been waiting for!" Dr. Om tucked into a box with a Swiss Army knife, but between his excitement and his injuries, he fumbled with the blade, and it fell to the ground.

"Here," Bertie said. "Let me help you." He held up the knife, narrowing his eyes at Dr. Om just long enough to make the guy nervous. Then he bent down to cut the box.

This is your heart, Dr. Om, he thought as he cut the box lengthwise. And this is your liver, as he cut the box the other way. Once it was opened, he stabbed the ground. That, my friend, is your big toe.

He looked up, with sweat in his eyes. Dr. Om laughed nervously.

It was Hessy's turn to look at Bertie funny.

"Well!" Dr. Om said, swallowing his last giggle. "Take a look at that feed! Just take a look!"

They all bent forward. The feed looked just like Lucky Charms cereal.

What a loon.

Hessy glanced at Bertie as though to say that she, too, thought he was crazy, but Bertie averted his eyes.

"Look, look!" Dr. Om said. "We don't just have regular feed. Open this package, Dr. Vole. This one!" Dr. Om pointed to one of the smaller boxes.

Bertie opened the box. Tucked inside were . . . cereal bars? "What are they?" said Bertie.

"Bars! Bars! For the kids to feed the unicorns," Dr. Om said. He waved his one good arm around excitedly. "The kids will love it!"

Bertie imagined a tiny child lifting up the glorified candy to Termite's mouth and losing an arm in the process.

Some souvenir.

"Yummy!" Bertie said under his breath.

A unicorn neighed behind them.

"Well, I've got some . . . paperwork to do," Lester said. He rushed away from the clearing.

"Don't you want to watch the first feeding?" Dr. Om screamed after him. "It's a momentous event!"

Lester sped up. He screamed over his shoulder. "I'd love to but, you know, paperwork."

"You're a security guard," Dr. Om screamed back. "What paperwork do you have?"

But Lester was either already out of earshot or didn't want to hear.

Dr. Om turned back to Bertie and Hessy.

"Dr. Vole, it's time for their first feeding. I've got the portion instructions here." He felt his jacket pockets, tucking his hand in one, then the other, to find the papers. "There! Now Dr. Vole, come here and listen carefully."

Bertie looked over Dr. Om's shoulder. "This is the exact amount they should get. Exact amount! My top scientists worked very hard on portion sizes. Make sure to follow this —this!—exactly. Do I make myself understood?"

"Completely, sir."

"Good." Dr. Om handed the instructions to Bertie. "You, Miss Beauregard. Help him feed my baby-poos."

Hessy nodded. She looked over at Bertie, but he glanced away. Bertie could tell that Dr. Om noticed. He smiled right at Bertie as though to say, "I have you right where I want you."

"Ah, one more thing," Dr. Om said before he left. "We are in the final push before we open in one week and six days! I love countdowns. Love them. There will be a lot of construction crews coming in to finish it all. The pen will be off-limits. Off-limits! If you see anyone nosing around here, shoot him with a tranq gun." Dr. Om laughed. "I'm joking about that, of course. Just make sure there is no snooping."

Dr. Om walked away. Bertie wanted to scream, "That's Lester's job!" But he held his tongue. Don't rock the boat. That was his north.

No rocking of the boat.

Bertie was still staring after Dr. Om when Hessy bent down and picked up a bag of feed. The sound woke Bertie out of his reverie.

"Here, I'll take that," he said. Then he walked briskly to the pen with Hessy following at a jog.

"Let's get this done!" Bertie said too cheerfully. He noticed Hessy didn't answer.

Bertie poured the required amounts in buckets, and Hessy carried them to the unicorns.

Dr. Om and his crew of scientific portion geniuses hadn't stopped to think that the unicorns may share buckets, which is, of course, exactly what they did. Only they didn't share nicely. Gila Monster Man was going to need a big Band-Aid after this meal.

Termite was the only unicorn who didn't nip at her compatriots, given that she really liked the feed. Really liked it.

Meaning that it probably tasted just like wood.

Bertie signaled to Hessy to back up towards the door. Just in case.

They watched.

The unicorns were quiet.

"It reminds me of my Uncle Carl," Bertie said. For a moment, he forgot he was mad at Hessy. "He'd visit at Christmas. He'd get really calm. As in calm, calm."

"Huh," Hessy said.

"Then he'd raid the kitchen big time."

"Fun family."

"Yeah, my parents didn't let us get too close."

They stood in silence. For the next fifteen minutes, Bertie watched the unicorns. No slow-motion gore fest took place.

Not yet, anyway.

Bertie pulled out his vet bag and slowly walked forward, signaling to Hessy to stay back. The unicorns didn't react. He took their temperature. He checked their breathing rate and their eyes. He noted the information on his chart.

Everything was back to normal.

Whatever normal was for a unicorn.

Bertie walked back to the exit. He grabbed his walkie-talkie. "Dr. Om?" he said.

Static came through, then a voice. "Yes, Dr. Vole. How are my baby-poos taking to the feed?"

The unicorns didn't react to Dr. Om's voice.

Bertie hated to admit it. "They're calm."

Dr. Om's voice crackled through the static. "It worked! It worked!"

"Don't uncork the bubbly yet. I'm going to need a couple of cameras posted here, so we can continue to monitor throughout the night."

"Why? Why? This is working! I've never met such a pessimist. Never!"

Hessy rolled her eyes.

"Dr. Om, any change in diet can cause stomach upset," Bertie said. "I want to make sure they don't get diarrhea."

'Cause guests would just love that.

"Ah, ah, ah! Of course, of course. I will talk to maintenance about getting the security cameras online ahead of schedule. They will do that today."

"Great. Out," Bertie said. He didn't say it, but Dr. Om should have had those cameras up and running from the start.

But then again, maybe he didn't want people to see stuff.

"Hessy," Bertie said without looking at her. "Go make sure maintenance actually does something."

"Sure, Bertie."

"And if they don't, bring in Saint. He'll know some hacker teenager who can get them online."

Bertie bent down and picked up a handful of feed. It all looked so inoffensive.

But was it?

Bertie stayed most of the day in the pen, alone with the unicorns. They remained calm. Every couple of hours, he'd examine them. He took more blood samples to compare to the pre-feed results and checked them all at his lab.

They seemed fine.

Around noon, he heard movement around the pen as people went back and forth getting security cameras online. No one came inside, though.

Not even Hessy. Apparently, Bertie's weirdness was keeping her away.

He was relieved.

One week and six days.

Maybe this would all work out.

When night fell, Bertie confirmed the cameras were up and running and that there was enough light to film the unicorns. He left the pens.

A unicorn neighed. The night fell silent.

For three days, Bertie and Hessy fed the unicorns their new diet. For three days, they remained calm. Normal.

Well, as normal as a genetically engineered mythical creature could be.

Bertie tracked their progress as before, noting it all down. He sat around for hours, watching the video feed from the night before. He noticed nothing worrisome.

Aside from feedings, he didn't have to worry about seeing Hessy. She was too busy helping Dr. Om deal with the construction crews and final preparations for the V.I.P. opening. Dr. Om trotted about, full of excitement. Each day, he'd remind everyone of the countdown.

One week and five days.

One week and four days.

One week and three days.

Despite Dr. Om's stated confidence that the feed was a complete success, Bertie noticed that a couple members of the park maintenance crew reinforced the slats of the pen with more metal strips and that the construction crews were adding bars to more windows around the park.

Given that the tropical cabañas of authenticity were wood, Bertie didn't know how much good that would do.

Especially against Termite.

But even Bertie was starting to feel a little optimistic.

On the fourth day ("one week and two days!" Dr. Om screamed over the newly installed PA system), Bertie entered the pen with Hessy. The unicorns retreated nervously.

Bertie put his hand out to Termite. She bucked.

"Calm down, girl," he said, still holding his hand out.

Termite approached, but she neighed skittishly. Bertie

signaled to Hessy to stand back and checked her breathing. It was fast again. Her eyes were dilated. Not a lot, but some. He tried to check her temperature, but the unicorn brayed and ran away.

He crept from unicorn to unicorn, trying to check as many of them as he could. Those who would let him get near were as skittish as Termite. He touched their hides to check for temperature.

It was spiking.

He looked back at Hessy, who was standing by the door, and shook his head.

Dr. Om wouldn't hear any of it.

"It's all the noise from the work crews!" Dr. Om said over the walkie-talkie. "It's making them edgy. That's all."

"I looked at the footage from last night," Bertie said as he watched the unicorns through the cutout in the fence. "They got agitated around three in the morning. There were no work crews then."

"It's the noise! They'll be fine. Fine!" Dr. Om said.

"Let's assume that's true for a second. You're going to muzzle the tourists to keep them quiet?"

Dr. Om paused. "The unicorns love people! People noise won't bother them. They'll be fine."

"You're not getting it."

"Dr. Vole. I'm sure you'll remember that you are welcome to leave. If you do, it won't affect you. Not at all."

Bertie screamed silently at the walkie-talkie before chucking it on the ground. From his feet, he could hear Dr. Om say, "One week and two days!"

Two hours later when he tried to go in to examine the unicorns, they kicked and growled.

Even Termite wouldn't let him get close.

CHAPTER 31

BERTIE COULD FEEL the hot sun on his eyelids when he woke up the next day. One week and one day.

He kept his eyes screwed tighter than ever.

Because once he opened them, it would be time to face . . . even more stuff.

Bertie really didn't want to see Hessy at breakfast. She was avoiding him almost as much as he was avoiding her. It was awkward when they were in the same place. Bertie got dressed and checked his supply of Ramen noodles. He was out.

He'd have to go to the dining room. Or starve, but then he'd get grouchy. And there was more than enough grouchy going down already.

He dragged himself to the dining room.

He took a deep breath, opened the door, and stared.

Hessy wasn't there. The room was empty.

Well, except for Lester, but his personality wasn't really something that populated a room.

"Hey, Lester?"

"Yes?"

"Have you seen Hessy?" He hoped she had come and gone.

"I sure did!" Lester seemed pissed. "She took the last of the bacon."

"She must have been hungry," Bertie said distractedly as he grabbed a tray. News you can't use. He didn't have time for chitchat about breakfast food.

"And when I say last of the bacon, I mean all of it," Lester said. "She cleared the whole refrigerator. The cook is about to blow a gasket."

It hit Bertie what she was up to. "Oh, no," he said. He passed his hand over his head, trying to get his brain cells working. This was not according to plan.

The tray clattered to the floor, and he raced down the stairs and ran as fast as he could to the unicorn's pen. He turned and ran down the narrow path. Out of breath, he ripped open the side door.

And there was Hessy, flinging bacon to the agitated unicorns.

"Hessy!" Bertie said as quietly as he could. "Hessy, what are you doing?"

She turned around, surprised. "Oh, Bertie, there you are. You're speaking to me?"

"What do you mean?" Although Bertie knew exactly what she meant.

"You've been, I don't know, out of sorts." Hessy tossed one more slice of bacon to Dragon Breath.

"You can't . . . you can't do that," he said.

"What do you mean? Do you want them going all crazy again? The feed isn't working."

"It isn't safe." Bertie looked behind him to make sure no one was nearby. He scanned the pen; the security cameras were working.

"If Dr. Om sees that video feed—" Bertie moved to grab the bacon from her, but she stepped out of his reach. "You're making this really hard on me," he said.

"What are you talking about?" Hessy looked annoyed.

"We've got to keep Dr. Om off our backs," Bertie said. "You of all people—"

"Dr. Om can bite me. We're supposed to be taking care of these animals."

"Listen, what can we do? Huh? What difference can me make? In one week, Dr. Om will bust the park doors open wide. We can't stop him. And a whole slew of tourists is going to come filing in expecting to see docile, kid-friendly magical creatures that will nuzzle their ears and eat out of their hands. Instead, they'll get meat-hungry mythical lab rats with horns who want to poke them to shreds. How likely is it that the park will stay open after that?"

"That's not the point." Hessy flung more bacon.

"Then, no matter what we do, we're out. It's just best to keep Dr. Om on our good side for the aftermath."

Bertie tried to keep his voice calm, to not agitate the unicorns even further. It was getting hard.

"What? We're supposed to placate the guy?" she said.

Black Mamba and Captain Viper kicked the dirt and shook their manes.

Bertie grabbed the rest of the bacon from her hands, threw it to the unicorns, and dragged her out of the pen to the narrow path outside. He looked around, but no one would be able to see them through the tunnel of trees. The growls of unicorns fighting over bacon punctuated their conversation.

"It's not safe in there," he said.

"So that's our main goal now? Watch out for our own

skin? We're supposed to care for them." She pointed at the pen. "That's why we're here."

Bertie didn't say anything for a moment. "That's not why you're here."

"What do you mean?"

"Dr. Om told me." He took a step back from Hessy.

"Told you what?"

"About the deal."

"What deal?" Hessy looked confused.

"The deal. The deal that has me in a bind because, for some reason I can't figure out, I'm the only one worried about not pissing Dr. Om off. Because if we keep sneaking around behind his back, he will find out. He will fire us. And your end of the deal goes down the toilet."

"What deal?" Hessy took a step forward, but Bertie gently pushed her back.

"Don't pretend," he said. "You've done enough of that."

"I have no clue what you're talking about."

"The fine print," Bertie shouted, then lowered his voice again. "That's what I'm talking about. The fine print. About your mother."

Hessy just stared at him.

"Dr. Om told me all about it."

"Dr. Om?"

"Yes," Bertie said.

"What about my mother? What did he say about my mother?" Hessy bit her lip, looking worried.

"Don't pull that on me," Bertie said. "He told me all about it. How he made a deal to get your mother in treatment."

"What?" Hessy said.

"How could you be that manipulative, by the way?" Bertie said.

Hessy shook her head. "What are you talking about?"

"Why didn't you tell me? And why is it that I'm the one making sure we don't get in trouble?"

"Again, what are you talking about?"

"I just wish you had told me. I'd have stayed anyway."

"My mother isn't in treatment," she said. "What's up with you?"

"That's not what he told me," Bertie said. "He offered you the deal, and you manipulated me to stay."

"I never manipulated you. Do you know how stupid that sounds? I told you from day one the decision was up to you."

"That's not what he said. Do you think I want to stand by and let Artie play games with the unicorns? I don't. But I'm not going to be the cause of your mother getting booted. I have no choice."

"There you are again," she said.

"What do you mean?"

"Of course you have a choice," she said. "If you really don't want to be here and you think I'm such a liar, leave."

"I can't," Bertie said. "I'm stuck. How is it that I have to explain this? If I leave or you leave or we get fired—any combination of those things, and Dr. Om pulls your mother out of the program. I can't do that to you."

Hessy didn't say anything for a minute. Her hands were shaking. "What will it take for you to believe me? I don't do things like that. How can you think that of me? There is no program. No backroom deal. No fine print about me manipulating you to stick around. You were the one who said you had to stay, not me. I never made you stay."

"Sure. You made it seem like you didn't care one way or the other. It was a good play," Bertie said. "Dr. Om showed me the contract."

"You—" She then pulled her phone from her back pocket and flicked through the screen. She held it up to Bertie's face.

"Is that the contract you saw?"

Bertie looked. "I guess, yeah. You took a picture of your contract?"

"Read the fine print." She shoved the camera close to his face. "Go on, read it."

Bertie read it, once, twice, a third time. He scrolled all the way to the top, then back down to Hessy's signature.

Nowhere did it say anything about Hessy's mother.

He'd been played.

After Hessy had stomped off, Bertie knew he should probably follow her, but he was too stunned.

How had he managed to let himself get so duped?

He spent the next few hours standing at the pen. He alternated between watching the unicorns through the cutout to hitting his head against the slats and mumbling, "Stupid, stupid, stupid," to replaying his conversation with Dr. Om over and over and over again, then back to hitting his head against the pen.

"Stupid, stupid, stupid."

He thought about his conversation with Hessy the day after they had gotten here. Once Dr. Om had swizzled his finger in his brain, it seemed perfectly logical to find it fishy that she hadn't said more about the meeting. It was easy to conclude she must be hiding something.

Looking back on it now, it was probably normal she didn't have had tons to say to him about the contract. It's not like contracts were riveting topics of conversation. And they hardly knew each other anyway.

As Hessy would probably point out, he didn't know her very well now either. Not if he thought such awful things about her. And then she'd flip her hair and stomp off again, little hands held in tight fists.

"Stupid, stupid, stupid."

As Saint would probably point out, it would be her prerogative to resent that to the grave too.

Dr. Om had played him good. He had literally put it all on the table and counted on Bertie to be too stung to think logically or see straight.

And it had worked.

"Stupid."

The sounds from the pen had quieted down. He looked through the cutout.

The unicorns were calmer. Gotta love bacon.

From behind, Bertie could hear the final phases of construction whirr and whine. He opened the pen door and snuck inside.

The unicorns didn't react.

Attracted by the smell of meat that lingered on Bertie's hands, several unicorns approached. He took the opportunity to examine them.

They weren't quite back to normal, but for the time being, it was probably safe to stay in the pen. He paced in the center for several minutes, hands on his head, trying to get his thoughts straight.

He heard a noise behind him.

Termite was back to licking a slat of wood.

"Well, I stuck my foot in it," Bertie said to Termite.

She whipped her tail and kept licking the wood.

"You know, Termite," Bertie said as he approached her. "Your name may not be as scary as the others. I mean, 'Termite' is no 'Dragon Breath,' but don't let that fool you. You are equally scary. I mean, a termite can bring a house down." Termite neighed. "Yeah, it can. It might take you forty years, but you can do damage." He paused. "You and me both, we can do damage."

Termite nibbled Bertie's hand before going back to the wood.

"Ow," Bertie said. No doubt the bacon effect wouldn't last for long. He sat on the ground next to Termite.

"Might as well enjoy your company while I can."

CHAPTER 32

ONE WEEK LEFT. Bertie and Dr. Om were standing by the pen, listening to the unicorns growling and butting the enclosure. Even Dr. Om couldn't deny that things weren't going so hot.

"Dr. Vole, tranq those beasts," he said.

"Is that the grand plan?"

"No, that is my directive," Dr. Om stared up into Bertie's face and poked him with his finger. "You are not in charge of the grand plan. I am."

"What about when the tourists get here? What's your grand plan for that?"

"The unicorns won't roam free for now." He looked disappointed for a moment, then defiant. "I'll figure something out. We'll tranq them—keep them good and medicated—until I work it all out."

"Constant sedation? What kind of life is that?"

"They are my unicorns, Dr. Vole. This is my island. It's none of your business how I handle this." Dr. Om turned to leave.

"Why not just feed them—?"

"Enough with the meat! These unicorns are obviously defective, but I will do everything I can to make this grand opening work. Everything!"

"Delay the opening, at least." Bertie knew that he was grasping at straws. A delay wouldn't be enough, but something was something.

"Delay? Do you know what delaying will do to my reputation?"

"And if they escape and hurt someone? What will that do to your reputation?"

"I have that handled too."

Dr. Om started to walk away again.

"I know about Hessy," Bertie said.

"What?" Dr. Om whipped around. He looked stunned.

"Her mother, she's not in any experimental treatment. You can't hold her over me anymore."

"Go ahead!" Dr. Om shouted. "Go ahead and release all the information you want. You know what will happen? The authorities will come in and exterminate the unicorns. Is that what you want?"

Dr. Om had him. He was right.

"No. No, I want to find a permanent solution."

Dr. Om laughed. "Permanent solution. You little upstart. I've been working on this for almost my entire career, and you really think you can waltz into this and find a permanent solution? You're just a vet."

"I thought you hired me because I knew something?" Bertie said.

"I thought you would be enthusiastic about what I'm trying to do. But every step of the way, you want to delay or dither or obsess about diet."

"You're the one who's obsessed about diet."

"I didn't work all these years—years when people made

fun of me or ignored me or called me crazy—to make bloodied monsters that would scare people!"

"You are way too obsessed about your reputation."

"You know what it's like to be disrespected," Dr. Om said. "To be a nobody."

"Oh, so you're saying we're basically the same?"

"No, no, not at all, not at all." Dr. Om got in Bertie's face. "We aren't. We never will be. Because I go big or go home. I do what it takes. You never will."

Dr. Om made to leave, then turned around. He took a deep breath and forced a smile.

"Let's make the best of this unfortunate hiccup. It's just a hiccup. We've stopped taking new reservations. I'm having productive conversations with my team. In the meantime, you tranq the animals, and I keep doing what scientists do."

Dr. Om stomped off.

What a nutcase.

A screech pierced the air. Bertie looked through the cutout. Princess Piranha took a bite out of Barracuda. Red stained Barracuda's white and beige hindquarters.

Like it or not, he was going to have to tranquilize them for their own good. But how could he get close enough?

He thought about tossing more meat into the pen. Now that he knew Dr. Om's deal with Hessy was phony, he figured he could risk sneaking in as much meat as he wanted. More screeches and growls, though, told him meat wouldn't be enough at this point. But maybe if they ate some meat, they'd calm down just enough for him to sedate them.

Hornet shrieked at Tasmanian Devil for trying to eat her leg.

On second thought, probably not.

Bertie grabbed a tranq gun and aimed through the cutout. But he stopped himself.

If he tried to tranquilize them from this vantage point, he'd only be able to reach about a third of the unicorns. At first blush, that may seem better than nothing. But what if the unsedated unicorns went after the sedated ones?

He couldn't risk it.

He looked up at the zipline. It wasn't ready for use yet, though. (How Dr. Om planned to get it inspected without revealing bloodthirsty unicorns to the world, Bertie had no clue.)

There was a third option.

He pulled out his phone and dialed Saint.

"Come on. Pick up." But there was no answer.

He'd have to take the Jeep out to Saint's shop. Maybe he was there.

Bertie crossed the park. He didn't have to go far when he heard voices coming from up in the dining area. The front window was still missing. He was able to make out who was talking.

It was Hessy. He couldn't quite hear what she was saying though. He crept up the stairs and stood flat against the wall so she wouldn't see him eavesdropping from the veranda.

". . . think that of me?" Hessy said.

Another voice came through. It was Saint's.

"Dr. Crazy Man is very manipulative," Saint said. "Repeat something many times, and everyone will believe you. Dr. Crazy Man is very repetitive."

"But still," Hessy said.

Was she crying? Oh, gosh. She was crying.

Or maybe she just got a cold. Yeah, a cold. Bertie liked that explanation better.

"It was good of him to watch out for your mother's fabricated welfare," Saint said.

Hessy didn't reply right away. "I know."

Snot. Bertie heard snot.

Bertie hated snot.

"There, there," Saint said. "Why don't you go wash your face. Then we can go smuggle some rotted meat. You like that, nah?"

She must have said yes, because Saint said, "There's my girl."

A chair scraped against the ground. Bertie moved around the corner to hide. Once Hessy's footsteps receded, Bertie snuck into the dining room.

"Hello Bertie," Saint said, his back to the door.

"How'd you know it was me?"

"Who else would want to eavesdrop on our conversation?" Saint said. He laughed.

"Hessy's mad at me again," Bertie said as he switched the weight of the tranq gun.

"Don't hurt your head. She'll get over it," Saint said.

"Wait, I save her life, and it's her prerogative to resent me into the afterlife, but I'm an idiot jerk, and she'll forgive me?"

"The turbulent mysteries of the mind, Bertie. In other news, I hear the horned natives have gone restless."

"Yeah, about that."

"Hessy and I will go by the butcher for rotted meat. We must divert Dr. Crazy Man's attention to feed the animals. Hessy says he will still open his madman's park."

"Yeah, and about that too," Bertie said. "I don't think meat will be enough right now. They're really bad. Before we can feed them, we have to tranq them." Bertie held up the gun.

"And the question is, how to tranq them without meeting your Maker?"

"Right."

"And you would like my help," Saint said, smiling.

"Yes. Also, do you still have that air balloon?"

Saint held up his finger. "As a matter of fact, I do. The vicious, evil smuggler won't pick it up till next week."

"Great. Let's go get that balloon."

Saint followed Bertie down the stairs and said, "This is what we do. You buy the meat so we have it ready for later. I go get the balloon."

"Great!" Bertie said.

Then Saint picked up his phone. "Hessy, it's Saint. There has been a slight change of plans."

Bertie looked at Saint. Hessy would probably be pretty mad at those change in plans.

"Yes, Bertie will get the meat. I have to run a quick errand. Meet us at the south exit."

Bertie shook his head at Saint. He mouthed the words, "No, no, no, no, nooooooooooo!" But Saint only laughed and patted him on the back.

"Yes, in about an hour. Bring some tranquilizer guns." Saint winked at Bertie. "We see you there."

"Awesome, Saint," Bertie said as they walked through the path leading to the south exit. "Let's arm Hessy with some tranq guns and put her in a hot air balloon with me. Great plan."

"Her aim is much better than yours, you know."

After Bertie hid the bags of meat near the pen, he headed back to the south exit to meet up with Saint and

Hessy. As he approached, the whoosh of hot air told him the setup was underway. By the time Bertie stepped into the back lot, the black balloon, bobbing in the breeze, was almost filled.

"Here's the plan," Bertie said. "We tether the balloon to that tree so that we don't float all the way to St. Carlota."

"Very bad people on St. Carlota." Saint nodded.

"Right," Bertie said. "Then we three go up in the balloon and . . . aim."

"Masterful plan, Bertie," Saint said as he patted him on the back.

"Right, then we head back to the pen, sneak in their meat, and make sure they're not injured."

"What if Dr. Om tries to stop us?" Hessy said. "Are the cameras in the pen still on?"

"Right. Well, yeah, they are." Bertie scrunched his eyes shut. Darn, why hadn't he thought of that? "Good thinking, Hessy. You go turn off the cameras in the control room, and we'll deal with the unicorns."

"I don't have the key," Hessy said.

"Forget that," Saint said. He helped Hessy into the balloon. "You two go up into the balloon, and I will deal with the cameras. I shoot the unicorns from down below."

"What?" Bertie made meaningful glances at Saint as though to say, "Don't you ditch me!" He wasn't crazy about being alone with Hessy and her tranq gun. "Why don't I stay below . . . ?"

But Saint pushed him into the balloon and released the ballast. Bertie and Hessy floated up as Saint jogged towards the pen.

"I wonder how he's going to deal with the cameras," Bertie said to make conversation.

"He's probably going to shoot them." Hessy didn't look at Bertie.

"Right, good idea, actually."

But Hessy still didn't look at Bertie.

He jumped as Dr. Om's voice came through the walkie-talkie. "What do you think you're doing?" The door to the administrative bungalow swung open, and Dr. Om's miniature was pointing at the balloon.

"We can't go inside the pen to tranquilize the baby-poos," Bertie said. "We have to do it from up here."

"That was supposed to be done already!" He stamped his tiny foot. "I have my zipline engineer coming in ten minutes—ten!—to do his inspection. I need the unicorns calm and YOU out of the way."

"Well, it's not like I have a hot air balloon in my underwear drawer." Bertie was relieved to hear Hessy laugh. "We had to get our hands on this."

The walkie-talkie squealed as Dr. Om raised his voice. "Don't make me come up and—"

Bertie lost his patience. He dropped the walkie-talkie off the side of the balloon and put his hand up to his mouth as though it were an accident.

Dr. Om waved his little fists. Bertie mouthed, "Ooooops!"

"Jerk," Hessy said.

"Me or him?"

"Both," she said. But she didn't look mad.

Or maybe she did. People were just so darn hard.

Bertie smacked his head a few times to boost his courage or cause a concussion or whichever came first. Then he took a deep breath.

"I'm sorry I believed what Dr. Om said about you." Bertie inspected his tranq gun more closely than necessary.

"Okay," Hessy said. There was a pause. "I guess you meant well, staying for my mother's sake and all."

"Yeah, I mean, I had no choice, right?"

Hessy rolled her eyes. "Of course you had a choice. It's not like someone dipped your feet in cement and dropped you in the ocean."

"Oh, so now you want me to have stabbed your mother in the back?"

"No, I appreciate you staying. But it's not just about that. It's everything." Hessy imitated Bertie's voice. "I'm stuck here. I can't do anything. I'm just going to have to rot in this job for the rest of my life or go back home and live in my parents' basement."

"My parents don't have a basement," Bertie hollered.

"Forget your parents' basement—"

"You're the one who brought it up."

"It's your attitude. About everything. Everything is a dead end to you. You're always stuck."

"What was I supposed to do?"

"Anything. Something. You didn't have to come here to begin with."

"I'm not sorry I came, but you've got to admit, this was one big fall from the fry pan into the fiery extravaganza below."

"Yeah, fell, just like that. Whoops!"

"What's that supposed to mean?"

"You didn't have to stay at Roderick's clinic or come here. You could have found a third or a fourth or a fifth option. You're not like me. You have an education."

"Like I could abandon you after I got you into this mess? I've told you this."

"I got myself into this mess. And I'm happy I did. You

didn't have to stay. Chivalry and inertia aren't the same thing."

"You two!" Saint screamed from below. Bertie saw they had arrived above the pen. "Stop bickering or I will shoot you both."

Hessy stomped to the other side of the balloon.

"Fine," Bertie said angrily. He noticed Black Mamba biting into Termite. Termite, he thought, I know what that's like. You and me both.

He aimed his tranq gun at Black Mamba, but the unicorn ran into the bushes too soon.

"Hold it," Saint called from below. "I will shoot the cameras in the pen to disable them first."

"Told you," Hessy said.

Bertie kept his mouth shut. He had had enough of the screaming.

"Nice shot," Hessy said.

"Don't tempt me," Bertie said. He screamed below to Saint. "Are you ready?"

Saint raised his tranq gun to confirm that he was.

"When you shoot a unicorn, say which one it is so we don't shoot twice," Bertie said.

Saint nodded and ran around the pen, smacking the sides to herd the unicorns away from the trees that would block Bertie and Hessy's aim.

"Captain Viper," Hessy said. She looked over at Bertie with narrowed eyes.

Bertie looked away and took aim below. "Gila Monster Man and Black Mamba." He turned to Hessy. "So there."

"How very adult of you," she said. And she shot Princess Piranha. "Princess Piranha."

"Takes one to know one," Bertie screamed.

"Hey, I got . . . that one," Saint screamed up. "Pay attention. I don't know their names."

"Termite," both Hessy and Bertie screamed.

They kept shooting. Bertie found it therapeutic, which was not something that could possibly look good on any future job application.

"Something's wrong," Hessy said.

Bertie threw his hands up. "Oh, sure, what did I do wrong now?!"

"Touchy, touchy. Take a look, why don't you? They're not calming down." Hessy jabbed her finger towards the pen.

Bertie was so caught up in shooting things, he hadn't noticed the passage of time. He hated to admit it, but Hessy was right.

"Do the guns take this long to work?" Saint screamed up to Bertie and Hessy.

"No," Bertie said. "Got Vulture, for what it's worth."

"Wait, I got Vulture five minutes ago," Hessy said.

"Why didn't you say anything?"

"I did!" Hessy stomped her foot.

"You two, stop! I tell you, I will shoot," Saint said.

"Fine!" Bertie said. "It probably doesn't matter. We may have to go into round two. Let's give it a few more minutes. If the general hysteria doesn't die down, we'll give them a second dose. Except for Vulture, of course."

"Brilliant call," Hessy said. She turned her back to him.

A few moments passed.

"It's not like you have it all figured out," Bertie said. His back was turned too.

"What's that got to do with anything?"

"Look at you. You put your life on hold for everyone

else. First for your mother. Then for magically enraged mutants."

Two minutes had passed, but all the unicorns, except Vulture, were still crazy.

"What do you mean, I put my life on hold?"

"You think you're sacrificing yourself for other people."

"It's called being generous."

"No, no, no. It's not just that. I'm willing to bet you're just . . . something. I don't know."

"Very deep. I'm not filthy rich, you know. I couldn't hire someone to take care of my mother."

The unicorns were still attacking each other and braying wildly.

"Do what everyone else does. Take out loans for school. Or ask someone to help you. But don't use other things as an excuse to put your life on hold."

"My life isn't on hold. Anyway, don't try to shrink me, Dr.   I'm-going-to-believe-any-lie-Dr.-Artie-says-about-Hessy."

"I said I was sorry about that."

"Fine," Hessy crossed her arms. "And maybe my life is on hold, just a little bit."

"Fine," Bertie said.

"But at least I don't blame fate."

"Oh, we're not done yet. Great. Well, I don't blame fate either, whatever that means."

"You might as well."

"I recognize limitations."

"Is that what you call it?"

"Yeah." He couldn't wait for the balloon to land. But the unicorns were as violent as before.

Bertie pointes his tranq gun at the unicorns. "Okay, time for round two. Keep track like before."

"Oh, so you mean shoot unicorns I've already shot?" Hessy said.

Bertie sighed. "Keep track better than before." He turned to Hessy. "Happy?"

"Got Tasmanian Devil," Hessy said.

"Got the smelly one," Saint said.

"That'd be Dragon Breath," Bertie said. "Got Barracuda."

"Got Jaws," Hessy said.

"Termite!" Bertie said.

"Got Hornet," Hessy said.

By now, all the unicorns had gotten a second dose of tranquilizer. They were no longer fighting, but they were still trotting around. "Okay, so this is not good news," Bertie said.

"What are we going to do?" Hessy said.

"I don't know yet. I've got to think." Bertie rubbed his temple. He had a headache. "Saint!" Bertie shouted below. "We're heading back to the back exit. Meet us there."

Saint nodded and ran for the lot.

The balloon lifted in the breeze in time to dodge the palm trees.

Below, Bertie could see Dr. Om standing next to a man with a clipboard, getting smaller and smaller as he pointed somewhere in the distance. Bertie turned around. That way, he'd have an excuse to ignore Dr. Om if he started hollering at him from below.

Because all the screaming, you know? He'd had enough of it.

Apparently Hessy had as well. She was on the other side of the balloon staring at the horizon.

Bertie looked back to the northern coast stretching out

before him. He could see a tiny, ocean-front building. The Last Resort.

Then he stared straight down to the south. For the first time, he saw a carpet of little houses that led right up to the wall of the park. An old lady putting up laundry looked up and waved; a young boy peeked under the hood of a car next to a man Bertie figured was his father.

If the unicorns escaped and went on a murderous rampage—

He pushed the thought down. He didn't want to think about what could happen if things got all out of control.

"I'm sorry I rubbed your parents' basement in your face," Hessy said. She sounded begrudgingly contrite.

"My parents don't have a basement," Bertie said. Why didn't people listen? "I rent a basement from someone. And technically, it's a half-basement."

"A half-basement. Got it," Hessy said. Bertie could hear a smile in her voice.

"And it has a window. Well, a half-window."

"Look, forget the basement already. What I was trying to say is that either you make decisions for yourself, or life makes decisions for you. Either way, they get made."

Bertie hated to admit it, but Hessy was right. "I'm starting to see that."

He tinkered with the fire to begin landing. "Actually, screw that. IT'S A WINDOW."

"Fine, fine. Window." Hessy looked down as the balloon touched down. "Truce?"

"Truce," Bertie said. He desperately wanted to avoid any more Hallmark moments, the "I'm not bitter" collection. "Definitely truce."

"We'll probably need to tranq them again soon," Bertie said once they were safely on the ground and Bertie was keeping Saint in between him and Hessy, just in case. Bertie noticed she hadn't put her tranq gun down yet. Truce or no truce, he was playing it safe. "Any way we could keep this air balloon close by?"

"Yes, over there is a shed that is big enough to fit it all in," Saint said.

Between the three, they hauled the balloon and basket into the shed. Saint rummaged around in his truck, saying, "It is always good to have a few extra around in case . . . Aha! In case you need to lock up someone else's property." He held up a padlock.

Saint slipped it on the door.

Bertie said, "You do that a lot, lock up other people's property?"

Saint laughed. "Don't ask if you don't want an honest answer."

Hessy grinned. "I bet Dr. Om would hit the roof if he knew you did that."

"Not at all," Saint said. "I am doing the fine loon a favor. If this balloon gets lost, a very angry Carlotian smuggler will have Dr. Om's head."

"All about that Christian charity, Saint," Bertie said. "You are an example to mankind."

"I do my best," Saint said. Saint gave the padlock a final tug and they jogged to the pen and peeked through the cutout.

They're calmer," Bertie said. "But not as quiet as they should be with that much tranquilizer in their systems."

"How quiet should they be?" Saint asked.

"Quiet, quiet," Bertie said. "As in, zonked out quiet."

"Saint and Hessy, you'll wait outside the door over

there," Bertie said, pointing to the small door on the pathway. "I'll go inside with the meat and treat their injuries."

"Oh, no you don't. I'm going in too," Hessy said.

They started carting meat to the side door.

"Hessy, please," Bertie said. "Saint, back me up on this one."

Saint put his hands up. "No, Hessy's aim is better than yours. I don't want to make her mad."

"I wouldn't want to put my life on hold," Hessy said.

"This truce thing is really working for you," Bertie said. "You two, I need you at the entrance to shoot if any go postal."

"Oh, look!" Hessy held up her gun. "I've got a portable tranq gun. What a relief. I can go in after all."

Bertie sighed. He didn't want to fight. "Okay, be ready to run."

Saint opened the door and walked in with a hunk of meat.

Bertie grabbed his shirt collar. "Saint, what are you doing?"

"Well, the faster we get out of here, the faster we get out of here," Saint said. He lowered his voice. "I'm less concerned about the unicorns and more concerned about you two killing each other."

Saint escaped Bertie's grip. "I will serve dinner, and you two treat injuries," he said.

"Okay, glad I worked so hard on the details of that plan," Bertie said.

"It was very intricate," Hessy said. "Must have taken a lot of Excel sheets."

Bertie rolled his eyes. Termite trotted up to them. Her hindquarters had teeth marks on them, and bloody strands of hair were hanging loose from her tail.

"What have we gotten ourselves into?" Bertie legs and arms felt heavy, as though he hadn't slept in days. Everything they'd done just now was a Band-Aid. What would they have to do to actually solve the problem?

One by one, they checked the unicorns and cleaned their wounds. Saint passed around all the meat.

A yell interrupted the calm. The zipline whirred as the inspector flew over, screaming, "How can I inspect this thing with a blindfold on?" He passed over without a glitch and disappeared from view.

"So that's how Dr. Om planned to keep the unicorns a secret," Hessy said. "The man is completely cuckoo."

They tiptoed from the pen, careful to avoid any commotion that would agitate the unicorns. "Tomorrow, let's inject the tranquilizers right in the meat," Bertie said. "That may save us another trip in the air balloon."

"Yeah," Hessy said. "But how long are we going to be able to keep this up?"

Bertie rubbed his hand over his head. Another question he didn't know the answer to.

CHAPTER 33

THERE WERE four days left till the grand V.I.P. opening, as Dr. Om announced for the fifth time on the PA system. Things weren't looking good.

For the past three days, Bertie, Saint, and Hessy had been tossing tranquilizer-laced meat into the unicorn enclosure. The best results they got were grouchy unicorns that didn't let them in the pen but weren't doing any damage. Bertie decided not to up the dose, though. They were already getting way too much as is.

In other news, Bertie and Hessy's truce held. It was cordial enough that Bertie sensed all was not well on the Quichan front, but he'd take cordial over frothing-at-the-mouth scream fests.

The one silver lining was that Dr. Om was so busy with final preparations, he didn't pay attention to anything Bertie, Hessy, and Saint were doing, including the ongoing sabotage of security cameras.

Then two bad things happened.

Or badder, when you consider that bad stuff was already going down.

First, Badder Thing Number One.

Bertie had gotten up early to go check on the unicorns. Hessy was headed the same way, and he had to run to catch up. He was already hot and sweaty, and he had only left his room a few minutes before.

"How is it that you never seem to get lost?" Bertie said when he reached her.

"You can't get lost here. The layout won't let you. You turn wrong, you just go in circle till you get to the point you need to be."

Bertie didn't have time to reply, though. They were at the pen.

Or what was left of it.

The slats of wood were pocked with holes all around. Bloody holes. The unicorns inside were butting their heads against the pen and, from the sound of it, biting each other.

The tranquilizer wasn't working. They hadn't eaten the kids' cereal in days and were on a 100% diet of preferred meat, and they were still going bonkers.

Bertie and Hessy cautiously approached the cutout. They looked inside the pen. Bertie couldn't believe what he saw.

The unicorns were frothing at the mouth. Pink and blue and orange saliva dripped from their jaws and left streaks of slobber on the grass. Their eyes were bugged out, and they nipped at anything they could get their teeth into. Barracuda, his white and beige flank covered in green goo, charged at Captain Viper, sending a string of pink froth through the cutout. Bertie pulled Hessy away before she could get splattered.

Who knew what that stuff would do?

"Listen," Bertie said to Hessy. "Do me a favor. Stay

back." Hessy nodded with huge eyes. Even she was freaked out.

Bertie tiptoed back to the cutout and looked down to where Termite often sat nibbling on wood. She was there, taking huge bites out of the tree next to her. Any minute now, and it was going to fall.

He took a penlight from his pocket and managed to shine a light at her eyes. One pupil was a pinprick. The other was all-out dilated.

She looked completely deranged.

All of them did.

Tasmanian Devil charged in his direction. Bertie plastered himself against the wall just in time for her to spit through the opening.

Bertie's nightmare, the one where Berta had eaten him, flashed before his eyes.

Just like in the dream, the unicorns had become zombies.

Okay, technically, this was looking more like rabies. Zombies didn't exist.

Right? Dr. Om didn't have any zombies tucked away, ready to star in a side exhibition?

"What is this?" Hessy said.

Bertie rubbed his forehead. He was getting a headache. "Beats me. The most technicolor case of fantasy rabies on record, maybe? It's got to be the food that caused this," Bertie said. "Or some interaction between the feed and the sedative."

"What could make that happen?"

"Who knows? We're dealing with made-up creatures, so the science is made up too."

The unicorns had gone rainbow rabid, and Bertie had no plan.

Well, no new plan. But an extension on an old plan. He didn't like it, but the risk of having diseased unicorns hurting each other or escaping and gnawing on the island population was forcing his hand. "Forget the tranqs," Bertie said. "We're going to have to somehow put them under. It's time for full-blown anesthetic. If this is rabies or something else contagious, we don't want any biting going on."

"Dr. Om will like that," Hessy said. "Sleeping unicorns. His V.I.P. crowd will be captivated."

"Well, as of now, it's official. Unicorns are nocturnal creatures," Bertie said.

"Was that in your book?"

But Bertie didn't have a chance to answer because the tree Termite had been chewing finally gave way. Bertie heard a groaning sound and then a "thump."

Great. Termite could start on the wall now.

Bertie looked back through the cutout. Gila Monster Man charged at Princess Piranha. He soon regretted it.

If Bertie didn't do something soon, there would be no unicorns left.

And if they got out, people would become scarce too.

There you have Badder Thing Number One. Bertie and Hessy ran to his lab. On the way, they saw Lester.

"Lester! Lester!" Bertie screamed. But Lester didn't stop.

"Lester!" Hessy said. Lester turned around, slowing his gait. "Lester, we need your help!"

Still, Lester didn't stop. For the first time, Bertie noticed how haggard he looked. Bertie couldn't help thinking this job wasn't very good for him. And if Lester looked that wrecked, how bad did Bertie look? I mean, even on a good day, he wasn't exactly GQ model of the year.

Bertie ran after him. "You want the unicorns to get out? You won't be able to walk fast enough to escape them then."

That made Lester stop. "What?" he said.

"Listen, go get the maintenance crew. They have to reinforce the pen," Bertie said.

"Uh-oh," Lester said. He grabbed his walkie-talkie.

"And let's keep Dr. Om out of it," Bertie said. "It's just easier that way."

Bertie could hear Lester telling maintenance to get to the pen. He wasn't sure what they could do, but he hoped they could do something.

But the day was still young, so there was plenty of time for Badder Thing Number Two to happen.

As they got into the lab, Dr. Om walked by with about twenty people behind him. He seemed ecstatic.

Obviously, he hadn't been to see his baby-poos.

Bertie and Hessy watched as the group passed by below. There was something odd about them, but Bertie couldn't put his finger on it.

He went back to trying to brainstorm a brilliant plan, or at least a better one than he had. "Okay, think, think, think," Bertie told himself. But the only thing that came to mind was his imminent mental breakdown.

Hessy paced around the lab as though trying to come up with something herself. She stopped in front of the freezer door.

You know, the one with Berta's corpse stuffed into it.

"No!" Bertie said, but it was too late.

She pulled.

Out rolled the table with Berta.

Hessy stared with wide eyes.

Oh, man. Bertie was sure the truce was swimming with

the fishes now. He ran up to the table and tried to pull Hessy away. She didn't budge.

"I . . . I was going to tell you . . . about Berta," Bertie said. "I was doing a necropsy because I wanted to see whether —" But Bertie couldn't think of anything to say that would make it sound better. "I'm sorry."

Hessy didn't say anything right away. She leaned forward and slid the cloth from Berta's face. All the unicorn sparkle was gone by now. "You did—" Hessy swallowed. "You did what you had to do. Did you find anything useful?"

"Not yet," Bertie said, surprised she was taking it this well. "I didn't have time to finish." He covered Berta up, but Hessy kept staring at her form anyway.

"Berta never ate that new feed," she said.

"Well, no . . ." Was Hessy feeling bad that Berta never ate Lucky "let's turn our unicorns into rabid zombies" Charms?

"It's too bad the others had," Hessy said.

"Sure, I agree," Bertie said.

"What if we—" Hessy got a disgusted look on her face. "We could some of Berta into the others? Maybe that will counteract the crazy?"

Bertie didn't say anything for a bit. Besides the fact that the thought of turning Berta into a Sloopie turned his stomach, he didn't think it would really work.

"Hessy, this isn't the movies. You can't just turn blood and gore into magical anti-rabies serum. Or whatever it is they have. Stuff like that doesn't exist."

Hessy turned to Bertie. "Neither do unicorns."

Before Bertie could answer, the thunk, thunk of footsteps on the stairs made him whip around. A frantic knock at the door followed. Hessy pushed Berta back into the freezer while Bertie rushed to the door.

"You two!" Dr. Om hollered. He knocked again. "Why is this door locked?"

Bertie gestured to Hessy to join him. He unlocked the door, and they stepped out on the veranda.

Dr. Om's arm was out of a sling, giving his arms a more expressive range of bossiness. "Why are you hiding out? I want to introduce you to the new members of our team!"

"Uh, hello," Bertie said. He waved to the crowd standing below. "We're kind of busy now."

"Not too busy to meet the team! Our crack team!" Dr. Om pointed at Bertie. "This is Dr. Vole, Bertram Vole. The author of the book I told you about. The only veterinarian in the world with experience in unicorns. It's astounding."

The new employees didn't look impressed. They all stood with their hands clasped behind their backs.

Weird, thought Bertie.

"And this is Miss Beauregard, interim manager and helper extraordinaire," Dr. Om said, smiling. He rubbed his hands together as though he hoped for an enthusiastic response from his new team. He got none.

Bertie looked at the new crew again. They were all in safari uniforms, but they didn't have the same nervous excitement most new employees have.

"Hey, haven't I seen you before?" Bertie screamed down to one in back. "You've worked here for a while?"

"Negative," the guy said.

But Bertie couldn't help thinking he recognized the voice.

"This team includes maintenance, store clerks, and tropical safari tour guides," Dr. Om said. "As you know, our first guests arrive in four days—countdown four days! I love countdowns."

"Uh-huh," said Bertie.

"We're about to go meet my baby-poos," Dr. Om said.

"No!" Hessy said before she could stop herself.

"Excuse me, Miss Beauregard?" Dr. Om said.

"I mean . . ." Hessy said.

"What she means is . . ." Bertie said.

"That . . . that's the . . . grand finale!" she said.

"Yeah, yeah," Bertie said. "Shouldn't they see that last?"

"Drama!" Hessy said.

Dr. Om was silent for a moment. He narrowed his eyes.

"And anyway," Bertie said. "We need to go get their weekly . . . stool samples."

"Yuck!" said Hessy with way too much enthusiasm.

"Poo?" said Bertie. "Is that the first thing you want the newest members of our happy family to see?"

"When you put it that way," said Dr. Om, "we'll go see the Tropical Paradise Souvenir Shoppe." He narrowed his eyes at Bertie and leaned into his ear. "You should have gotten the stool samples earlier. Hur-ry."

Dr. Om stamped his foot and walked away with the workers.

Bertie and Hessy rushed back into his lab.

"Do you notice something strange about those people?" Hessy said.

"Yeah, I recognize one of them," said Bertie.

"They're all stiff," she said. "Look how they walk."

Bertie peeked out the window. Hessy was right.

They didn't walk like tour guides or maintenance people or shop clerks. Most especially, they didn't walk like new employees on a casual tour.

They walked like the military.

Bertie looked closer. A sudden explosion from the direction of the pen made Dr. Om jump. But none of the new employees startled. The one nearest to Dr. Om pulled a gun from an ankle holster and inspected the area before putting it back.

They weren't regular park employees. Not really.

That's when Bertie remembered where he had seen that other guy.

Dr. Om had hired the private security back.

"Oh, no," Bertie said. "This is bad. When I asked him what he'd do if the unicorns escaped, he said he had it handled. 'Handled.' That was his word. I don't think those people are here to sell knickknacks. I think they're here to shoot and kill."

Hessy's eyes widened in horror.

"But what would make Dr. Om change his tune?" she asked. "He was dead set against killing unicorns before."

"No clue. That's got me really confused too. Unless you just chalk it up to his brand of crazy."

Either way, they had to do something.

But what?

"It's not going to be enough to administer anesthetic at this point," Bertie said. "Once those military types see the condition they're in, they may not wait for an attack to happen. Doesn't matter if the unicorns are snoozing."

"Once people find out about this . . ." Hessy said. She put her head in her hands.

If people found out about it . . .

That was it! Little Artie's Achilles heel.

"You're right," Bertie said. He put his fist to his mouth pensively.

"About what?"

Bertie didn't say anything right away. A slew of ideas

bombarded him all at once. He closed his eyes to focus. When he opened them again, he looked at Hessy and said, "That's it. You've been right all along. We're here to take care of them. No more half measures. No more Band-Aid solutions in response to the next emergency. No trying to put off the arrival of guests."

"What do you mean, exactly?"

"I mean I'm ready to fight. We're going to save them. I don't know exactly how yet, but we're going to save them. But first, we're going to need a lot of meat."

Shrieks erupted from the pen.

"And lots of anesthesia," he said. "Lots and lots of it."

CHAPTER 34

BERTIE AND HESSY finished lacing the meat with anesthesia in the kitchens, now free of employees thanks to the universal currency of bribery. They had to make sure the unicorns could eat it up as quickly as possible so they had blenderized it and then lugged the precious slosh to a cart, covered it from prying eyes, and made their way to the south exit.

Bertie hoped the rabid unicorns were as fond of meat as regular unicorns were.

However you define "regular unicorn."

"Okay," Bertie said. "The cafeteria is doing 'Ocean View Caribbean Tropical Catering' to the gift shop to delay Dr. Om and his crew. Check. The meat is out of sniffing range of the unicorns, check. Lester gave us access to the PA system. Check."

"We just need to get Saint onboard," Hessy said. "I'll call."

"Thanks. Make sure he brings Bartholomew."

"Bartholomew? But he's just a kid."

"No," Bertie said, looking at Hessy. "He's not just a kid. He's a juvenile delinquent."

It was times like these that Bertie wished life came with a soundtrack.

The stage was set. It was a rickety one at best, but as Saint would say, when you ain't got horse, ride car.

Or something like that. Bertie couldn't quite remember.

A really iffy variable was whether the unicorns would hold off till the right time to play their part. All the way from the south exit, Bertie could hear the animals screeching and ramming into the pen walls.

He wasn't so sure that they would wait. Or as Dr. Om would no doubt say, time was a-wasting.

Hessy said, "Saint's on his way. He's got the intel from his hacker."

"Yes!" Bertie said. "Tell him to bring it. All of it."

He had never been so relieved to hear Lady Mathilda cough her way up to the south exit. Saint stuck his head out the window. "Sorry for the delay. Lady Mathilda isn't used to chauffeuring this many people."

As Bertie caught Saint up on the details, he looked at those who had come to help. Percival the rum plant guy was circulating glasses of oh-be-joyful to the others. The pastor was reminding Agatha, Bartholomew's mother, that Uahula wasn't going to jump out at her so she could stop wailing. Bartholomew stole the pastor's wallet before his mother made him give it back.

None of them knew why they were there yet. The surprise was vital to the plan. But they came on down because Saint had asked them to.

Such was the power of Saint.

"Do you have the stuff from the hacker?" Bertie said.

"I got the papers," Saint said, handing them over. "DNA and finances all there."

Bertie skimmed the documents. His pulse raced. "That's why Dr. Om changed his tune about exterminating the unicorns."

Saint looked confused, but Bertie said, "I'll explain later." He put the papers in his back pocket.

It was show time. Not that he was ready. A crack from the pen reminded him that, ready or not, something was going to happen. He could get in front of it or wait to be trampled. He took a deep breath to steady his voice and clapped his hands. "This is how it's going down." His voice cracked. "Agatha, Percival, and Pastor. You go with Saint. Saint, you know what to do."

Saint held up the key to the hot air balloon shed and smiled. He nodded, almost imperceptibly, as though to say, you can do this, my boy.

Bertie nodded in return. "Remember to wait for Bartholomew before taking off."

Saint gave a thumb's up and signaled for his team to follow.

Bertie turned to Hessy. "You Hansel and Gretel this yellow brick road with the meat all the way from the outer edges of the park to the pen," Bertie said.

"On it." She darted away.

"Bartholomew," he said, "I've got an important job for you. Come with me."

Bartholomew nodded and followed Bertie towards the center of the park. By now, the delay tactic at the shops had worn out, and Dr. Om was standing in the clearing in front of the pen briefing the new team on the unicorns. Bertie breathed a sigh of relief. Based on Dr. Om's smile, he hadn't seen the unicorns yet. The employees all stood along the path in a straight line, hands behind their backs, eyes forward.

"Bartholomew." Bertie crouched down to his eye level. "You see that line of people wearing stupid uniforms?"

"You are wearing the same uniform," Bartholomew said.

"Yes, but I look less stupid. What you're going to do is lift the hem of their right pant leg. The right one. Got it?

"Yes."

"Then you're going to take their guns."

"May I keep the guns after?"

"No, you may not. You're going to empty the bullets and tuck them into your pockets."

"May I keep the bullets after?"

"We're going to need to have talk later. And no, you may not. Then you're going to put the guns back."

"Okay."

"And they can't know you've done anything."

"Dr. Bertie, I am a professional."

"That's my man," Bertie said, slapping him on the back. "On my signal, get to it."

Bartholomew waited where he was while Bertie walked up to Dr. Om. Bertie punched him on the shoulder. Really hard. "Hey, Dr. Om," he said.

Dr. Om swiveled towards Bertie. That was Bartholomew's cue.

"Not now, Dr. Vole."

Bertie glanced at Bartholomew. He was crouched next to the first employee's leg. For this to work, Bertie needed to distract Dr. Om for as long as possible.

"I know this isn't the best time—"

"Right you are, Dr. Vole. Move along—"

"But I was thinking, in a spirit of goodwill towards the locals—"

"Now is not the time to worry about the locals."

Bertie gripped Dr. Om's elbow to keep him from turning. "I know, but I was thinking, they really should get the first sneak peek of the park."

"What?"

"Well, it's their island. I mean, it's your island, but they live here. And I think they'd be just tickled pink to see what you have going on here. They've heard so much about it."

"What? Did you feed your brain to the unicorns this morning, Dr. Vole? Did you? Because I have work to do!"

Dr. Om was about to turn, but Bartholomew still had ten more guns to empty. Bertie rested his arm around Dr. Om's shoulder in what he hoped was an amicable side hug.

"You know what the locals say about you? Do you?" He stretched a pause out to give Bartholomew as much time as possible. "They call you Uahula, which in local parlance means 'savior of our economy and culture.'"

"Really?" Dr. Om looked equal parts flattered and skeptical.

"That's—" Bertie glanced at Bartholomew. Almost done. "A loose translation."

Bartholomew slipped the gun in the last holster and dashed back to the south exit just as Dr. Om looked back at the line of employees. Any second now, Hessy should arrive ready to play her part. He crossed his fingers and hoped she got here soon.

"Dr. Vole, if you don't mind—"

"Oooops!" Hessy yelled.

Atta girl, thought Bertie.

She had accidently on purpose spilled maroon meat slop from a bucket as she dragged it towards the pen.

"Dr. Om! I am so sorry," Hessy said. She lugged the

container towards the line of employees, tripped and spilled some more.

"Oh, I am so clumsy!"

Dr. Om's face went red. "What are you doing? What is that? What is that?"

"Dr. Om. I am so sorry." Hessy leaned in towards Dr. Om. "I'm afraid—well, Dr. Vole. This really is your area."

"Yes, um, I'm afraid the baby-poos have had some diarrhea," Bertie said.

"That's . . . that's . . . ?" Dr. Om said, pointing at the slop with big eyes.

"Their stool sample, yes," Bertie said.

'That doesn't look like any stood sample I've ever seen!" Dr. Om said.

"Unicorns the world over are known for colorful stool samples," Bertie said. "Miss Beauregard, you should be getting those back to the lab."

"Yes, Dr. Vole. Dr. Om, again, I'm so sorry. This is a terrible time for this to happen." She looked over sheepishly at the guards, who despite their normally steely gazes, were crinkling their noses. "Especially with the guests coming."

"Guests? Guests? What are you talking about, you silly girl?" Dr. Om looked from Hessy to Bertie and back to Hessy.

"Bertie? You haven't told him his surprise?" Hessy said as she spilled more slop.

"You!" Dr. Om pointed to the employee nearest to the most recent mess. "You! Get that cleaned up."

The employee ran to get cleaning supplies.

"Well, Dr. Om, here's the thing," Bertie said. He looked towards the south exit. Still nothing.

"What Bertie means to say, Dr. Om," Hessy said as she

spilled sludge on his shoes, "is that he feels bad about dragging his feet."

Bertie took Dr. Om's arm and walked with him towards the pen.

"Yeah, so I took some initiative," Bertie said.

The unicorns had stopped fighting. In the presence of meat, the growls and howls had been replaced by the sound of sniffing and snuffling. Bertie was relieved that meat still held its attraction over them.

"You know what I did, Dr. Om?" Bertie said.

"What? What did you do? Spit it out already!"

"I got a small, exclusive group of locals to come as part of a V.I.P. pre-showing!" Bertie stuck out his shoulders to show how proud he was.

"You did what?!" Dr. Om said.

"I got a small, exclusive group of locals to come as part of a V.I.P. pre-showing!"

"When? When?" Dr. Om spit. "When?"

By now, the three had reached the pen. Bertie positioned Dr. Om by the cutout so he could see the unicorns. When he glanced into the enclosure, his eyes bugged out and he went pale.

Bertie continued nonchalantly. "Oh, they're on their way. T-minus, like, a couple of minutes, tops." He slapped Dr. Om on his back. "Isn't it exciting? I love countdowns!"

But Dr. Om didn't seem to be listening. He was staring, transfixed, at the unicorns, sputtering, "What? What? What's happened to them?"

"Not sure," Bertie said with a smile. "Probably just a cold. Or a case of the rabies. Who knows?"

"Rabies, rabies?" Dr. Om faced Bertie head on. "Unicorns can't get rabies."

"Think again!" Bertie pulled the wireless PA microphone from his front pocket. "Countdown: Zero days!" He pointed to the black air balloon approaching from the south.

Dr. Om turned. His jaw dropped.

"A warm welcome to our first tour!" Bertie said. "Beneath you, you will see Dr. Om, the founder of the Mythical Unicorn Something Featuring Something Zipline Something. Heck, let's just call it a park."

Dr. Om tried grabbed at the microphone, but Bertie held it out of his grasp.

"No, no," Dr. Om said. "You can't do that now. Not now."

"As you can see, tourists," Bertie said, "the animals are safely held in a pen."

The wall shuddered from another unicorn onslaught.

Dr. Om reached for mic again. "This is not how this is supposed to be. Not like this. Do you know what this will do to my years of work? My reputation! I'll be ruined. Ruined!" When he couldn't get the mic from Bertie, he towards the balloon, as though he could somehow stop it with the force of his babbling. Any second now, and it would clear the ring of trees and descend to reveal the mutant insanity. The locals would know all about the unicorns.

"Dr. Om," Bertie said. "I thought you'd be happy. You've been working towards this point for years."

Hessy slopped the last bit of meat on the path and dashed back towards the pen. Wooden slats cracked under the force of another unicorn headbutt. Bertie really, really hoped the unicorns went for the meat and not for the people standing right outside the enclosure.

Another thunk, thunk, crack, and the ballooned cleared the pen. Dr. Om sank to his.

From above, Bertie heard someone—probably Agatha—

shriek. But he didn't look. He was too busy peering through the cutout. Barracuda, foaming wildly at the mouth, kicked off from his back legs and lunged at Gila Monster Man, who growled ferociously. Yellow, orange, purple foam splattered all over the place.

"As you see, V.I.P. tour," Bertie said, "Dr. Om here is a premier geneticist who worked for years to create the first unicorns the modern world has ever seen."

Agatha hollered from above. "What is the matter with those . . . those creatures?"

Dr. Om jumped up on his feet. "They're having a bad day! Really, it's just a bad daaaay!" He held his hands aloft helplessly. "They have colds."

"Should they be frothing at the mouth?" the pastor's voice reached below. "And not to say, 'I told you so,' but I told you Uahula wasn't up here."

"Oh, Pastor," Agatha said, "this . . . this isn't safe."

"We are high up, nearer to the Lord," he said. "We will be fine."

"What if they can fly?" Agatha wailed.

"Oh, Agatha," the pastor said, "you and your constant worry. Do you see wings?"

"Dr. Bertie!" Bartholomew screamed as he pointed to the pen. "Unicorns exist! And they are the coolest animal ever."

"I gotta agree, Bartholomew," Bertie said with a smile.

Hessy grabbed the microphone. "As a bonus, just for our very special guests today, Dr. Vole has for you the official documents containing the genetic makeup of these not-so-mythical creatures."

Bertie pulled the pages from his back pocket and waved them.

"No, no!" Dr. Om said. "Those are proprietary secrets! No!"

The wall heaved. The guards slipped their guns out of their holsters and stood at the ready.

"Yes, I do have those documents!" Bertie said. "Courtesy of our good friend Saint. Thanks, Saint!"

Saint waved back from the balloon.

"Now, Dr. Om, I may have some questions for you. But first, let's take a look at these ingredients. Let me see . . . we've got horse. That makes sense."

"What conspiracy is this?" Percival leaned over the edge of the basket and hollered. "Are we sure those horns aren't glued on?"

"No, Percival," Bertie said. "I checked. And we also have a dash of rhino. That's for the horn. Makes sense. Hyena too. Now we see where their fine taste for rotten flesh comes from. Ooooh, and mongoose. Maybe the mongoose had a nasty case of rabies. What do you think, Dr. Om? And now for something really interesting." Bertie paused, hoping to create some suspense.

"What? What?!" Dr. Om craned his neck to look at Bertie. "You think genetic innovation is clean and simple and straightforward? You don't understand what it takes—"

"Yeah, blah, blah, blah. Who wants to know the next ingredient?" Bertie looked up at the team in the balloon and waved the papers teasingly.

They all leaned over and raised their hands.

"Are you sure?" Bertie asked as Dr. Om tried to grab the papers from his lifted hand.

"Yes, get on with it, you doltish boy," Agatha screamed.

Bertie looked at the page, even though he knew what came next. "Crocodile" Bertie said in the voice of a game show host. "Loads and loads of crocodile."

Dr. Om looked shocked. "Crocodile?"

Bertie looked down at Dr. Om. "Why crocodile DNA, Dr. Om? Why not a dash of Godzilla DNA too? Or King Kong DNA? Or DNA from that alien, human-eating blob from that 1950's movie that was boring as heck?"

"Croc-crocodile?" Dr. Om said weakly.

"That's what it says." Bertie held the page close to his own face and read it again. "Croc-o-dile. Why would you use crocodile when you wanted animals for a petting zoo—I mean, park?

Dr. Om grabbed the pages and skimmed through, mouthing the words nervously. "I told them giraffe! Giraffe! For an elongated, elegant neck. They must have gotten confused. Oh, no, no, no."

"Maybe you should neaten up your handwriting," Hessy said.

"Now, Dr. Om. I'm the one who's confused," Bertie said. "Please clarify for our guests. How is it that you didn't know what was in your unicorns? Didn't you make them?"

"You don't just make unicorns!" Dr. Om said. "They're not a bunch of Legos. It's a complicated process that involves the collaboration of many brilliant minds—"

But Dr. Om never got the chance to finish. As though timed on purpose, the wall finally collapsed.

The pastor, Percival, Agatha, and Bartholomew all shrieked when the unicorns, as one, surged forward.

It was just like in a movie, all slow-mo. Only Bertie wasn't afraid. He knew what the unicorns would do. Hessy and her big bucket of meat slop had made sure of it.

Or anyway, he was pretty sure he knew what the unicorns would do.

But Dr. Om had no idea. He screamed, "Shoot, before

they eat us all! Shoot! That's what I paid you for! Shoooooooot," and he ran towards the guards.

The crew took a step forward. The guard at the head screamed, "Ready!"

"Don't stand on ceremony. Shoot!" Dr. Om screamed.

"Aim!"

"What are you waiting for? Shoot!" Dr. Om stamped his foot.

"Fire!"

But the guns, of course, didn't fire.

The unicorns followed the meat-strewn route, stopping every few steps to nosh on the vilest Sloopie St. Quiche had ever seen. Their mouths dripped with foam and left a trail of reds, blues, purples, pinks, oranges, and yellows.

Bertie would never eat another Starburst again. It was disgusting.

The guards took one look at their emptied, useless guns and ran as fast as they could towards the exit, followed closely by Dr. Om.

Bertie looked at Bartholomew. They gave each other a thumbs-up.

Bertie watched as the unicorns followed the path from one puddle of meat to the next. If all went as planned—and who could tell whether it would?—they would all fall asleep by the time they reached the outer wall of the spiral.

Bertie realized all sorts of things could still go wrong, but Dr. Om, well, at least he was no longer in control. And that was progress.

CHAPTER 35

THE SHARP NOONDAY sun made Bertie squint. He had to go check up on the unicorns, but first, he needed to deal with the overly helpful pastor, Percival, Agatha, and Bartholomew, none of whom was interested in marching back to the safety of their homes.

"You have given us a good show," the pastor said. "We want to stay and help."

"You're just happy to be proven right about Uahula," Saint said.

"I have won many a bet," the pastor said.

"Go on home," Bertie said. "It's not safe here."

"Bertie," Saint said. "This Dr. Crazy Man took over our island. They want to stay and take it back."

Before Bertie could reply, Agatha poked him in the chest.

"You, young man," she said.

"Ow," Bertie said.

"I'm not going anywhere. You think this is not my home too?"

"Miss Agatha—"

"Answer me!"

"Yes, but—"

"Don't back answer me!"

"I think it would be safer—"

"I didn't want to do this, but you make me, you know. Go for the slipper. Go for the slipper!" Agatha said.

"I don't know what that means," Bertie said.

Hessy leaned in to his ear. "I think it means she won."

"Dr. Bertie," Bartholomew said with big eyes. "You think the unicorns were bad? You don't want the slipper. You don't."

The rest nodded in agreement.

Bertie squeezed his eyes shut but realized the hard-learned truth, namely that there was no use fighting against the well-intentioned. "Well, okay. We're going to need that pen fixed as fast as possible. We don't know how long the meds will hold, and we'll need a place to put the unicorns."

"Put me to work!" Agatha said.

"I'll supply the rum!" Percival said.

"Lester!" Bertie screamed into his walkie-talkie. "LESTER! Get your keister over here. We need supplies to fix the fence."

Saint slapped Bertie on the shoulder. "I will go find that good-for-nothing Lester. You go collect the unicorn zombies."

"Technically, they're not . . ." But Bertie didn't bother finishing. After all, at this point, who knew what these unicorns were?

Bertie and Hessy followed the path, littered with pastel-rainbow froth and blenderized meat, towards the outer edges of the park. They advanced cautiously. Bit by bit, the sound of snoring reached their ears. Bertie felt relieved.

The unicorns were knocked out.

"Any ideas on how to get the unicorns back to the pen?" Bertie said.

"We can make a harness and attach it to the bottom of the balloon," Hessy said.

"Yeah, good idea." Bertie grabbed the walkie-talkie. "Saint, we're going to need to get a unicorn harness attached to the balloon basket and get it back up in the air for transport."

"On it," Saint said.

A noise—a noise that wasn't snoring—made Bertie and Hessy turn around slowly.

The unicorns were still asleep, but they were starting to seize.

"Oh, no, oh, no, oh, no," Bertie said. He leaned down and touched Termite. Her skin was on fire.

"What's going on?" Hessy said.

"I don't know," Bertie said. "But their temperatures are spiking."

He looked under the eyelids. Termite's irises were crazy concentric circles of reds, oranges, blues, every color of the dratted unicorn rainbow.

"Saint!" Hessy screamed into her walkie-talkie. "Saint, come in."

Bertie checked Barracuda, Gila Monster Man, Dragon Breath. The same. They were all the same.

"Saint, change of plans," Hessy said. "Get everyone out as fast as you can. Then seal the park. Now!"

Bertie kneeled, transfixed. The unicorns twitched. Froth started to seep from their mouths again. Jaws opened his eyes. Then Black Mamba and Captain Viper and Princess Piranha. They were waking up. Over the walkie-talkie, he heard Saint telling everyone to board the balloon.

"Bertie," Hessy said.

Everything he had tried had failed.

"Bertie!"

Made things worse, even.

"Bertie, we have to go."

Bertie didn't know what he had expected. What, say a few rousing words and stampede onward with some ridiculous plan, and everything was supposed to magically work out?

Hessy touched his shoulder and whispered, "Bertie."

He had put people in danger. Bartholomew. The pastor. Agatha. Percival. Saint, Hessy—

Princess Piranha growled and struggled to her feet. Vulture tried to hoist himself up and fell, then tried again. Captain Viper nipped at Termite's behind.

"Bertie, now!"

Termite stood over Bertie, opened her mouth in a growl. Bertie grimaced under her hot breath. She dripped froth— red, blue, orange, pink—on Bertie's clothes and the ground he kneeled on.

It was his nightmare, all over again.

Termite lunged forward, snapping her teeth. Hessy pushed Bertie out of the way. He came to his senses and screamed, "Run!"

"What do you think I've been trying to get you to do?" Hessy said, gasping for breath.

They scrambled to the office building. The uneven rhythm of stumbling hooves followed close behind. As Bertie turned to slam the door, he saw how the unicorns, too weak to walk on their hooves, were dragging themselves on their knees, falling, foaming, getting back up again. They were coming right for them.

Bertie and Hessy hit the floor, their backs against the cool metal of the door.

"Saint! Saint!" he screamed into his walkie-talkie.

"Bertie, we are in the air now, safe. What happened? Are you and Hessy okay?"

Bertie peeked over the window sill. The unicorns were ramming into the bars on the windows, spattering the glass with rainbow froth and blood.

"Uh, not exactly."

"I will be back for you," Saint said. "Don't—"

Another explosive head butt cut Saint off.

"Those poor things," Hessy said. "They've got to be in pain."

"Yeah." Bertie slid to the floor and put his head in his hands. He had to do something, but what?

Bertie and Hessy jumped at the sound of breaking wood and got out of the way just in time for one of the unicorns to smash his hoof through the wall.

"The glass isn't breaking. It must be bullet proof," Hessy said.

Then the glass shattered.

"I take that back," Hessy said.

Bertie pushed himself up. There was no point just sitting there. He grabbed Dr. Om's desk. Hessy saw what he was doing and grabbed the other side. They put it up against the hole in the wall. Bertie could feel the heat radiating from the unicorns, even from inside.

What was wrong with them? How did this happen?

Another unicorn hoof came through the wall. Bertie and Hessy looked around the room. The only other big piece of furniture was a bookcase.

"Hessy, let's head upstairs. We'll pull that bookcase in front of the stairwell. If they break in, it may stop them long enough so we can—"

"So we can what?" Hessy screamed. "Climb to the roof? Jump? Take flight?"

"Yeah, all good plans."

"Saint!" Bertie said into his walkie-talkie. "Any update on the rescue?"

"I am already on it, Bertie," Saint said. "But we got a problem."

"Oh, another one? Great! Consistency is a good thing." Bertie tucked the walkie-talkie between his cheek and shoulder and helped Hessy manhandle the bookcase towards the stairs.

Saint's voice came through static. "I tried to get the helicopter. It would be much faster. But it would appear Lester stole it."

"How do you know?"

"I saw him take it."

"Great! Just great. And the balloon?"

"About that."

"Oh, Saint, whatever you do, please tell me there's more bad news!" Bertie signaled to Hessy to start climbing. The sound of a hoof breaking through the wall echoed through the office.

"Your friend, Dr. Om, got a hold of a tranq gun," Saint said.

"And?" Bertie said.

"And he burst the balloon."

"That's super news," Bertie said. "Give us a moment to barricade ourselves in. Don't go anywhere."

Bertie and Hessy tugged the bookcase over the entrance to the stairwell and ran up the stairs.

"Saint?" Bertie said.

"Yes, I am fixing the balloon."

"I figured."

"It will take a while for the patch to dry."

"Thanks, Saint."

Hessy, her eyes huge, looked out the window at the unicorns.

"There is some good news in all of this," Saint said.

"What is it? 'Cause I could really use some good news."

"Our evil Carlotian smuggler will be really mad at Dr. Om for damaging his balloon. And do you know what happens when evil Carlotian smugglers get mad?"

"They eliminate problems just in the nick of late?"

"Yes, way too in the nick of late," Saint said. "But better late than never."

Bertie jumped as a crack thundered through the downstairs.

"Thanks, Saint," Bertie said. "Over and out."

Hessy started rummaging through drawers. Bertie followed suit.

"What are we looking for?" Bertie said.

"Tranq guns. Not that they'd work. Or anything that could help, really." She fumbled through a drawer full of files and slammed it shut. Bertie yanked open another drawer full of office supplies. Hessy opened a closet stocked full of colorful balloons and other party stuff. They were marked "Opening Day!!!"

"Nothing," she said. She sank to the floor. Bertie kept looking, but didn't see anything of use either.

Eventually, he slumped down next to Hessy. From downstairs, he heard a unicorn slam against metal. If the bars gave way . . .

He looked over at Hessy, who was sitting with her head propped up on her hands. "You know . . ." he said.

"Hmmm?" Hessy's dazed eyes were fixed on the door opposite.

Bertie looked towards the door too. He didn't say anything right away. Downstairs, a metal bar fell to the floor with a clang. Any minute now . . .

"I didn't stay for your mother."

Another metallic clang made Hessy jump. She looked at Bertie.

"I know," she said.

One last clang and the breach was complete. The thump, thump, thump of unicorn hooves drummed against the floor downstairs.

"Okay, just saying." Bertie said.

Bertie stood up, grabbed hold of a chair, and stood ready at the door.

Like a chair was going to do any good.

A ruckus of hoof steps followed. The floor slats shook beneath Bertie's feet. Any minute now, and the unicorns would take to the stairs.

Hessy, chair in hand, stood next to him.

They were goners.

He held his breath. It was weird. Bertie felt calm, like, really calm. All these weeks of worry, and the anxiety all came to a screeching halt, right when he and Hessy were about to be the world's first unicorn fatalities.

Maybe because, for the first time in a long time, Bertie didn't have to worry about making a choice. The maze stretched out before him. Left, right, forward, backwards. It didn't matter.

It was official. He was unicorn food.

He wished he could go back to the old days.

The bookshelf slammed into the floor below. Bertie breathed out. Seconds later, the unicorns stormed the stairs.

But then . . .

Bertie tilted his head to listen.

The noise, it was different, quieter. It was like . . . ? Bertie looked at Hessy, whose forehead was wrinkled in confusion. The noise was kind of like a flock of really big birds were caught in a hurricane and had taken refuge in the office below, only to find that the hurricane had tagged along with them.

Bertie took a step towards the door.

And suddenly, all went quiet.

Bertie and Hessy didn't move.

Had the unicorns left?

Or died? Sadness squeezed Bertie's chest tight. Yeah, it was more likely they had died. The mutation, whatever it was, had overtaxed their systems and—

Bertie pushed the thought away. He inched towards the window and looked outside. There were no unicorns.

"I don't see any unicorns," he said.

"Maybe they collapsed again," Hessy said.

"Stay here."

Bertie tiptoed to the door with Hessy right behind.

"Or, you know, come," he said.

They tiptoed down the stairs, careful to not make a noise. Halfway down, wooden slats from the bookcase littered the floor.

"I still don't see any unicorns," he said.

"Shhhh," Hessy said.

But still no unicorns.

They got to the bottom of the stairs. Bertie stuck his head out. Nothing.

They inched toward the front door and peeked.

Zip.

They stepped outside.

"Where'd they go?" Hessy said.

"They're gone."

"I see that."

Part of Bertie felt relieved. But the other part screamed, "You think they were bad before, you loser? What are they going to be like now that you can't even see them?"

Bertie closed his eyes and lifted his head in frustration. "Now what?'

Then he opened his eyes.

And he couldn't believe it.

"Uh, Hessy . . . Hessy."

Flying above the park were a bunch of—

"I'm going to go look for them out back," she whispered.

What do you call flying unicorns anyway?

"Don't bother." he said, pointing. "Look up,"

She did.

And she didn't say anything.

"Uh, Hessy?" Bertie said. "What do you call flying unicorns?"

"Flying unicorns don't exist."

"Right . . . Well, then this all makes sense then."

He pulled his walkie-talkie from his shirt pocket. "Saint, change of plans."

"Good change or bad change?" Saint said.

"Take a wild guess. You have to alert everyone—everyone—to stay indoors." Bertie dodged pink unicorn saliva that fell from the sky. "Those rabid unicorns?"

"Yes?" Saint said.

"They're flying rabid unicorns now."

"Eh, eh, I agree. That is bad."

Red and green saliva dropped on Bertie's shirt. It stung. Now what? This was definitely not part of his vet school curriculum.

"What are we doing to do?" Hessy said.

Bertie racked his brain. If Dr. Om were here, he'd order

a bunch of guards to shoot down the unicorns. No doubt, he'd consider the problem solved.

Lots of people would probably consider the problem solved.

Bertie shook his head.

One thing he knew for sure, he couldn't wait around for someone to make that kind of decision. He needed to get ahead of the game, even if it was deadly, to save the unicorns.

An idea, a memory, floated to the forefront of his mind.

It made absolutely zero sense. None whatsoever.

Which made it potentially the perfect plan after all.

He turned to Hessy. "Reality, meet zombie fantasy land. Zombie fantasy land, meet reality. Looks like we're heading back to the lab."

Because when reality turns into zombie fantasy land, you reconsider the impossible options.

CHAPTER 36

BERTIE AND HESSY were in the lab, staring at Berta, now completely uncovered on the table. Hessy's idea of dosing the unicorns with Berta was crazy, but desperate times call for chucking your veterinary school education out the window and following the script of every bad sci-fi show ever made.

Because who needs real science, you know?

Bertie had tried to get Hessy to leave. He didn't think she'd like to see the gutting, but she had wanted to stay, of course.

One by one, Bertie took out all Berta's organs and stuck them in the blender that Hessy had brought from the kitchens. He blenderized Berta's organs in batches. Her liver. Her heart. The gastrointestinal tract he had written so much about in that dumb book that got him into this mess. He tried to recover as many fluids from her body as he could.

"What about the brain?" Hessy said. She was pale.

Bertie sighed. "Okay, might as well. But really, Hessy. You're not staying for that."

She glared at him.

"Or you are. What was I thinking?"

Bertie put his hand on Berta's head. "Sorry, girl. I really hate doing this to you."

They didn't say anything for a moment. It all was coming to this.

"Are you ready?" Bertie said.

"No," Hessy said.

"Me neither." Bertie took his knife and cut as cleanly as he could. He knew it wasn't logical, but he figured she deserved some respect.

She was going to be dinner, after all. Cannibal Charms: the funnest new cereal on the market.

Shut up, thought Bertie. That's just gross.

Before taking the electric saw to the skull, he examined the horn. "I think I'll add the horn."

"Do you think it will be of any use?" Hessy said.

"No idea."

"It couldn't hurt."

"That it could not," Bertie said. He cut off the horn from the head, sliced it into smaller pieces, and put all but one in the blender.

Thank the good Lord that Dr. Om splashed out on Vitamixers.

He gave the remaining piece to Hessy, who took it without asking questions.

She was sentimental that way.

"And now for the brain," Bertie said. He carved it from the skull and added it to the blender.

St. Quiche, meet your newest Sloopie flavor, Bertie thought as he turned the blender on. He didn't say it out loud, though. It would upset Hessy.

He may never be able to drink a Sloopie again. Not without thinking of poor Berta.

They mixed all the batches together, adding ground meat to the mix, and carefully poured it in containers. They spent a moment standing over Berta before covering her up again and putting her in the freezer.

There would be time for a proper good-bye later.

They stepped outside, lugging the containers on the cart. Bertie turned to Hessy. "That was officially the worst memorial service ever."

"I hope you don't do weddings and Bar Mitzvahs," Hessy said.

Bertie looked surprised. Hessy said, "If you don't laugh, you'll cry."

"Gotcha."

They looked up to look for the unicorns. They couldn't see any.

"Great! The baby-poos are officially released on the population," Bertie said.

"So it's a good day, then."

Bertie grabbed his walkie-talkie. "Saint? Hessy had an idea. We just need to get airborne to deliver it."

"Hessy, my girl! Good to hear," Saint hollered. Screams of horror from the Quichan population escaped from the static. "People are upset down here."

"Right, can't blame them," Bertie said. "Why aren't they inside?"

"They all putting photos on Facebook," Saint said.

Bertie rubbed his tired eyes. "Of course they are. Is the balloon repaired?"

Another scream erupted from the walkie-talkie before Saint could answer. "It will have to do."

"That's what I love to hear before entrusting my very life to a flying machine," Bertie said. "Head over as fast as you can. Hessy and I will find a way to deliver the . . . treatment."

"Be there directly," Saint said.

If this didn't work—But no, Bertie would have loads of time for pessimism when he was dead.

A final scream pierced Bertie's ear just before the walkie-talkie went silent.

Bertie and Hessy jogged back to the office to acquire what every task force facing a flying-rabid-zombie-unicorn-or-whatever-the-heck-these-creatures-were attack.

Party supplies.

"Apparently,' Hessy said. "Artie's grand opening included animal balloons and balloon guns. There was a closet full of the stuff."

"I see where you're going with this. We'll mollify them with balloon self-portraits."

"Right, flattery into submission is the heart of my plan."

"See?" Hessy said once they were in the office upstairs. She filled a balloon with water. "We'll pretend for now that the water is . . . the stuff. And then we aim for their mouths."

"There's nothing that can go wrong with this plan," Bertie said.

She put the water-filled balloon in the toy gun and shot Bertie's head. "Sorry, the balance on this toy gun is different from the tranq gun. I've got to learn to readjust my aim."

Bertie wiped water from his eyes. "This is looking really hopeful. Well, let's do this thing."

Saint's voice came through the walkie-talkie. "I am almost there. Meet me at the south exit."

Bertie and Hessy grabbed all the stuff and headed out as fast as they could. A unicorn flew crookedly and slowly overhead, growling and dripping foam.

"We're on our way," Bertie said.

The balloon had a rocky landing, and out came Saint.

Followed by the pastor, Percival. Agatha, and Bartholomew.

"Wait?" Bertie said. "What are you all doing here? You're supposed to be holed up at home avoiding enraged flying . . . whatevers."

Agatha stomped up to Bertie and poked him in the chest. Bertie was getting tired of that. "You listen, young man. You reach St. Quiche only a few weeks ago, and you bossing everyone around. Stay holed up in our homes? I don't think so."

Percival bobbed his head in agreement while the pastor leaned in to Bertie and tapped his nose. "Remember the slipper."

Bartholomew nodded.

Saint laughed and started loading the toy guns in the car. "They will take Lady Mathilda and shoot from below. Bartholomew will run reconnaissance, and we got people throughout the island who will be calling in with unicorn sightings. I will go with you in the balloon for the air assault. Will we use tranquilizers?"

"No, and before we can do anything," Bertie said, pointing to a pile of colorful party balloons, "we have balloons to fill."

CHAPTER 37

BERTIE AND HESSY tied the last party balloons while Saint carted them to the air balloon and Lady Mathilda. So far, the sightings were concentrated over Rumstad, thanks to an open-market butchers' festival.

"Let me tell you, those butchers weren't happy about the unicorns eating their wares," Saint said.

They'd have to hurry to restrain the unicorns before they scattered.

"The wind is blowing to the south," Saint said. "We will attach the balloon to Lady Mathilda since we will be going North. She will pull the balloon along after her."

"Right," Bertie said. "Sounds like a plan."

They tied Lady Mathilda to the balloon and Saint, Hessy, and Bertie climbed into the basket.

"Listen up, everyone!" Bertie said. The pastor, Percival, Agatha, and Bartholomew looked up. "We don't actually know whether this will work. But here goes. Aim for their mouths. With any luck, they're going to want to eat this sludge. If that's the case, it will make our lives a lot easier. You in the car, concentrate on the unicorns who are on the ground or close to it. Saint, Hessy, and I will focus on those in the air. And Bartholomew?"

"Yes, Dr. Bertie?"

"Whatever you do, don't engage. If you see a unicorn, let us know and run the heck out of there."

Bartholomew held his hands up in triumph. "Yes, Dr. Bertie! You know me! I'm a professional!"

Bertie rubbed his head. "Okay, not a good sign." He raised his voice. "Let's do this."

Lady Mathilda coughed into action and descended the path from the park to Rumstad. Saint slowly raised the balloon as Lady Mathilda pulled onto the road into town. Below, the cobblestones and smashed, evacuated kiosks were splattered with rainbow unicorn drool.

As they reached the edge of town, Hessy pointed and said, "There's Princess Piranha."

"Gila Monster Man is close by," Bertie said.

Princess Piranha and Gila Monster Man, both airborne, were heading right at them, growling, frothing at the mouth, and flapping their wings frantically. If this didn't work, there would be a very tough landing in just a few seconds.

Bertie looked at Hessy. "Are you ready?"

She nodded. "Ready! Aim! Fire!"

Hessy shot her water balloon gun at Princess Piranha, but it missed her. Bertie took a turn. His pink balloon curved through the air. Princess Piranha suddenly charged at it, apparently drawn by the smell, and swallowed it whole. Gila Monster Man came in closer, nipping at Princess Piranha. Hessy took another shot, and Gila Monster Man gulped the green party balloon.

"It's working? Bertie said. "Is it working?"

Hessy looked over and smiled. "Maybe!"

A scream from below made Bertie, Hessy, and Saint

look down. Vulture was kicking the wooden railings on the veranda of a yellow house. A lady screamed, backing up through her front door.

The pastor stuck his head out of the back of the car and aimed. "Don't get worked up, Charlotte. We are here!" He shot Vulture, but hit him in the flank instead.

Vulture turned in anger and charged Lady Mathilda. Percival stuck his head out of the car, and he shot Vulture right in the mouth.

It worked. Vulture ate up the Berta sludge. He sniffed his flank, where the pastor had hit, and licked himself clean.

Bertie felt a wet, slimy nudge at his elbow and a breeze at his back. He turned around.

Princess Piranha and Gila Monster Man were rooting around in the basket containing the Berta balloons. Although they looked as deranged as ever, they snuffled contentedly.

"Uh, Hessy," Bertie said.

"They're following us?" she said.

Bertie looked up. Vulture had joined. He was sniffing around the basket, presumably for more sludge.

"Okay, interesting development," Bertie said. He searched for unicorns. A scream told him more were nearby.

"Great job staying indoors, people," Bertie yelled. "You're making this job so much easier!"

Captain Viper (or was it Barracuda?) turned a corner and flew up the narrow street. His dirtied wings got caught in the electrical lines. Bertie took aim, but his shot went wide. Hessy shot next, but the balloon grazed his tail. "I can't get in close enough," she said.

"Just keep shooting and hope he smells it," Bertie said. "Ready, aim, fire!"

Another round of party guns went off, and the balloons exploded on the unicorn's side. He howled in rage. Trying to make a quick turn, he got tangled in the electrical lines and crash-landed on a fruit cart.

Bertie aimed for his mouth, open mid-howl. "Got him!"

By now, Saint had managed to get Black Mamba, who joined the others in poking around the basket's Bertie sludge supply.

"Eh, they are blocking us," Saint said. "How can I maneuver the balloon with these unicorns flying around?"

"I know. I can't frikking aim with all of them shoving their faces in here," Bertie said. "Shoo, shoo!" He tossed a bunch of balloons on the sidewalk, hoping to attract the unicorns' attention elsewhere. A store owner poked his head out the door to see where the slop was coming from and took a balloon right in the head.

"Sorry!" Bertie screamed. But he didn't have to worry about a scolding. The man ducked back in his shop and slammed the door as the unicorns congregated in front to nosh on the sludge.

With a clearer, unicorn-free view, Bertie was able to see below, where Agatha leaned out the window and took some shots. He couldn't tell whether she hit anything, but he heard her yell, "Sorry, Mr. Vanderpeel. That will come out with Clorox. Why aren't you inside?" As Lady Mathilda lurched away, she screamed louder. "See you in church on Sunday."

As the balloon inched forward, Jaws came into view. He was licking his lips as an elderly gentleman, covered in pink sludge, cowered behind a bicycle.

"We've got seven of them," Bertie said. "Any word from Bartholomew?"

"No, I will call him," Saint said.

Saint raised the flame so they could get a better view and dialed Bartholomew. "Bartholomew, what are you seeing?"

"I shot three!" he said. He was out of breath. "They are following me now! I am heading towards you."

Bertie grabbed the phone. "Bartholomew, I told you, no engaging!"

"I didn't ask them to marry me! I just shot them," he said.

"You know what I mean! How'd you get the water gun anyway?"

"Like you said," Hessy screamed above the din. "He's not just a kid. He's a juvenile delinquent."

Bertie huffed, but before he could say anything else, Bartholomew threw himself out of a side street and dove underneath a chummy cart. Close behind, Tasmanian Devil, Hornet, and Dragon Breath flew between the narrow buildings. They were licking their lips and sniffing around, looking for more sludge.

From behind, a yelp drew Bertie's attention. Another unicorn was flying in low through the street, heading towards Lady Mathilda.

"Agatha," Saint screamed, pointing at Barracuda (or was it Captain Viper?). "Left of the signpost, behind you! Take aim."

Agatha stuck her head out as the unicorns growled. "I would prefer Area 51 aliens," she screamed, but she got her shot in. The unicorn chewed on the balloon, forgot to flap his wings, and crashed into a wooden kiosk.

The pastor lifted himself out of the window and looked at Bertie, Hessy, and Saint. "Margaret won't be happy about that kiosk. I am counting ten unicorns! Which one is left?"

Bertie scanned the scene and said, "We're missing Termite. Where is she?"

Hessy craned her neck. "I don't see her anywhere. With any luck, she's chewed through half the wooden structures on St. Quiche by now."

Bartholomew dragged himself out from under the cart and pointed up the street. "I see her!"

Everyone looked where Bartholomew had pointed and raised their balloon guns. Sure enough, there was Termite. She was half walking, half flying through the narrow street. Her wings knocked down carts and got tangled in hanging laundry. Foam—yellow, red, orange, pink—dripped from her mouth, her eyes were bugged out of her sockets, and she was howling in what looked like fear.

She looked completely deranged.

And soon everyone could see why.

Dr. Om, his jacket askew, his head covered in colorful foam, was chasing after her and screaming, "I'm going to get you!!!"

He was shooting a gun wildly.

"Noooooo!" screamed Bertie. "Those in the car, aim for Termite! In the balloon, aim for Dr. Om."

"What good will that do?" Hessy said. Her eyes were huge.

"Blind him!" Bertie said, shooting a balloon at Dr. Om, who was gasping for breath but still running. It missed. "His aim is bad enough when he can see. Blind, he won't be worth anything."

Bertie loaded another balloon while Hessy and Saint aimed at Dr. Om. A balloon grazed his head. Another grazed his side.

The third hit him right in the chest.

"Darn," Bertie said.

He reloaded again and aimed.

But he didn't shoot.

He didn't need to.

Because Dr. Om had stopped running. Slowly, he looked down at the pink covering his chest. His eyes widened. The gun clattered to the cobbled street. He gazed at the air balloon in disbelief.

"You . . . you . . ." Dr. Om he staggered on the slimy cobblestones. "You . . . killed me."

He collapsed on his knees and fell forward, leaving himself, apparently, for dead.

Saint shook his head. "That man is an imbecile."

Termite finished her serving of the Berta Sloopie and sniffed around for more. She spotted Dr. Om and stumbled towards him. She nudged him onto his back and chewed on his stained shirt.

"Aaaaaah!" Dr. Om screamed. "This brute is eating me aliiiiiiiive!"

But before anyone could intervene, Black Mamba, Barracuda, Jaws, Princess Piranha, Dragon Breath, Captain Viper, Gila Monster Man, Vulture, Hornet, and Tasmanian Devil, attracted by the smell or the cries of agony or both, limped over to Dr. Om and licked him from head to foot and back. They whinnied in contentment.

Saint lowered the balloon and landed by Lady Mathilda. Bertie, Hessy, and Saint climbed out and stared at the unicorns. The pastor, Percival, and Agatha joined them.

Bertie grabbed more balloons and crept towards the herd. Hessy followed suit. As tempted as Bertie was to dump the sludge all over Dr. Om, he deposited it in a circle around the unicorns instead. One by one, they left Dr. Om behind and ate through the new sludge. They appeared calm.

Cautiously, Bertie put his hand on Termite. She no longer radiated heat. He checked her eyes. They weren't normal yet—whatever normal was for a flying unicorn—but they were no longer deranged. She was frothing less at the mouth. Which was good, thought Bertie, because all that saliva?

It was disgusting.

Termite whinnied happily, nudged his elbow, and then went back to eating.

"Hessy," Bertie said.

"Yes?"

"Science be darned. You're a genius."

"Who'd have thunk?" she said, looking just as stunned. "Although, technically, we don't know whether this will hold."

"Party pooper," Bertie said. "But we'll keep our fingers crossed."

Somehow, in all this crazy, Bertie had a feeling this solution would work. After all, when dealing with mythical creatures come to life in a madman's lab, you don't use real science. You fall back on fantasy.

He laughed. He knew it would be wrong, but he couldn't help himself. He lifted his last balloon and threw it right at Dr. Om. The unicorns whinnied happily and went back to licking him.

"Nooooo!" Dr. Om cried as he struggled to his knees only to be knocked down by Dragon Breath's slimy, foamy, multi-colored tongue.

"We'll have to cancel on the first guests and eliminate these . . . beasts," Dr. Om said. "All those years of work. All those sacrifices. My reputation. We'll have to eliminate them."

Hessy stepped between the unicorns and grabbed his arm. "You will do no such thing, Artie."

He cackled. "There's nothing you can do. Nothing. I own this island. I own it. All of it."

"Not so fast." A new voice rose behind them.

They all turned. It was from one of St. Quiche's finest, Police Officer Gerland.

"Gerland, so nice of you to make it," Saint said. "How is the wife doing?"

"She is as always," Gerland, said. "Gives me lots of good incentives to work overtime. And how is Lady Mathilda?"

Saint gazed at Lady Mathilda. Riddled with bullets from Dr. Om's gun, she had hoof-shaped dents on her hood and was covered in saliva. "I am afraid she is not at her best today."

"She will perk up," Gerland said. "She always does."

Dr. Om looked up at the police officer with big eyes. "Is now . . ." He gasped for breath. "Is now really the time for pleasantries?"

"Excuse me, Dr. Om," Gerland said. "You own the park up on the mountain?"

"Yes, I own the park. I own the park, and the mountain, and this entire island, in fact. All of it."

"I had some complaints from neighbors about disturbance of the peace here," Gerland said.

"Yes, yes, officer," Dr. Om said. He pushed the unicorns away and limped over to the policeman. The unicorns trotted after him. "Yes, these creatures—these creatures you see right here—they're dangerous. They need to be put down." Barracuda walked up to Dr. Om and licked his hair.

The police officer cocked his head and lifted Barracuda's filthy wing. "They don't look dangerous to me."

"No, no, you don't understand—"

"Let's see here." Gerland pulled out a little notebook. "I have a complaint from Charlotte. She is very upset about her broken railings on her home. I also have a complaint from Anita. Her fruit cart was destroyed. And Frank is vexed about the state of his chummy kiosk."

"Let me explain," Dr. Om said.

Gerland turned to Lady Mathilda. "And Saint, who did this to Lady Mathilda?"

"Dr. Om's weapon," Saint said, looking sad.

"Also," Gerland said. "This black air balloon, it looks familiar."

"Balloon? Balloon?" Dr. Om said. "Who cares about the air balloon? We have here a flock of deranged—"

"Oh, yes!" Gerland said with a smile. "I remember now. This black balloon belongs to the evil Carlotian smuggler, Luke Rative." His smile disappeared and he looked sternly at Dr. Om.

Saint looked at the balloon. "I think he's right."

"Dr. Om, are you an associate of Luke Rative?" Gerland, said.

Dr. Om put his hands on his head. "Wh-what? I don't—"

"I found it in a shed at the Dr. Crazy Man Park," Saint said.

"Dr. Om, I now arrest you for collaboration with Luke Rative." Gerland placed cuffs on Dr. Om's wrists.

"Hey, Dr. Om!" Bertie said. "You said you were big on collaboration!"

"And also, public disturbance, reckless use of a firearm, ownership of unlicensed exotic . . . pets." Gerland clicked his tongue at Barracuda. "You should bathe them more often. Oh, and, you have the right to say as much as you like. It will make the Crown prosecutor's job much easier, as he leaves for vacation next month."

"What? How can . . . ?" Dr. Om said. "Dr. Vole! Say something!"

A light rain started to fall. "Dr. Om," Gerland said. "I am afraid we will have to walk. My wife borrowed the patrol car for her kalooki game."

It was then that Bertie remembered. He grabbed the papers he had in his back pocket and leafed through till he found what he wanted.

"Officer Gerland!" he screamed. "Wait up! I've got something else for you. Take a look."

Gerland read the pages quickly and looked at Dr. Om.

"Oh ho ho, very interesting," he said. "Hacking. Skimming from bank accounts. St. Quiche's justice system will have a party with you."

"I own this island," Dr. Om said. "I own it! All of it. I own you and you and you and you. All of you!"

But the effect of Dr. Om's tirade was dulled by the fact that he was in handcuffs, covered in pastel-colored foam, and slipping on the cobbled street while unicorns licked his face as he passed.

Officer Gerland looked at Saint. "You, leave the air balloon here. I will be round to pick it up. And no borrowing. I know you!"

Saint laughed.

"Bye, Dr. Om!" Bertie said as he waved.

Officer Gerland and Dr. Om's voices got farther and farther away. "You had your fun, Dr. Crazy Man," Officer Gerland said. "What sweet in the goat mouth does sour in the bam bam, eh?"

"What does that even mean?" Dr. Om wailed, but his voice was finally taken away by the wind for good.

Bertie, Hessy, Saint, and the rest took stock of the mess around them.

Bertie turned to the group.

"Now what?" Saint said.

Now what? That was a great question. "It's time to get the unicorns home," Bertie said. "How are we going to manage that?" He looked at Hessy, Saint, all the people who had helped him today, and finally at the flying unicorns. Everyone was tired and sticky with rabid unicorn goo. The thought of walking up the mountain with a bunch of flying unicorns in tow didn't sound too appealing.

Bartholomew rolled his eyes. "You blind?"

"Bartholomew, your mouth," Agatha said.

"Look," Bartholomew said. He flapped a unicorn wing and pointed.

"Um . . ." Bertie said.

"What are you suggesting, young man?" Agatha said. Bertie took cover behind Hessy in case she planned to come for him next.

"Saint," Bertie said. "Do you think Lady Mathilda could handle driving us back?" Maybe the unicorns could form a caravan behind her.

Saint shook his head sadly as he looked at Lady's Mathilda's injuries. "She needs a rest."

"Okay, flying unicorns it is," Bertie said. Great. Another opportunity to fall to his death.

He wasn't the only one who wasn't enthused by the idea.

"I am not riding that thing," Agatha said. She grabbed the pastor's arm.

"Pastor, back me up on this one," Bertie said. But Percival stepped in before the pastor had a chance.

"Don't want to come back with us to the park? That's more rum for the rest of us."

Agatha let go of the pastor.

"Did you say rum?" Agatha said.

Agatha planted herself next to Viper. "You going to help me get on this thing or what?"

With rum sending out its siren call, they gathered the rest of the Berta-filled balloons. They would need them to entice the four unicorns who wouldn't have riders. Then the seven of them climbed on Captain Viper, Barracuda, Black Mamba, Gila Monster Man, Tasmanian Devil, Hornet, and Jaws. No one wanted to ride Termite because she chewed on too many things. Princess Piranha wouldn't obey to save anyone's life. And Dragon Breath, well, he smelled really bad.

Even worse than the others, that is.

As Bertie kicked off on Black Mamba, his stomach bottomed out, just like in that helicopter ride that brought him to this insane job. He clamped his eyes shut.

"For the love of all things holy," Hessy screamed from Tasmanian Devil. "Open your eyes, Bertie. It's not every day you get to fly a unicorn."

Hessy was right. Bertie opened one eye. The red, blue, yellow, and orange buildings blurred beneath them. He opened his other eye. The buildings were left behind, and the kiosk-lined road out of Rumstad pointed them back towards home. Black Mamba and the rest flew higher, and Bertie caught sight of the wooden houses dotting the hills. Bartholomew whooped from behind, and Agatha shrieked, "Pastor, if I fall, you will catch me?"

"Remember the rum, Agatha," he hollered. "It will give you strength."

From below, neighbors waved and pointed. It seemed like months had passed since the day he had walked down the mountain in the rain, feeling stuck.

And now, here he was, holding the reins of a flying unicorn.

Well, metaphorically, anyway, 'cause technically he was clutching onto Black Mamba's neck for dear life.

When they landed at the park, Bertie watched as the others dismounted from their unicorns. How was he going to put this on his résumé without being carted off to the crazy bin? He sort of knew what Artie felt like now. He almost felt bad for him. Bertie was the last to climb down.

Dr. Om hadn't even had a chance to fly one of his own creations.

Using Berta sludge, they enticed the unicorns back to their pen, which the team had pegged back together as best they could. With a smile, Bertie noticed an awful lot of duct tape involved.

"What was in the papers you gave to the policeman?" Hessy asked.

Bertie came out of his reverie. "Just the reason why Dr. Om was willing to kill the unicorns. You know how he had someone skim money from people's bank accounts?"

"Yes," Hessy said.

"Well, he found a hacker who was willing to do it again, to fund another round of unicorn creation."

Hessy turned to Saint. "How did your hacker friend find out?"

Saint smiled. "He was the hacker who agreed to do it."

Hessy nodded. "How did the unicorns sprout wings?"

Bertie pulled the DNA documents from his back pockets. He hadn't had a chance to read through the whole ingredient list yet.

There, at the bottom, he saw it.

"Caterpillars?" Bertie shrugged, too tired to question how any of it made sense. "He included caterpillar DNA."

"What?" Hessy said.

"Dr. Om included caterpillar DNA in the mix."

"Crazy, crazy man," Saint said.

"But the unicorns didn't make cocoons," Hessy said.

Bertie raised his hands. "No clue."

"Maybe he included microwave DNA," Saint said. "You push a button and poof!"

As far as Bertie was concerned, that was as good an explanation as any.

CHAPTER 38

THE DAY WAS FAR from over. Apart from having to monitor a bunch of flying unicorns and give them baths, there was lots of work to do on the pen. They put a huge net over the opening to prevent the unicorns from flying off and terrorizing the population. A more permanent solution would have to come later, though.

They stored the remaining Berta Sloopie in a fridge. Just in case the unicorns escaped and had to be lured back.

As Bertie, Hessy, Saint, and the rest worked into the night, Percival circled with glasses of rum.

Finally, the work was done. There was just one thing left to do.

Because they had never given a proper funeral to Berta.

You know, at least one where she wasn't gutted and blenderized.

Bertie wasn't too keen on burying Berta yet. She was the only specimen he had on hand to examine from the inside out, and the good Lord knows he needed all the help he could get to learn about these animals.

So instead, Hessy retrieved the remaining piece of horn from her room.

"Berta never did get to fly," Hessy said. She looked pleadingly at Saint.

He narrowed his eyes, then laughed. "Oh, no, no, no. Let me guess. You want me to go to our good friend Gerland and get him to release a smuggler's air balloon from custody so that you can give Berta a final send-off."

"This is correct," Bertie said. "Or we could just steal it. Whatever you think will work better."

"Bartholomew has been a bad influence on you," Saint said. "We will need to talk."

In the end, they didn't do either. While Bertie and Hessy took one last ride in the air balloon, Saint held the tether in the police station yard. After all, as Saint explained it, the balloon isn't stolen if it never loses contact with the ground.

For a moment, Bertie imagined his old half-basement with the tiny half-window. Now, here he was, floating in an air balloon owned by—according to Quichans—the Caribbean's most evil and dangerous criminal. Because Berta deserved the very best.

They floated over Rumstad where, just today, rabid unicorns had painted the town red, pink, blue, purple, orange, every color of the rainbow. The balloon carried them towards the East and hovered off shore. They had The Last Resort to their backs. The sun dipped, streaking the horizon with an orange band of light. Hessy fished the piece of Berta's horn from her pants pocket, took one last look at it, and threw it overboard. It fell with a plop in the ocean.

"To the unicorn who ate my pants, we will miss you," Bertie said.

"Ate my pants? Is that the best you can do?"

"Okay, Take two. To the unicorn who left a mark, we will miss you."

"To Berta."

"To Berta."

CHAPTER 39

SO, what do you say at a press conference, thought Bertie as he climbed up the steps to the podium, when you have just a bunch of unanswered questions?

Bertie didn't really want to be here, mostly because he and Hessy still had a whole herd (or was it flock?) of flying unicorns that could still very well be unpredictable. He wanted to keep his eye on them, make sure they were all right.

Granted, they seemed fine. Aside from some pink, blue, yellow, red, purple and orange stains from their full-on postal stage, they were calm. Hessy and Bertie kept plying them with extra portions of meat to keep them not insane.

But then, this morning as he and Hessy were feeding the unicorns, his phone had rung. It was the governor, and he was none too happy.

"What is this I hear about the opening of a unicorn park?" he said.

"Um, well, I, uh . . ." Bertie didn't even know who the governor was. He really needed to get out more.

"Why didn't I receive an invite to the grand opening?"

"I wasn't in charge of invites, sir," Bertie said. At least he knew the answer to that question. "I certainly would have invited you, but I'm just the vet."

The governor seemed mollified. "There will be a press conference in half an hour," he said. "Come by Government House. As the premier expert on flying unicorns, you must be there."

"I don't actually know . . .uh, sure," Bertie said.

He turned to Hessy. "We have a press conference to go to. Darn."

"I'll call Saint," she said.

"Right, so where's Government House anyway?"

So now Bertie, flanked by Hessy and Saint, was on stage, waiting to answer questions he didn't know the answers to.

"Dr. Vole, Bastian Best from the *St. Quiche Ledger*. Are these flying creatures safe?"

"Well, as far as we can tell, as long as we give them an adequate diet, they are," Bertie said. He looked at Hessy for support, who took to the microphone.

"They respond to our calls and seem content to stay in their pen," she said.

"Yeah," Bertie said. "We'll, you know, build something more permanent to keep them from flying around uncontrolled."

"Bastian Best from *Agence Sainte Quiche Presse*," Bastian said. "Dr. Vole, as the uncontested expert on these creatures, what is your next step?"

Bertie hadn't had much time to think long-term, but somehow, he knew the answer. "My next step is to stay and take care of them. I think we need to respect the fact that no one here or anywhere is any kind of expert on unicorns, or pegasi, or unipegs or whatever they are. We still have lots to learn." He looked at Hessy out of the corner of his eye. "But I've decided to stay and figure stuff out."

"Bastian Best from *El Semanal de Santa Quiche*. Are you in charge of the park?"

"No, I'm the vet. Miss Hessy Beauregard has been manager, but she'd have to say what her plans are."

A blond reporter grabbed the microphone from Bastian, who was about to ask another question. "Cynthia Priss from *The Economist*. Miss Beauregard, what are your plans?"

"I will stay on as interim manager for the next couple of months," Hessy said, "and then was going to offer the job to John 'Saint' Castle, if he wants to accept."

Saint smiled, of course, because that's what he always did, but Bertie wondered what was up with Hessy. Was she really going to leave St. Quiche?

Bastian wrested the mic from Cynthia Priss. "Bastian Best from the *St. Quiche Gossip Rag*. Miss Beauregard, why are you leaving St. Quiche? Has the pressure been too much? Are you afraid for your life because of dangerous genetically engineered creatures and a former boss who has been implicated in fraud, theft, illegal pet ownership, public disturbance, and ill-fitting suits?"

Before Hessy could answer, Officer Gerland jumped to the stage. "Pardon my delay. As you know, my wife uses my patrol to get to her kalooki games. The matters of Dr. Om's alleged crimes are under investigation. We can make no comment for the moment."

"Is he in custody on St. Quiche?" Cynthia Priss asked by putting her head up to the mic in Bastian's hand.

"No comment can be made at the moment," Gerland

said, "except to say that I was the one to arrest him." He smiled.

Bertie's mind was starting to wander.

"Bastian again. Miss Beauregard, will the park ever open again and, if so, when?"

Bertie sure didn't know the answers to these questions. No one did really.

"My turn," said Cynthia, shooting daggers at Bastian. "How will the park be funded now that it has been revealed it was opened with stolen money?"

And, if he were to be honest, there were other questions that were more important to him.

"No comments!" Gerland said. He straightened his shoulders and looked happy to have his turn in the spotlight.

Like why did the unicorns need meat? And what was in that feed? And why did it make them go rabid? Was it even rabies that they had?

"Bastian here! Will ticket prices go down to make the park affordable for the average Quichan?"

And the wings? Where did those come from?

But none of the reporters were asking those questions.

But then, a stout man in a cream-colored suit walked onto the stage and cut Bertie's thoughts short. The reporters went crazy.

"Governor, governor!" Bastian said.

"Governor! Cynthia Priss from *The Economist*." She stressed the name of the magazine and smirked at Bastian.

The governor put his hands up in the air. "Excuse my tardiness. I was taking an important phone call from the prime minister. He flies home today."

Bertie said, "Does this mean Dr. Om doesn't own the island anymore? Sir?"

Gerland jumped to the front. "As that involves money from an ongoing investigation, no comment can be made."

"Quiet, Gerland," the governor said. "Dr. Om no longer owns the island."

Bertie leaned in and whispered "Because, um, Hessy and I don't have our passports, so—"

"Not to worry, Dr. Vole."

"Or work permits, for that matter."

"Not to worry. That will be dealt with. Dr. Vole, your mother is mailing your passport express. She says to call more."

"Sheesh, ma," Bertie said.

"And Miss Beauregard," he said. "We can have some papers drawn up for you. I am sure Saint can help with that."

Saint smiled.

"Bastian Best from the *St. Quiche Ledger*. As illegal immigrants, do you experience persecution? Did you arrive in leaky boats?"

The governor put his hands up for silence. "I have also just got off the phone with the rector of the University of St. Quiche. As you all know, our nation has an orphan park with great touristic and research potential. St. Quiche's own premier educational institute will be taking it under its wing." The governor laughed and winked at Bertie. "Ha ha, wing. Ha! How à-propos, do you not agree, Dr. Vole?"

"Yeah," Bertie said, forcing a laugh. "Right."

"To continue, the University of St. Quiche will help turn the park into a research institute." He looked at Bertie and Hessy. "I believe Mythical Unicorn Land Featuring the Rainforest Zipline Extravaganza is no longer an appropriate name."

"I guess not," Bertie said.

"And finally, they have made an offer that can't be refused," the governor said. He turned to Hessy. "Would you mind if I announced it?"

"Not at all," she said. Bertie looked at her, wondering what was up.

"The premier educational institute has offered its first Flying Creature Scholar Grant to Miss Helsinth Beauregard, who will be starting school there in the August term."

The governor turned to Bertie while clapping. "Once you decide what to call these creatures, please let the university know so they can settle on a proper name. 'Flying Creature' lacks a je ne sais quoi."

"Will do," Bertie said, clapping Hessy on the back. "Happy to do that."

Bertie saw Cynthia Priss try to extract the mic from Bastian, but the governor put his hands up again.

"No more questions! We are to have a celebratory lunch at St. Quiche's premier restaurant—"

Saint poked the governor on the shoulder and whispered something in his ear.

"Or rather, at The Last Resort, as the premier restaurant needs repair. Apparently, a wild creature destroyed its brand-new roof sometime yesterday."

The governor looked sternly at Bertie who, in turn, looked at Hessy.

"Termite?" he mouthed the words.

She nodded and suppressed a giggle.

"Off we go to lunch," the governor said as he waddled down the stairs.

But Bertie, Hessy, and Saint didn't go straight to The Last Resort.

The four of them (it is always best to not leave out Lady Mathilda) made a quick stop at the butcher and headed back to the park. Black Mamba, Princess Piranha, Barracuda, Jaws, Dragon Breath, Captain Viper, Gila Monster Man, Vulture, Hornet, Tasmanian Devil, and Termite would be wanting their mid-morning snack.

Because it's best that such creatures not go hungry.

EPILOGUE

TWILIGHT HAD COME to St. Quiche. A small, brown lizard peeked out from under the brush. He turned his head to the left, then to the right.

The world was finally quiet again.

He skittered out of his hideaway into the fading light of the day. A bird flapped his wings above; the lizard startled, again watchful. A flutter of wings alerted the lizard to the bird's departure, and the twig he took off from shook.

A glop of pink foam fell on the lizard's back.

The lizard shook his head. He tried to lick the foam away. It burned. His lungs felt like they were on fire.

In the darkness of St. Quiche, no one was around to hear the cough, a pop, as if a tiny engine backfiring, or to see the quick lick of flame from the lizard's mouth.

To be continued in *The Veterinarian's Field Guide to Smelly Dragon Breath*. See the preview at the end of this book!

PLEASE REVIEW!

As independent authors, we don't have the multimillion dollar promotions budgets the big corporate publishing conglomerates do. Did you know that for every 100 people who read this book, only about 1 will leave a review? Help us beat those odds! Please leave your review today on Amazon.

CLICK TO LEAVE REVIEW

Or in your browser: https://amzn.to/2LljWdO

FREE GIFT!

Freebie alert!

Get the free short story sequel,
"Driving Lady Mathilda"

A missing car. A tyrannical
police officer. A juvenile
delinquent. Did Saint's car, Lady
Mathilda, survive the mad
unicorn rampage only to perish
in a chop shop?

Find out by clicking here. Or, if
you have the book or a Kindle
that is old like mine, paste
http://eepurl.com/dhMaf1
into your browser.

ACKNOWLEDGMENTS

First, thanks to you, the readers. I hope *The Veterinarian's Field Guide to Rabid Unicorns* provided you with a nice escape from your everyday as much as writing it let me escape from mine.

Also thanks to Hurricane María for knocking out power for months. It freed up lots and lots of time to work on this book.

A huge thanks to Dalan Decker, my husband, for his help in editing, running down stray typos, generating ideas (to him goes all the credit for naming the "chummy"), marketing, and all the rest. You know, we should take a vacation to St. Quiche sometime. What do you think?

SNEAK PEAK: ST. QUICHE 2 - THE VETERINARIAN'S FIELD GUIDE TO SMELLY DRAGON BREATH

Bertie charged through the leaves in pursuit of the unicorn. Her black form jumped out of his reach, onto the sun-baked beach. The superheated sand burned as it wedged itself in his tennis shoes. Bertie picked up the pace just as the unicorn braked. He rammed into her hindquarters.

Princess Piranha had escaped again.

Bertie grabbed her reins and made sure he had a firm grip on the rough leather before sinking to the hot sand and gulping in deep breaths. Princess Piranha flapped her wings. The breeze gave Bertie some relief from the heat.

"You could have at least parked in the shade," Bertie said. But all things considered, he had lucked out.

She could have flown away.

"You realize you got wings, right?" he said between breaths.

Bertie looked across the sand to The Last Resort bar. He checked his phone.

He had enough time for something cold before the meeting, right?

A message bleeped. "Bertie, where are you?"

It was from Hessy, doing her managerial duty to make sure he got to the meeting on time.

As in The Meeting, The Meeting with the new board of the unicorn park.

Yeah, he had time for something cold.

Bertie shoved his phone in his pocket as it bleeped again and tightened Princess Piranha's reins around his knuckles as he pulled himself to his feet. He rubbed the sand off, ignoring another bleep from his phone, and clicked his tongue at Princess Piranha to follow him to the bar.

He would keep her close. There was no way he was showing up to the meeting and telling his bosses the he had lost a winged unicorn mutant thingy. No way.

His phone bleeped again.

"Not again, Hessy," Bertie said. He dug out his phone. "Hey, star vet," the first message said, "you haven't forgotten the meeting, right?" Then the next one. "You're avoiding???" And another. "You're avoiding."

Which was so not true.

He was searching and rescuing. And sipping.

Or would be sipping soon.

He tied Princess Piranha to the flaking blue porch of The Last Resort and stepped inside. But before he could make it to the bar, a thunderous crack made Bertie whip around.

Oh, no, no, no, no, no.

The post of The Last Resort dangled in the breeze. Princess Piranha had run off.

Bertie ran into the hot sand.

He looked to the left.

Nothing.

He looked to the right.

The sun bounced off Princess Piranha's sparkling black hide. Bertie ran to catch up, but she was galloping too fast, kicking sand up into Bertie's face.

She made a sharp turn left onto the northeast pier. Bertie rushed after. He stopped to get his breath where the sand met the worn slats of the pier. There was no reason to keep running. He had her. When she looped back, he'd cling onto her reins for dear life and drag her back to the park. It's not like she was going to fling herself into the ocean.

A rush of air skimmed Bertie's head.

No, no, no, no, no.

Bertie let out a breath of frustration. Princess Piranha was flying.

He ran inland, across the sand, trying to keep up. She made a beeline for the mangrove forest.

Not the mangroves, Bertie thought. Not the mangroves, please not the mangroves.

Just as she was about to breach the forest, she dove to her right and galloped across the field towards—

"Not the town!" Bertie called.

That's worse. So, so, so much worse.

The road into town met at a crossroads. Bertie hoped she'd turn left, away from town. He sped across the grass, his footsteps matching every ragged breath. He wasn't going to reach her in time. There was no way.

He was a few car lengths behind when she reached the

road. As Bertie feared, she turned right. A line of stalls swallowed her up.

Unicorn on the loose. What would the bosses say?

Bertie lunged forward. He skidded on the road, regained his balance, and followed Princess Piranha's retreating heinie.

"Is that your unicorn?" A vendor stopped Bertie. "Can I have a picture?"

"If I can catch her." Bertie pulled himself out of the vendor's grasp. Today of all days, Rumstad decided to put up kiosks everywhere. Bertie didn't have time to ask why.

He dodged smiling shoppers who pointed at him as he straggled along. He overheard the commentary: "That's that vet" and "He runs the unicorn park" and "Autograph?"

At least all the crowds were slowing Princess Piranha down. He was so close now. So close.

He threw out his arm and just about snagged her reins, which were whipping behind her, when she made a sharp left into a narrow street. Bertie slid on the cobblestones.

"Grab her," Bertie said, but everyone was too busy taking pictures with their phones.

"There goes Dr. Unicorn," someone screamed as Bertie dashed after Princess Piranha. The red, orange, green, yellow, and purple of the Spanish colonial buildings bounced in front of his eyes as he tried to keep up his speed. The street curved towards the old fort. Just then, Princess Piranha rammed into a t-shirt stall.

"No!" Bertie screamed. He caught up to her just as she slipped on the broken wooden slats and shook the t-shirts from her back. With a red shirt still swinging on her horn, she bucked down the street.

"Eh, toreador!" The vendor laughed. Bertie stopped for an instant, wondering if he should help clean up the mess, but the vendor didn't seem to care that his kiosk was in pieces. He would probably put up a plaque that said, "Unicorn was here."

Bertie stumbled over the slats of wood in pursuit of Princess Piranha. He almost had her. A bicycle shot in front of him. When Bertie regained his balance, she pushed off her hind legs and flew into the blue sky.

Bertie bent over, gasping for oxygen, and watched as Princess Piranha, with a red shirt flapping in the wind like a sail, disappeared from view.

Purple, green, orange, yellow t-shirts interspersed with black unicorn feathers littered the ground at Bertie's feet. A bead of sweat dripped on the bluish cobblestones. Bertie sucked in humid air.

"Bertie?" Hessy's voice came at him from above.

Crap, he was probably late for the meeting.

Bertie straightened his back, but before he could explain why he was late, a flash blinded him. He shielded his face with his hands.

"Bastian Best from the St. Quiche Ledger." Bastian snapped another picture. "From underdog to unicorn superstar. That is what all of St. Quiche is calling you. How do you balance it all?"

Bertie looked over at the demolished t-shirt stand. He grimaced at the stitch in his side.

"Maybe you could give Bertie a minute?" Hessy said. Bertie found her in the crowd, her red head all fiery in the sun. She was standing in front of the fort's giant double doors with what Bertie assumed was the unicorn park board. The governor, looking particularly broad in his cream suit, smiled. "Indeed, our star veterinarian has arrived."

Hessy stood next to Bertie and whispered, "Smile."

Bertie stretched his face into what he hoped was happy.

"Okay, maybe not," she said.

"Miss Beauregard relayed your message," the governor said.

"My message?" Bertie said. He looked to Hessy for help. Message? What message? Hessy kicked him.

"As to the reason for your delay," the governor said.

"Yeah, totally, my message," Bertie said.

"Dr. Vole?" A man with way too much product in his hair and gold chains peeking out of an open collar stretched his hand out to Bertie. Bertie seemed to remember that he ran illegal horse bets from his pharmacy. "Once matters settle down at WURRIEA, are there any plans to create another genetically engineered animal?"

"UREA?" Bertie said. Hessy whispered something in his ear, but he didn't catch it on account of a lady bellowing.

"More mutants?"

That was Miss Celestina.

As in president-of-the-board-boss Celestina. She raised her finger at Bertie. A red handbag, like a cannonball, swung slowly at her elbow. "You! Do not let me catch you making more mutants."

"I—"

"Celestina, dear," the governor said, "Dr. Vole was not the one to suggest the creation of more mutants."

Celestina grabbed Greasy Man's collar. "I told you, don't you go putting crazy talk ideas into this boy's head. Or did you not see what just happened?" She pointed at the vendor who was picking up all his stray t-shirts. "Bull in a China shop."

"I believe you are crushing Anton's windpipe," the governor said.

"Anton," Celestina said, "if I find out you push anyone to make more monsters—"

Bertie said, "The unicorns aren't—"

"Monsters, you hear?" Celestina put her finger in Greasy Anton's face. I will push you off the board."

Greasy Anton smiled, showing a space between his front teeth. "Celestina, dear—"

"I will push you out of your business. I will push you off St. Quiche." She pointed to the fort behind her. "I will push you off the top of this building."

"Do you want me to continue supplying fertilizer for your mother's prize lilies?" Greasy Anton said greasily.

Celestina pulled back her finger. "Fine. I will pay your hospital bills after I push you!" Celestina rounded on Bertie. "You made me miss my kalooki game."

Bertie gulped. Was she waiting for an apology? Maybe she was waiting for an apology. "I'm sorry, Miss Celestina."

"Everyone thinks you are a star, but I have been watching you these past few weeks." She leaned in. Her voice became a hiss. "I. Know. Better."

Bertie worked really hard at not blinking as she stared up into his face. Then she growled.

He was sure of it.

When she turned away, her red handbag thwacked Bertie in the ribs. Bertie hunched over in pain just as Bastian snapped another photo.

By the time the floaters cleared from his vision, Celestina was stomping away. Pedestrians cleared a path for her. It was like watching the parting of the Red Sea, only scarier.

"Governor!" she hollered. "I will go pick up the new veterinarian."

"New vet?" Bertie said.

"Tell you later," Hessy said. "And read your e-mails."

"Eh, eh," a happy voice separated itself from the crowd. It was Saint. "Did I miss the meeting yet?"

Bertie nodded. He took advantage of Hessy talking to the governor about some festival or something to say, "You came late on purpose."

Saint smiled.

"You were avoiding Miss Celestina, weren't you?" Bertie said.

Saint smiled wider. "O-ho, she hits hard."

"Some hardened smuggler you are."

"These are mechanics' hands. I need to keep them safe."

Hessy looked over at Bertie and Saint funny. "What did you two do to Miss Celestina?"

"Nothing," Saint said with big eyes.

"Different story," Bertie said.

"Dr. Vole," the governor said, "we did not discuss it in the meeting, but I am curious about WURRIEA's role in the Mango Sloopie Cup."

"UREA?" Bertie said.

Hessy whispered in Bertie's ear. It tickled. "Winged Unicorn Research Reserve and Institute for Educational Advancement. Park's new name. Read your e-mails."

"Cup?" Bertie said.

"Bertie has delegated festival preparations to Saint," Hessy said.

Saint smiled.

"Yeah, totally. On account of Saint replacing Hessy when she goes off to study." Bertie smacked Saint on the back, probably too hard. "Might as well start on-the-job training now."

The governor nodded once. "I am pleased to see how you have successfully taken the reins from Dr. Om. It is gratifying to see it all come together."

The vendor from the demolished stand stuck a broken slat of wood in Bertie's face. "Can I have an autograph? Just write 'To Vincent.'"

"Thanks," Bertie said to the governor as he signed the slat of wood before anyone saw him doing that. 'Cause it felt really stupid. He breathed out in relief when the governor took his leave and waddled through the crowd.

Vincent threw his arms around Bertie's shoulder. "Bastian, you rascal. Snap a picture of us two."

Bertie was pretty sure he looked constipated in the photo.

"Bastian Best from *El Semanal de Santa Quiche*. Have you found your prognostications about unicorns to be true?"

"Prognostications?" Bertie was starting to feel dizzy.

Bastian held up tattered pages. Bertie squinted. They were some sort of bootleg copy *of The Gastrointestinal Tract of Unicorns: Part I of the Anatomy of Rare Creatures Series.*

Hessy whispered in his hear about how he should admit the book was a practical joke. It tickled.

"Uh, define true," Bertie said.

"Are the allegations true?" Bastian said.

"Allegations?" Bertie glanced at Hessy. She shrugged. "What allegations?"

Had Bastian found out about the book being a joke? He should have confessed. He should have—

"Reports have surfaced—"

"Reports?" Bertie said. "Surfaced?"

"—that you have been nominated to be the Mango Sloopie Cup King."

Relief washed over Bertie. It was only that. Actually, Bertie felt kind of flattered. He'd never been nominated for—

And then panic.

He had to be Mango Sloopie Cup King? What was that? What did he have to do?

There wouldn't be photo ops, would there?

'Cause he wasn't That Guy.

"Do you have a quote?" Bastian said.

Saint slapped Bertie on the back. "His quote is, he is honored." He whispered in Bertie's ear. "Don't worry. You will not win. Lady Mathilda will."

"A car can win?" Bertie said.

"Three years consecutive," Saint said. "Bastian, include that in your article. Lady Mathilda has won three years in a row."

Bastian scribbled like a maniac.

"Don't worry," Saint said. "Lady Mathilda will give you advice if you win. But you won't win."

"She's a car, Saint." Bertie was feeling dizzy.

"Dr. Vole needs to get back to WURRIEA," Hessy said. She gave Bertie a look that said, you're not going to faint, are you? "We have an errant unicorn to catch."

"Toreador!" Vincent laughed.

Bertie let Saint and Hessy pull him through the crowd towards Saint's car. People pointed as they passed. Miss Bernice, head of the Temperance League, waved her cane at him and smiled. This was all so weird.

What if he couldn't hack it?

He couldn't quite put his finger on it, but when Celestina was all up in his face, he couldn't help thinking she had the real scoop on him. She was like this handbag-wielding Jiminy Cricket telling him what was really going down. Hessy would say he was being stupid. Get caught up on e-mails, she'd say. You'll do great, she'd say. If Saint were in his shoes, he'd be soaking up the glory, planning all sorts of cool stuff for the park, half of them illegal, but he'd have such a big smile on his face, pretty much no one would care.

Except for Celestina.

At the thought of her, Bertie grimaced. They reached Lady Mathilda, Saint's VW Rabbit, her rusty green hood soaking up the rays. As Lady Mathilda hacked to life, Bertie tried to find the right way to ask Hessy what kind of vibes she'd picked up from the board. Was Bertie's job secure? Or was the governor being nice to him while secretly planning to toss him off the highest building of St. Quiche with a pink slip stapled to his forehead? He needed to be chill enough so they didn't think he was some namby-pamby who couldn't hack his job but hysterical enough to get an honest answer.

But as it turned out, Bertie didn't have to ask anything. Hessy gave him everything he needed to know when she turned around in the front seat and said, "About your replacement . . ."

"They're not firing you," Hessy said as she, Bertie, and Saint walked towards the unicorn pen at the mountain-top unicorn park. The mountain was called Mt. Om back when Dr. Om ran the place, but now it was back to being Mt. Sugarcane. "How many times do I have to say that?"

"Replacement," Bertie said. "That's what you said."

"If you'd read your e-mails or bothered to show up at the meeting, you'd know you're head of WURRIEA—"

"That's a stupid name—"

"The new vet is replacing you in your old role."

"Why bring in someone new?" Bertie said. "And you said, 'replacement' to scare me into reading my e-mails, didn't you?"

Hessy said, "If you'd read your e-mails—"

"If they weren't so long—"

"You'd know about the new vet."

"And they send so many."

"And then you wouldn't be so paranoid."

"Do you read the e-mails?" Bertie asked Saint.

"Stop fighting, you two, or I will shoot you both," he said.

Bertie was anxious to get to work, to look busy before the vet—whoever he was—showed up. He needed to look in control, in charge, in—"

" . . . capable of reading your e-mails," Hessy said. "Stop avoiding."

They reached the pen.

"Doody head," Bertie said.

"Avoider," Hessy said.

"Yeah, well . . ." Bertie couldn't think of anything. "You smell bad."

Hessy looked at Bertie in that way that headmistresses do, you know, over the rim of their eyeglasses? Only she didn't wear glasses, so it looked even scarier.

Right, 'cause you're not supposed to tell girls they reek.

Hessy peeked through the door. She whispered, "Told you he was already here. Oooh, he looks like that actor from the 80's. Easy on the eyes."

Saint jostled for position. "Is that Celestina giggling?"

"Giggling?" Bertie said.

"She never giggles," Saint said.

"Give her a chance, you two," Hessy said. "She's not so bad."

"She hits hard," Saint said. "Just look at Bertie's black eye."

Bertie clicked his tongue. "It's not black anymore. Let's get this over with." Bertie elbowed Hessy and Saint out of the way and tugged the door open.

His heart sank.

The new veterinarian was standing in the middle of the pen in the only puddle of light available. The guy leaned over to coo in Tasmanian Devil's ear, and a ray of sunshine bounced off his red locks in freaking slow-mo. He spun towards Bertie, Hessy, and Saint. In one smooth movement, he flipped his hair like they do in dandruff commercials. Only the guy didn't have a speck of dandruff in sight. He leaned against Tasmanian Devil's silver-spotted rump, and she whinnied happily.

That unicorn never whinnied happily.

Celestina giggled.

Some sort of cologne mixed with the unicorn scent.

Hessy was right. He was the spitting image of that red-haired actor from the '80's. Bertie peeked at Hessy out of the corner of his eye. Her mouth hung open.

For pete's sake.

How could anyone compete with that?

How could Bertie compete with that?

"Sheez," Bertie said, and Saint nodded.

But something else niggled at Bertie. Something he couldn't put his finger on.

"Hessy," Celestina said. Bertie noticed she didn't even look at him and Saint. "Meet our new veterinarian." She smiled up at him. "And author of The Gastrointestinal Tract of Unicorns."

Bertie did a double take.

Author?

Bertie leaned forward to get a better look. "Tim-Tim? It's you?"

"Surprise! Buddy, long time no see. And actually, it's Timothy now." He kicked his head back in laughter. "Nobody has called me Tim-Tim in, oh, ages! Celestina, what do they say here? Is it 'It is time to stop drinking sweet ginger?'"

Celestina laughed like an overeager foghorn. "Dr. Grett. You're one of us already."

"How have you been, Bertram?"

"Actually, it's Bertie still. Still just Bertie."

"How you've been doing, Bertie? It's been too, too long."

"You could say that."

Hessy gave Bertie a funny look.

"Celestina, have I told you how we met?" Timothy said.

And Celestina giggled some more.

While Tim-Tim gasbagged about what best friends he and Bertie were, Hessy whispered, "How could you not recognize him?"

Before Bertie could answer, Timothy took Hessy's hand and kissed it. "Is that, hmmm, butterfly jasmine I sense?"

Hessy giggled.

Bertie was going to tell Hessy that this Timothy looked nothing like the Tim-Tim he had known. Nothing. But Timothy was still strangling her hand and staring into her eyes.

"You're a redhead too," Timothy said to her.

She giggled. Again.

Bertie stepped next to Hessy to break up the little party. "It's funny. Did you know red hair is caused by a mutation?"

"So you're calling me a mutant?" Hessy said.

"No," Bertie said. This wasn't going as planned. "Well, sort of, but no."

Saint rolled his eyes.

Timothy said, "Bertram—"

"Bertie."

"Bertie always did have a sense of humor," Tim-Tim said. "You and I, Miss Beauregard, we make a cute pair of mutants, don't you think?" He winked.

"Dr. Grett," Celestina said, "they don't make gentlemen like you anymore."

Timothy finally freed Hessy's hand and greeted Saint. Bertie leaned into Hessy's ear. "He was pimply and slouchy and kind of like that round kid from Goonies, only rounder. Like much rounder."

She scrunched her face up, as though to say, that's rude.

"No, I mean, that's why I didn't recognize him. You know? 'Cause he's changed."

Hessy went back to ogling Timothy. Her gaze was blurry. "I'll say."

How could Bertie compete with that?

How could anyone compete with that?

"You," Celestina said. She rammed her handbag into Bertie's ribs. "Introduce Dr. Grett to the creatures."

Bertie gasped for air, and by the time he took his next full breath, Timothy had already reclaimed his position in the spotlight next to Tasmanian Devil. He was cooing in her ear.

"She is some kind of wonderful, isn't she?" Timothy said. He went back to cooing.

"Yeah, totally. But Tasmanian Devil likes to nip. You want to be careful."

"Oh, Bertie, you don't need to tell me. After all—" He looked straight at Celestina. His voice came out all breathy. "I wrote the book on unicorns."

Celestina sighed. "Oh, Dr. Grett. We are so lucky to have the doctor who wrote the book on unicorns working with us."

"Hey," Bertie said. "I wrote the book on unicorns too. You know, Timothy, it'd be great to chat with you about you and this job and your weird, weird decision to come here. So weird we both ended up here."

"How could I not seize this opportunity?" Timothy said.

"So, so weird," Bertie said.

Tasmanian Devil nuzzled Timothy hair.

"It's a once-in-a-lifetime defining event." Timothy glanced at Bertie, and for one instant, Bertie thought he looked cautious. Or threatened? He wasn't sure.

It was no wonder, considering what Timothy had—

And then, like a switch, Timothy went back to that misty look laundry soap commercials go for.

Or maybe Bertie was just being paranoid.

"Uh, well, you've met Tasmanian Devil," Bertie said. "That unicorn over there, the light bluish one, is Termite. She likes to eat wood. Watch out for your fingers. And that one over there is—"

"No, no!" Timothy said. "Let me guess their names. I've been studying." He winked at Celestina, whose ensuing guffaw must have scared the unicorns because—

Whump.

Bertie landed in a puddle of mud. He couldn't breathe. His ears rang. He swiveled his head as much as the pain would allow. Termite was staring down at him from behind.

Termite had kicked him.

His head buzzed. Was this what death was like?

From a distance, he heard a dreamy voice sigh, "Bertie, are you okay?"

It was Hessy.

So he wasn't dying. Or maybe she sounded dreamy because he was dying, and she was talking to him as he floated off to the great celestial beyond.

When Bertie looked up, he saw Timothy's hand reaching down. He tried to get up without help but fell back in the mud, so he grabbed Timothy's hand and struggled to his feet. Bertie was covered in mud, but not a spot had gotten on Timothy. Even his hands were miraculously, impeccably, pristinely, impossibly clean.

How could anyone compete with that?

How could Bertie—

"You!" Celestina said, extending her finger again and clucking her tongue. "Take a bath. Filthy."

"You know," Timothy said, his chin in his hand, "they're not technically unicorns. Now that they can fly." He waved his hands around as though imitating the shape of wings. "Bertie, we should form a committee to come up with a better term."

"I already—"

"Dr. Grett, that is an excellent idea," Celestina said.

"—have an idea," Bertie said. "Or two. Or one."

"Celestina, maybe we can discuss this while you show me the rest of WURRIEA."

"Unicorny pegasus," Bertie said. Only he blurted it out, kind of loud. Louder than he had intended.

Celestina looked Bertie up and down like he was slime.

"I like that one," Saint said.

Timothy turned to Hessy. "Miss Beauregard—"

"Call me Hessy."

"Hessy. Would you like to join us?" He put out his elbow and leaned down. "You know, I think I sense some ginger as well, don't I?"

She giggled.

Again.

Timothy ambled out of the pen, Celestina on one arm and Hessy on the other.

As they walked away, Bertie heard Timothy asking Hessy whether she had seen Celestina's mother's prize flowers.

No offense, Hessy, but you don't smell like jasmine or butterflies or sweet ginger or anything but Benzalkonium Chloride.

Which was absolutely fine with Bertie.

The last of Timothy's voice ("Your hair, it reminds me of her flame lilies") floated away on the breeze.

"What are you doing, you doltish boy?" Saint grabbed Bertie's elbow. "Don't leave Hessy with that man for a minute."

"What can I do about it?"

"Did you see the man?"

Of course Bertie had seen him.

How could he . . .

But he was too out of it to chase after anyone. He still hadn't caught his breath, and pain shot up, well, everything. He leaned against Tasmanian Devil.

She nipped him.

Bertie said, "Why does Celestina like him and not me?"

"Look in the mirror, will you?"

Bertie gazed at the mud puddle, then at the blue sky, then back to the mud puddle. "Saint?"

"Yes."

"How long since it's rained?"

"A few days."

"So that mud . . . ?"

Saint looked from Bertie to the puddle and back to Bertie. He took a step back. "Yes."

Bertie smelled his shirt.

Crap.

Click here to buy *The Veterinarian's Field Guide to Smelly Dragon Breath* – Available for Kindle now!

Made in the USA
Monee, IL
10 May 2020

30232513R00187